Miguel the Barber

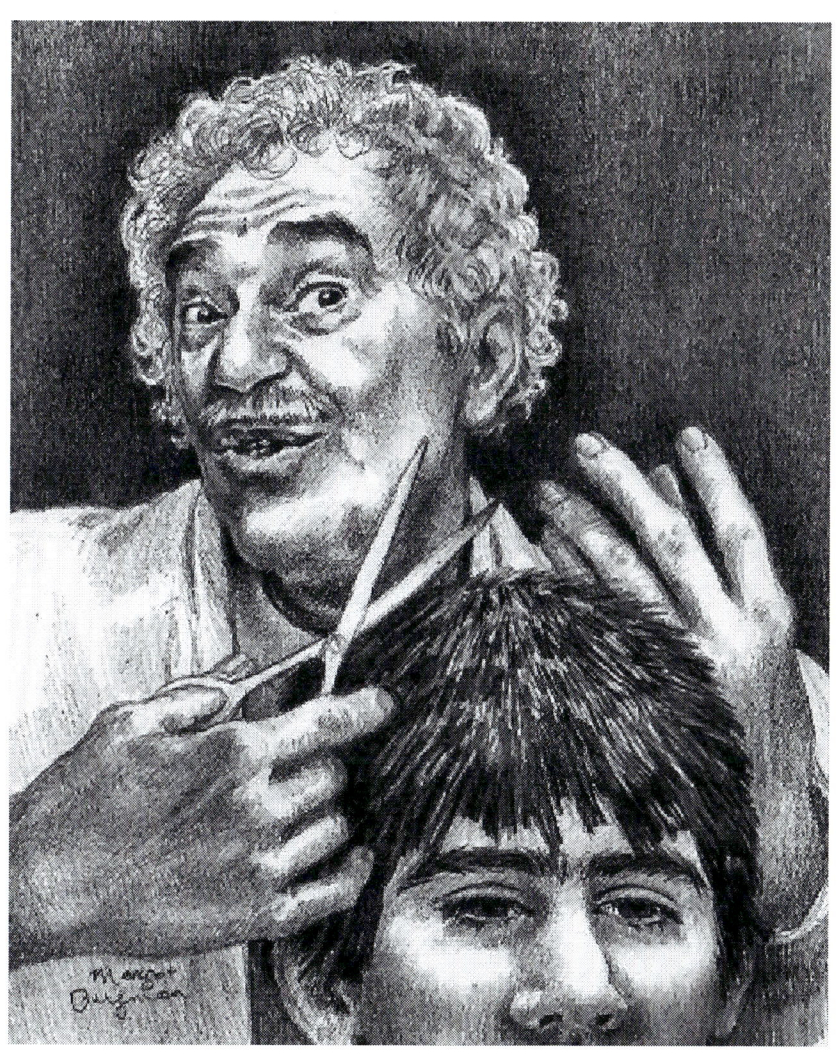

A Novel By

Vitae Bergman

Burkeshire Press – Virginia, U.S.A

Also by Vitae Bergman

Take Sylvia's Case
AFGA: A Mystery Set in Harrisonburg
Berkeley Tales: A Collection of Stories
Open the River: Memoir of a Grieving Heart
Numerology for Soul Awakening

*In Memory of Sorrel,
Ridgley, Helen, and Shannon*

Published by Burkeshire Press
Copyright © 2009 by Vitae Bergman
Cover Art Copyright© 2009 by Vitae Bergman
Ink Drawing Copyright © 2009 by Margot Bergman

All rights reserved under International and Pan-American Copyright Conventions, including the right of reproduction in whole or in part in any form.

This book is a work of fiction. Names, characters, places and incidents are either the product of the author's imagination or are used fictitiously. Any resemblance to actual events or locales or persons, living or dead, is entirely coincidental.

Manufactured in the United States of America.
First Edition

ISBN 1448629233
EAN-13 9781448629237

ACKNOWLEDGMENTS

      I very much thank the following persons for their enthused participation in the making of this book:
      Margot Bergman, my wife, my best friend, my best critic, who encourages me to write, write, write.
      Lydia Maes, my proofreader and dear friend, who enjoys my work, reads with a steady eye, and freely offers good critical advice.

Miguel the Barber

Old Miguel Guzman (not his real name) sprawled in his barber's chair, half in stupor, half in a state of perplexity. Lately, anxiety over his granddaughter gripped him day and night.

It was siesta time in the shantytown where he and his granddaughter lived. His pleasant morning of hair clipping and gossiping while taking occasional sips of fragrant coffee had turned into a stifling afternoon. August heat—brutal, debilitating—filled his now empty shop. His tiny shack, where he lived and conducted his business, steamed under its tin roof like a Dutch oven. There were four rooms: two small bedrooms, one for himself and the other for his granddaughter, a main room with a passageway to an outdoors kitchen, and the barbershop that took up the front portion of the house.

Today, the heat was astounding. As was to be expected, he reminded himself. He had wrestled with this oppressive climate for a long time. He could have gone outside, he knew, and climbed into his hammock. It hung between two coconut palms, which he had planted years ago. He could have taken his old body outside, into the open air under a bit of shade. But what was the use? The heavy, humid heat of breezeless August sizzled your brains whether indoors or out. It made no difference.

But what bothered him more than the heat was the fact that his granddaughter, Manuela, was growing up too fast. She had just turned sixteen. He was her sole family, her one and only guardian and protector—had been cast into this role when she was only six years old. Under his sentinel eye, she had grown into a young woman, and consequently subject to the blandishments of all the hot bloods in this shantytown where they were forced to live.

She came and went as she pleased.

He could no longer keep her within the softness of his wings. He had become a weighty old buzzard, weak and slow. Slow in every way except in snipping hair and rising to anger. His fanatical need to protect his precious Manuela made him quick to anger. Every morning at least two or three young swains came into his shop. They made a practice of congregating in the corner, squatting against the wall, their faces between their knees expecting to ogle Manuela while waiting for their hair to be snipped. Yes, he easily got angry. As soon as they walked in he boiled over. And he knew this boiling-over did no good. It did nothing but assault his thumping heart in insidious ways. Sooner or later, his ticker would give out, burst into flames, or cave in like one of the old copper mines in the hills behind the town. And then what would be Manuela's fate? This is what bothered him.

But two hours of stewing over his predicament was enough. "Enough!" He muttered. "Pointless trying to snooze any longer." With a groan, he hauled himself out of his barber's chair and staggered into the room behind the shop. Miguel and Manuela called this the back room. It served as their only living space where they ate their meals and where the granddaughter did her lessons under the barber's watchful eye. Their two tiny bedrooms flanked this main room, where there was also a closet of sorts dug into the hillside behind the shack for the sake of a bit of coolness in which was kept the larder and two jugs of water.

He found her in this back room, sitting at her kitchen worktable, mixing tortilla dough for their evening meal, a book opened in her lap. How could she read and make tortillas at the same time? He wondered, shaking his head, then found a glass and filled it with the cool water from one of the jugs.

Nevertheless, he was proud that she could read. There was no school in this forsaken shantytown. He was her teacher as well as her grandfather, her abuelito.

Thoughts of the evening meal, soon to come, calmed his mind.

But of course, he had not taught his Manuela how to cook. For this important skill she had ingratiated herself into the tutelage of the two older women who lived in each of the hovels on either side of the Guzman shack.

There was Maria Roybal, the fuzzy chinned widow who lived on the one side with her grown son. She was a figure of staggering proportions despite her short legs. She specialized in mouth-watering tamales. The barber couldn't stand her whimpering ways.

And there was Consuelo Diaz, thin boned with gray hair piled into a bun at the back of her head, with piercing huge eyes that stared at everything. She dwelled next door on the other side. Her culinary skill focused on curious ways to prepare the fresh seafood her husband brought home from the sea. In the sandy soil beside her house, being the shantytown's curandera, she managed to cultivate miracle herbs for medicinal purposes as well as for the table.

Perhaps one of these two shantytown mujeres had shown his Manuela how to read and make tortillas at the same time? He doubted it.

Miguel let out a sigh and sat down at the table across from his granddaughter. He sipped his cool drink and silently studied her face. She was bent over her book. Accustomed to his silence, she went on reading, idly forming a glob of corn masa into a round ball to be later patted flat when it was time to cook.

Had she looked up, she would have seen sadness written across his face, would have taken note of his puffy eyes due to lack of sleep over the constant worry, of which, unbeknownst to her, she was the cause.

He was a slender man of medium height, who held himself with a dignified air. He had a massive head with noble features, a full moustache and thick, gray curly hair. For her sake, he worried. Now that she was older, he was beginning to regret ever bringing her here in the first place. This remote village seemed like such a good place where they could safely hide. But that was ten years ago. Time changes everything. He sighed again. What to do, he wondered.

He stared at her profile. How beautiful she was! Those long silky eyelashes. Her braided ponytail, shiny and black, that looked so much like a snake curling around her slender neck. She wore a white peasant blouse that held her sweet young breasts with dainty modesty. He imagined her as a young woman of Crete.

No wonder the boys couldn't resist her. That was a given. To be expected. But the real question was could she resist them? She had lived here more than half her life. Had grown up with these rascals whose fathers taught them nothing else but how to fish, get drunk, and make noise. Aside from himself, and the librarian over in Guaymas, and of course, the Professor, these were the only kind of men she knew and was used to.

Ay! Caramba! This wretched place!

Over the years, the little shantytown, which had no name, grew to be the habitation for homeless fishing folk and a few others who came as fugitives of justice. It stood on solid dunes only a few yards from the narrow beach, situated on the edge of the Sea of

Cortez, in the state of Sonora. At the furthest end of a bay called Bahia Algodones, several miles distant from the nearest official principality—San Carlos, itself a tiny beach resort and fishing town—this unofficial fishing village clung to itself as orphans in an orphanage keep aloof, showing only as much interest in the outside world as necessary.

The men took their daily catch to a wholesale buyer just on the edge of San Carlos. With the money they collected, they bought whatever supplies they needed—flour for their tortillas, vegetables, beer, wine—obtained from the closest abarrotes. Then they scurried back home to their wives and children as fast as possible, by way of the sea using their fishing boats, their pangas for transport.

The town with no name had no official identity, stood on land that belonged to someone—no one seemed to know who, a personage, an hidalgo perhaps who had mined the copper veins and had died some time back. Ownership of the land was a mystery. No census taker had ever made a study of this nameless place. People came and went according to personal needs and desires; the population fluctuated; no one was required to supply proof of identity; there was no church, no priest; it was a pretty loose place. Nevertheless, it had become a standard saying among its inhabitants that the village was composed of 103 souls. And Miguel Guzman was considered the learned man of the town.

Suddenly, Manuela burst into ripples of laughter. Tears came to her eyes, full of mirth as she looked up, rolling her last tortilla ball. She roared, turning to her grandfather.

"What is so funny, child?" He asked.

"This book, abuelito. I can't believe what this man says. It's impossible, I tell you."

"What does he say?"

"He says that when a man and woman kiss, even deeply, a baby will not be the consequence. What an outrageous lie! Wait till I tell Consuelo this. Then we can both have a good laugh."

"What book is this? Let me see this book!"

Manuela handed it to him. He took one look at the title and banged the book on the table.

"You're reading this? Sex education?"

Manuela bit her lip.

"I forbid you to read such books!"

"But abuelito, I need to learn about life."

"You have plenty of time to learn about life!"

"But I am sixteen now, and all the time, I am feeling things."

The barber looked startled. He shoved his massive head halfway across the small wooden table. "What things?" He demanded.

"You know…things. I feel things…down here." She pointed to a place below her waist.

"Caramba!"

It was too much for him. He was too old and tired. He had no stomach for such problems. He ran his hand through his thick curly hair, dismayed. Raising a child was impossible. Was it now required of him to tell his granddaughter the facts of life? Such a thought made his body go limp.

Manuela, on her part, heaving a sigh of despair for the trouble she was causing her dear abuelito, removed herself from the conversation. It was impossible to get her grandfather's help. She could see that. He had taught her everything he knew. It was obvious to her now; there were some things he had no inkling about.

She stood up from her chair and stepped through the door that led to the cooking shed outside, taking her book and plate of uncooked tortillas with her. It was time to prepare their evening meal. She had already made pickled onions and cabbage. They rested in the cool of the larder. Now, she would fire up the cooking grill. From the pile of sun-baked drift wood, she chose just enough pieces that would toast the tortillas and grill the strips of fish—fresh filets of grouper, which Javier, dear sweet Javier, had brought to her earlier in the day.

It was Javier who caused her to feel those things down there in the region below her waist. Javier was not like the other boys. He was tender and sensitive. They were the same age. They had grown up together, had played as children in and around the swirling sea. He lived with his family at the other end of the shantytown, their shack tucked into the side of the rocky hill that marched into the sea. This hill rose up behind the town and grew to the size of a small mountain, its jagged formation pointing to the sky like the thick fingers of a man's hand. From early on Javier and Manuela had climbed among these fingers as easily and as swiftly as two mountain goats. They loved exploring the creases and crevasses, pockets of sand in which tiny plants with flowers of vivid colors nestled under the bright sun, protected from wind.

Manuela hummed to herself, thinking of her friend Javier. She watched the small sticks of wood burn down to charcoal. Then she laid the filets on the grill. They were oiled and seasoned with herbs that Consuelo had taught her to grow. The raw fish sizzled on the hot grill. Smoke rose to her nostrils; the smell of the food made her mouth water. After turning the pieces over to cook on the other side, she began toasting the tortillas now patted flat. They would have a tasty supper. She felt pleased with her work. The food would cheer up her grandfather.

The aroma and sizzling did not go wasted on old Miguel. He turned his mind away from brooding for a while, and set about in search of the bottle of wine he had brought home the week before from Guaymas, a small port city some twenty miles distant. Generally, the old man and his granddaughter went to Guaymas twice a month. They would always go to the biblioteca first. Miguel delighted in opening his granddaughter's mind to the wonder of books. At the biblioteca, while Manuela browsed the stacks, Miguel became acquainted with a certain Eugenio Escudero, a man of learning who always happened to be in the library whenever Miguel and Manuela were there. Actually, EhEh, as he called himself, spent several hours every day in the cool reading room of the library. A retired academic—sociología had been his field—EhEh relished the time he spent conversing with Miguel the hour or so they spent together every couple of weeks, a pleasant interlude from perusing his intellectual interest. Their talks ranged from current events, particularly the political scene, to pop culture, of which, while Miguel had no special curiosity, the sociologist had a keen interest.

In a short time, a friendship developed between the two old men, and Miguel began to hope he would find EhEh willing to consider taking Manuela under his wing to bring some order, so to speak, into her reading habits. From her grandfather, Manuela had learned to love books, yes. But he had no inkling as to how to teach her academic discipline. Miguel showed up with Manuela one day at the door of the professor's cottage, earnestly requesting this favor. EhEh promised to consider it; but after a few discussions with the girl, the matter seemed to evaporate. In any case, Manuela refused to go to the professor's house. She had her own will. She could spend hours pouring over old thick tomes. She loved to read history, and lately, novels about romance. But other kinds of stories captured her imagination as well. And she loved hearing stories told to her by her grandfather, stories of their ancient family.

This man, her grandfather, Miguel, whose real name must never be mentioned, was no ordinary man, no ordinary barber. No indeed. His lineage—and hers as well—was entwined with the history of illustrious personages. Their family descended from a long line of noteworthy barbers, men who had been personal attendants to princes and kings.

When she was a little girl, Manuela would often sit on her abuelito's lap while he told her stories of their intriguing ancestors, and the secret techniques that had been passed down from father to son. Miguel had a way of speaking with a dramatic flair that caused his granddaughter's wide eyes to sparkle. His words made vibrant images in her mind. And whenever she so desired, she could always visualize, for example, the figure of their illustrious great, great, great—she couldn't count how many—great grandfather, known as James the Barber.

This James lived in England where his barbering practice flourished during the Elizabethan period. Miguel told her this many times. In those days—Miguel would repeat—men took as much pride in their hair as the women did. And Manuela would nod gravely at her grandfather's words, gazing soulfully into his eyes, urging him to continue. And Miguel would obligingly continue, squirming in his chair to get more comfortable—caramba she was getting so heavy! "They would spend whole days sitting in the barbershop listening to music and talking to one another." It was this illustrious James, Miguel told, who, by sheer dint of instinct, had developed to a perfection never before attained in all of barbering history a high awareness for shaping hair in such a way as to compliment the contours of his patrons' heads. "Which only we"—and here Miguel would whisper the family name, the real name into Manuela's ear—"Which only we ____'s know how to do so very well. This is the secret of our success, you see."

Her abuelito was fond of explaining, "Ordinarily the Elizabethan barber—bah, such barbarians—stiffened, starched, powdered, perfumed, waxed, and dyed the hair, usually a fashionable red—caramba! The hair was worn shoulder length and curled with hot irons—ach! But not our James, Manuela. No indeed. He never resorted to such unnatural, barbarous ways. He knew how to make the hair come alive!"

Manuela had loved hearing about James the Barber, of his perfect ability in juggling the daily intrigues, the daring and romantic exploits among the Elizabethan royalty. He was privy to all the scandals of the court, yet managed to remain aloof and not get sucked into the eddies and whirlwinds. That her abuelito was prone to fabrication and exaggeration, Manuela was completely unaware. She believed every word that steamed through his bushy moustache into her excited ear.

Those were magical nights, when she was too frightened to go to sleep, and her abuelito softened her nerves with wondrous tales. And not just stories about James the Barber. There were other significant ancestors as well over whom elaborate stories got whispered into her ear. Miguel's grandfather, for instance. Philippe, the personal barber to King Alonzo XIII of Spain. And Miguel's own father, who arrived in Mexico at the beginning of the revolutions, who cut the hair of Poncho Villa.

But of his personal career, Miguel spoke not one iota. He was too frightened to speak of the monstrous, the deadly mess he had gotten into. Unlike his ancestor, James the Barber, Miguel had failed the test of aloofness.

Not only had he put himself in danger, but his family as well, and as a result, his daughter and son-in-law were no longer. Thoughts of their decease haunted him ever after. All because of his stupidity, his timidity, his monumental ignorance.

On a chic, tiny side street in the district of Polanco—a short distance from Bosque de Chapultepec—in the heart of old Mexico City, Julio Valladares, the barber, established his now famous Julio's Salon de Belleza. The year was 1957. He had just turned 25.

Julio, like all his hair-cutting forebears, was an ambitious man. The choice of location for his place of business had been carefully considered. Polanco, one of the most popular shopping and residential areas among the high classes of Mexico City, was a beautiful place to go walking, shopping or to eat in. And for Julio, beauty stood at the center of his existence. He loved the beautiful, adored making men and women beautiful. What better place to execute his art but here in Polanco where beauty, and the money required in maintaining it, abounded.

And because he was such a great artist, such an exquisite connoisseur of fine taste, so consummately able in his admiration of a lady-client's new frock for instance, cooing and fussing in colorful expressions and subtle nuances; because he was such a jolly good listener, and as well equally adept at telling the latest good joke or juicy piece of gossip, it was not long before the rich and the famous came to him for their stylish needs.

Julio offered all the latest high fashion and celebrity hair trends. Whether his clients had straight hair, curly hair, fine hair, thick hair or even difficult hair . . . Julio, with his snipping scissors and his slender comb, knew how to make every one look beautiful.

Movie stars, politicians, wives of wealthy businessmen, and their husbands to boot, even well known gangsters—celebrities of all kinds flocked to Julio's Salon. It was truly a house of beauty. A marvelous perfumed oasis. A place of quite, exquisite elegance. Elegant black and silver framed mirrors; elegant smoky black marble tops, elegant soft leather seats. Swanky black and white décor accented by flaming colorful flower arrangements brought in fresh daily made the perfect setting in which Julio's genius flourished.

And Julio himself was a marvel to anyone's admiring eye. He was tall, but not towering, slender, but not emaciated. He had gorgeous blue eyes, a Spaniard's noble head, with black wavy hair and a vivid jaw line. His broad smile and strong, even teeth completed the picture of one who could look quite fierce if so inclined. But Julio had not an angry bone in his body. His was an innate happy disposition. He enjoyed life to the utmost. He believed in goodness and beauty. Beauty most of all.

From early times, Polanco was the district where the Jewish community settled, and still today a great part of the community is Jewish. Although himself not of Jewish descent, Julio Valladares admired, even revered the ancient culture of the Jews. To him they were a mysterious and romantic bunch, perhaps even more emotional than his own people, which is saying quite a bit. Emotion and Beauty were just about synonymous in his mind.

And so it was no surprise to anyone with any powers of observation to see Julio thunderstruck when she, the Jewess who was to become his beloved wife, entered the salon one cheerless, rainy day. It was the month of October, only a few days after Julio's thirtieth birthday.

For all his successes as the premier hair stylist in all of Mexico City, two most important parts were missing from his life. One being his ambition in becoming, like his forefathers, the personal barber to the highest-ranking person of the country, in this case the President of Mexico, and the other being his desire for a loving wife.

Los Pinos, the official residence of the President of Mexico, stood only a twenty-minute walk from Julio's Salon of Beauty. Julio knew this for a fact. How many times had he walked through the Chapultepec Gardens and past Los Pinos, looking up at the window above the second story balcony, the room he believed to be the private chambers of El Presidente?

And always, after pausing for a moment to reflect, interrupting his weekly stroll through the park—his exercise for good health, he always proclaimed—Julio would patiently sigh and repeat to himself: '*Someday…someday, I will be called…*'

As for the other emptiness in his life, Julio remained even more patient. Of all the women who flounced before him, not one had managed to capture his brilliant imagination. Yes, they were charming in various, subtle and not-so-subtle ways; yes they were elegant, even beautiful—after all, hadn't he had his influence in that regard? And yes, many were intelligent, and even sweet, although many were blusterous and foolish. And of course he had had some engaging moments of passion with some of these ladies. But none had touched his heart; none had pierced him through and through.

Patiently, he waited. Just as he waited for his telephone to ring with El Presidente's call. He knew. Someday, it would happen.

And then…that rainy Friday, October of 1962.

The salon was buzzing with activity. The weekend was at hand, everyone, apparently, in desperate need of coiffeur repair. Julio had by now expanded his business to include six hair styling stations, three shampooing stations, two manicure stations, and two private rooms where patrons enjoyed relaxing deep body massages and clay facial cleansing. Julio's Salon de Belleza was on its way to becoming a full-blown spa.

His staff, carefully chosen, the best of the city, assiduously performed their tasks—snipping, curling, shampooing—in what seemed like a symphonic performance under the direction of the great maestro himself who strolled from station to station with an air of supreme confidence in his artistic genius, suggesting here, correcting there, averting a near disaster in one moment, complimenting, approving at another moment, moving about with utmost grace and charm, a ray of contentment emanating from his handsome, good-natured face.

That rainy day, the door swung open. In she stepped. The chattering clientele, sophisticated men and women, sitting in the black leather chairs in the waiting area at the front of the salon—all in an instant ceased their banter to stare at the homely girl.

Rusty brown hair clung to her face; rainwater streamed off her damp thick tresses. Perhaps no more than an inch above five feet, she looked, in her brown colored damp coat, the startled creature with the doe's eyes, as if, from confusion, she had entered the wrong establishment. Her shapeless, wet clothing hung around her body. Like a living mockery, an affront to the elegance of this fashionable establishment, she stood there in her dumpy appearance, a clump of brown clay.

Astonished eyes fastened upon her. All human sound ceased. In a matter of seconds, the clicking swish of snipping scissors died away. All that remained was the softened strains of a Viennese waltz that came out of Julio's sound system as it wafted unhurriedly through perfumed air.

Julio approached this statue of a young woman. She stood in the middle of the waiting area, all eyes shining on her, alone and surrounded by a small puddle of water.

He had immediately divined her reason for entering his shop, and it was not simply to get in out of the downpour outside.

With head bent sideways and with piercing eyes, he examined her figure, gazed upon her unruly hair, squinted at her plain face, while holding his jaw in his fist, slowly circumnavigating this outlandish person, this challenge to his art, that had sauntered into his establishment.

"Yes," he thought, "I can make you beautiful."

But actually, before this appraisal had even entered his head, he knew beyond a shadow of a doubt that this was the woman of his destiny. His heart was pierced through and through. His soul sang for joy. He had no idea who she was; nor where she came from. He only knew he was in love with her, at first glance totally enamored. He knew not that she was the daughter of a prominent rabbi, leader of an orthodox synagogue, and the English teacher at the Jewish School.

He lifted her chin with a gentle touch and looked deeply into her eyes.

As if wakened from a deep sleep, she was moved to speak.

"I want to be made beautiful," she whispered, speaking so that no one but he might hear.

"You are already beautiful," he said. "More beautiful than you could ever imagine. Come, I will show you."

And with that he led her to his work station, where he sat her down in the most comfortable chair she had ever experienced, a very plush chair that swiveled and articulated backwards and forwards, up and down, like the chair in a dentist's clinic.

Her oldest brother was a dentist. She knew from many visits during her formative years all there was to know about dentist clinics. No—even though it looked like a dentist's chair this was not one of those where sitting in one meant having long needles thrust into your gums and high speed whining drills grinding into your jaws, nothing like that, not intrusive, not threatening, but quite the contrary. There was an elegant quality to this chair that offered her the sensation of feeling happy and full of anticipation.

A smock of some sort, made of a colorful print like an abstract painting, was draped around her clammy skirt and blouse. Julio had removed her coat. She squirmed a bit in the chair getting more comfortable when suddenly she felt the sensation of being swirled around and thrown back so that her head was over a porcelain sink.

"First, we shall shampoo. Relax and enjoy."

She heard him softly speak, then the sound of faucets gurgling. She felt warm water penetrating to her skin, and then probing fingers pushing and kneading her rust colored yarn-like tresses. Then the foaming fragrance of shampoo was applied.

Gentle fingers massaged her scalp. She had never felt such wonderful sensations before. Her mind emptied of all thought. It seemed as though she were floating out of her body. Again the faucets gurgled, and warm water rushed through her hair as the rinsing began. And this brought her back to the present moment. She heard his voice expressing words of endearment—not to her precisely, but to her hair. Yes, he was talking to her hair! How extraordinary, she thought.

She was then wheeled to another place, where a cone shaped thing came down over her head, and streams of warm air descended upon her scalp. The tingling sensation was like nothing she had ever felt before. At home, a thick Turkish towel for drying her heavy tresses had been her only known procedure. The hum of the electric motor sent her mind into a trance state. A reverie took hold of her and in a wink she found herself in a narrow, intimate meadow sitting against an ancient willow tree. Its low hanging branches dipped down into a small pond, as if bending to slake its thirst. She could feel the willow's sad and soft vibration awaken a similar mood within her own body. Everywhere she turned, vivid shades of soothing green filled her eyes. Her inner sense drifted toward a semi-sweet impression, a kind of greenish melancholic state.

But the mood lasted only briefly; for the humming motor brought her thoughts back from this inner contemplation to more immediate questions constellating around the impulse that had brought her to this worldly place of vanity in the first place.

She had had no real idea of what to expect when she responded to that sudden urge. She had been hurrying home from the Jewish school where she taught English, when a sudden downpour fell out of the sky drenching her. It had been a difficult day. The man, a colleague, upon whom she had set her yearnings, had again slipped through the day without once taking notice of her.

There had been a meeting of the small faculty. These were weekly affairs held in a casual manner in the teacher's lounge. Hannah (for that was our heroine's name) had successfully positioned herself in the room so that it would be easy for him whom she adored to cast a glance at her as he spoke—and he spoke a great deal at these meetings. In fact it would have been almost impossible for him not to make eye contact with her while turning his view from one side of the room to the other as was his wont while emphasizing the point he was making—and he had many points to bring to the table—eager as he was to gauge the impact of his words upon his colleagues, and, of course, on the headmaster who always sat in the most comfortable armchair situated by the fireplace.

But Palti (for that was the adored colleague's name) was a master at avoiding her simpering gaze. As his head turned in search of agreement among his not quite fully attentive colleagues, his vision seemed always to blur when it came to seeing her; he squinted at the precise moment, or looked down at his gesturing hands, or up at the ceiling as if all his brilliant ideas were suspended from the white painted surface in easy to read words, yet invisible to all the others.

No amount of words could possibly describe the frustration Hannah experienced from Palti's lack of attention. She could be walking toward him in the hallway on her way to the lounge or some other destination, with no one else nearby whom he could suddenly decide to address, that is to say: with no way to avoid her; she could be about to say something to him, when suddenly a coughing seizure would grip him, and he would turn away, facing another direction, seemingly as a cautionary measure showing civility by not wishing to contaminate the young lady who taught the English, quickly extracting a handkerchief from an inside pocket and rapidly striding past her, mumbling the while something about schools and the preponderance of sickly kids and germs this time of the year, which could be actually any time of the year.

It was the rehearsal of the day's frustration that filled her mind when the cloudburst caused something similar to burst forth from the core of her being. It was unmitigated anger that seized her. In the gray afternoon of rain-filled light she suddenly saw her unhappy state mirrored in the sheet of glass of the establishment where she found herself standing, attempting to garner some protection from the downpour under the hanging marquee. Amazing that she noticed, full of anger as she was—anger at her colleague, anger at herself, bitter consternation over her impossible agonizing plight, a miracle almost that she noticed the place was a beauty parlor. A moment of coincidence perhaps, she thought, that she should find herself outside such an establishment at precisely the moment when she had come to the realization she must do something about her appearance?

It was like a message from the gods.

Just then, Julio, or someone, removed the machine from her head, and her thoughts evaporated. Her ears were still buzzing. But she could hear him engaged in conversation with another person, most likely a fellow stylist. They were discussing her case.

In fact Julio was in the throws of creative self-enchantment. Beside him stood his most gifted assistant, Alonzo. But Julio, it must be admitted, persisted in thinking of his assistant as his apprentice. In any case it seemed so, for the younger man always listened intently to Julio's mini-lectures, which actually Alonzo tended to receive as mini-sermons.

"The client is like the canvas of an artist's painting," Julio intoned, "with a rough draft already etched out. As hair designers, it is up to us to make that painting shine! Our scissors are our brush, and our hair color is our paint. Look at the client as a beautiful painting and your work will follow."

His speech over, Julio began snipping.

To Hanna's ears, these words were as thrilling as a Shakespearian sonnet. She was willing, for the moment, to consider herself to be this 'beautiful painting' of which he had spoken. Her barber! How marvelous of him to see her this way!

And as chunks of her hair drifted to the floor, her mind's eye drifted among graceful hanging vines, an inner landscape set in a garden that looked very much like what she believed an Elizabethan garden would resemble. Young men and women in elegant costumes sauntered among the flowerbeds. In the background, a minstrel strummed his lute. Soft music filled her ears. It came from Julio's sound system. However, the English teacher believed it was coming from her treasured garden.

"You see, Alonzo," Julio lifted his client's tresses above her head and glanced at his assistant, "when we expose her face, we see that its shape is essentially round. This long, wooly confusion she wears for her hairstyle makes her entire head look fatter than it truly is. Look how it hangs around her face and shoulders like a tent!"

Hannah attempted to pay attention to the maestro's words, but her mind would not cooperate.

"We must snip judiciously," Julio continued. "We shorten it and thin it, make delicate layers of it, taking away a strand here and a strand there."

Snip, snip the scissors went, and soon Hannah's face became miraculously narrower. A cunning strand of a curl wound its way around her cheekbone on one side, while on the other the thinned tresses barely covered her ear. Julio had taken notice of her delicate, well proportioned ears and so caused one to be accented in the design of his painting.

Julio stood back to admire his work. Alonzo stepped forward and ran his index finger across Hannah's almost straight eyebrows.

"These ought to be shaped, don't you suppose?" Alonzo addressed the maestro.

"Absolutely not!" Julio looked offended. "We want her natural beauty to come forth, not make her into a frippery movie star!"

And now laughter surrounded the two men and the apron-clad English teacher. Julio's staff of hair stylists—and some of the clients as well—had gathered behind the trio to observe. It was as if they stood in a gallery above the operating table in a hospital surgery attempting to learn something from the procedure. Well, not exactly learn, they might have murmured. Rather they were overwhelmingly curious to see just precisely what Julio could make out of this frump of a woman. And they were laughing because the idea of movie star quality being associated with her was just plain ridiculous.

Except…except…by golly! When he had finished with her, her face now framed in a soft mantle of dark brown hair, she did indeed look like a movie star. Not the glitzy kind, but the soulful kind, the Ingrid Bergman kind.

And now Hannah was granted a look, she saw her reflection in the elegant black and silver framed mirror, and she was totally amazed. In fact, she failed to believe she was seeing herself.

"Who is that?" Was her immediate reaction. Astonished, she closed her eyes, then opened them and looked again. And this time, she noticed the barber standing behind her, a satisfied grin on his handsome face. Yes, she had taken notice that he had a handsome face.

Their eyes met in the mirror; and at that precise moment, all thoughts of anything else existing in the world went completely out of their minds. For her, Palti turned into a sour apparition. For him, his persistent aching patience evaporated. No single word could describe what they felt, except the word love. Their eyes seized upon each other with such ferocity of love, one could imagine it shattering the glass of the mirror into a million pieces.

And everyone present took instant notice. A hush—not the kind that had occurred an hour or so before—not that, but another hush descended upon the room. It was a hush of wonderment.

Love, beauty, goodness filled the hair salon. Had someone entered the establishment at that precise moment, the impression would have been not unlike that of standing before a tableau vivant, as though in a museum, in front of an early Renaissance painting—of the sacred kind, rich in color and fraught with meaning.

And so began the unusual, almost scandalous courtship of Julio Valladares the Catholic barber and Hannah Ytzhak the Jewish schoolteacher.

Rabbi Isaac Ytzhak shuffled hurriedly along the avenida on his way home. It was the evening of the Sabbath, and he was late. Discussions at the synagogue had lasted longer than expected, and sundown was rapidly approaching. He must light the menorah before dark.

With no woman in the house to perform the rites, since the death of his dear wife eight years before, he practiced the Sabbath ritual for himself and his daughter, who—now twenty-five and the English teacher at the school and free to do as she pleased—seldom arrived home early enough to participate.

Nowadays, Ytzhak, the widower, lit his Sabbath candles alone, ate his Sabbath meal at the big oak dinning table alone, his tiny yarmulke almost hidden by his snow white bushy head of hair, his Prayer Shawl always slipping off his worn-down rounded shoulders.

The rain had ceased, but there were puddles to side step. Ytzhak hopped from one foot to the other as nimbly as a child. For all his years—he was sixty-seven and three months (he took pleasure in bragging about his age)—this roly-poly man, in height about as tall as a small bookcase, still retained an athletic pleasure of movement. He had been a vigorous sportsman in his youth, those days, so long ago, back in Kiev before the Stalin purge. Twenty-seven years old when he immigrated to the New World in 1930, Mexico was the only place of choice. The United States by 1924 had curtailed the flow of Russian Jewry into its Promised Land.

Ytzhak arrived in Mexico City penniless, alone, without family, and without even a vague notion he was destined to become a rabbi. His inclination had always leaned toward revolution. His father had been a Bolshevik. When the God-fire grabbed him by the throat, he was as surprised as anyone.

But that fiery incident was long ago. In his advanced years, Ytzhak maintained that nothing could surprise him anymore. God had thrown him all the surprises any man could dream up.

This would have been his belief, until now. For on this rainy Friday afternoon, an uncanny incident was about to take place.

The Rabbi was a familiar figure on the avenida. At least twice daily he bobbed past all the smart shops and boutiques, going to and fro from his flat to the synagogue, hardly aware of the glamour these establishments represented. The stylish ladies and gentlemen, on their part, took as little notice of the Rabbi as he of them.

However today, Ytzhak, jumping over a rather large puddle, found himself staring straight into the entranceway of one of those modish clothing stores he so fervently abhorred. Stylish dress to him constituted the height of frivolity.

He stood there balanced on his toes, riveted. What absorbed him so intently was the fact that he found himself staring at a young woman who appeared to be someone he felt he ought to know.

She had just stepped out of the shop in question facing the Rabbi, who happened to be her father. She bounced out of the shop, arm-in-arm with a young man who held in his free hand a shiny red shopping bag stuffed with a number of packages. They were laughing over some witty statement one or the other had just uttered. It was plainly obvious; they were enjoying each other's company.

With the agility of youth, they jostled themselves around the edge of the puddle, passing the old man without any notice of who he was. Ytzhak, on his part, shook his head in bewilderment. He felt certain he ought to know who these people were. The young lady looked vaguely familiar; however, he just couldn't quite match her appearance with anyone in his memory.

Shaking his head and muttering to himself, he let his puzzled thoughts fade, remembering instead the lateness of the hour and his Sabbath duties, and he rushed on.

The precise moment when it suddenly dawned on him that the woman he had seen coming out of that unbelievably absurd establishment dressed in an equally unbelievably frivolous costume was indeed his daughter is difficult to pinpoint. It could have been when he began the climb up the three flights of steps to his flat, or a short time thereafter.

In any case, in the shadowy light of the stairwell, somewhere between the first and third landing, could be heard the bellowing roar of an injured being. Some kind of animal had let loose the primal voice of agony. Isaac Ytzhak clung to the banister, rocking his body as though he were wailing before the ancient wall in Jerusalem. And here he remained for a long time—longer than he should have, for outside the building, night had descended, and in pious homes throughout Polanco candles were already blazing.

That night, he stayed awake in his library waiting for her to come home. But she never came home. He fell asleep, slumped in his reading chair. Ytzhak's assistant rabbi had to conduct the Friday evening services. And the same occurred on Saturday, and in the week to follow.

Hannah stayed with Julio that night. That night, she realized her sensuality. The door to the unknown had opened, and she found it an immensely absorbing exploration into the mystery of the flesh. Julio's ardor enflamed her own. There was no question: They were a perfect match. And not in the physical sense alone. Julio spoke of his love and his passion with the words of a poet. She soon grew to adore his charming mannerisms, his cheerful acceptance of life in all its most ordinary expressions. She loved the way he ran his fingers through his hair when he became excited over a particular theme he was giving speech to. And above all, she loved the way he caressed her—not possessively, but with a courteous and gentle ardor, acknowledging, as it were, her independent value, while at the same time laying claim to their interdependence.

She recognized that he hadn't thought out these distinctions with his intellect, as she, the schoolteacher and intellectual, had. His demonstration of love came from pure instinct, a high level of intuition at work. She was only beginning to know her own capacities in this aspect of her life. The sudden impulse to enter Julio's beauty parlor represented her first infant steps into the blurred territory of intuitive action.

And the consequences of her action dismayed her not the least. The very first day she attended her classes after her physical transformation, she was firmly and not too politely dismissed from her post. The school in fact was in an uproar. It was agreed by everyone, she had turned herself into a floozy. Look at the outrageous clothing she was wearing! And her hair! What in the world had possessed her to have that done to her hair?

Only one of her colleagues took notice of her new appearance with any sort of pleasure. It was Palti. In fact, Palti covertly ogled her with a lascivious intensity he had never felt before—for anyone. Was this the woman who had been stalking him all these months? It was unbelievable, but incredibly true. And now he wondered what might he do to gain her attention. She had walked right past him without so much as a glance. A tornado began to swirl in his psyche.

But her scandalous behavior did not end there.

Hannah had entered her school, as usual, at 8:30 in the morning, and by 10:00 she was out the door, all her personal possessions stuffed into a shopping bag. She went home and told her father she was moving out.

"What have you done to yourself?" He screamed.

"Poppa, its time we woke up to the fact that I am a woman, not a child."

"Never mind, this 'we'. What would your blessed mother be thinking seeing you like this? Oh, Lord of our fathers, what's to become of our house?"

He broke into tears, fell into his reading chair and began to pray. Hannah, stepped closer, kissed her father on the top of his head, while admiring the wavy similarity of his crown to that of her dear beloved.

"Dear Poppa," she murmured, "Momma would understand. I'm certain, she would be proud of me."

Then quietly she went to her room and gathered the very few things she would need for her new life.

Rabbi Ytzhak for his part remained seated in his library a lonely figure of crushed paternal confidence. He assumed she had left home in favor of a whorehouse.

Old Miguel sat at the water's edge on his customary rock cooling his feet in the roiling sea. This rock, smoothed out from eons of tidal wear, he regarded as his very own throne. Warm summer evenings like this, brought him here where he would face the west, and absorb himself in the colors of the setting sun. And as the sky turned to deep purple, he would cast his eyes into the foam that swirled around his ankles. He believed he could see his Hannah's face bubbling up from the foam. Shortly after arriving in this shantytown, Hannah's voice came to him in a dream. It seemed she was telling him to seek her image in the swirling water at twilight. He trusted the inspiration, and ever since, when conditions were right, he availed himself. He took his dream to heart and made out of it a ritual that became his principle source of solace.

This was the hour for his communion. And tonight, he needed her more than ever. Oh, how much he needed her advice, always so sensible, always so penetrating. He saw himself a young man again, kneeling before the old Rabbi, asking for the hand of his daughter, Hannah.

"Listen, Hannah. See the irony of my life? I am like the old Rabbi now. In the same predicament. One of these days, and probably sooner than we might expect, a young scamp of a fisherman's son will be stealing away our only granddaughter. Probably wouldn't even have the decency to ask for her hand. At least I had the guts to face the old Rabbi. I looked him straight in the eye and asked permission to marry the woman who dwells in my soul. But what good did it do us? You know how it all turned out.

"So, Hannah, what to do?" He pleaded. "Tell me what I can do. Give me the advice I need."

He listened to the gurgling water, straining to hear the words of wisdom he so yearned for. In their years together he had always respected her family decisions. Even the rift she had caused between her and her father, a gloomy cloud infecting their otherwise satisfying life, he respected. And all these years later, it still amazed him how the fireworks had exploded. A case of bad timing.

The timing had been all wrong. When had the timing ever been right, he wondered? Julio and Hannah had decided they need never get married. As far as they were concerned, their wedding had already taken place in heaven. No civil or religious authority could possibly sanctify or enhance the sublime connection they themselves had already made complete. But then, when it became evident that Hannah was pregnant, they decided differently. The baby ought to be viewed as a legitimate offspring. They would go public.

So, Julio presented himself before the Rabbi to ask for his daughter's hand in marriage. For this purpose, he donned his most conservative suit of clothing, armed with the knowledge from his beloved Hannah of the Rabbi's aversion to any kind of flamboyant sartorial expression. It so happened that the night Julio presented himself fell on the eve of the most holy of all Jewish holidays, Yom Kippur. In but a few hours at sundown the holy ritual would commence. Hannah's hopes were high that the spirit of the holy day might soften the old man. It had been her idea for Julio to make his appeal at this particular time. For, she reasoned, wasn't this the most holy of days in the Jewish year, the time of atonement, of reconciliation between man and God? And wouldn't her poppa deem it crucial that he first reconcile with his daughter before approaching his God?

Hannah had seen little of her father since the night she moved out. The few times their paths had crossed on the busy avenida proved disastrous occasions for her. She'd spot him skipping along in his customary fashion, and she'd rush up to him and try to hug him. But her father would push her aside and continue on his way, as if she were some kind of an insect fluttering around his neck. He refused to acknowledge her, let alone speak. She yearned to find a way that would lead to reconciliation. And when she discovered she was pregnant, she saw this as a hopeful sign.

A full year had gone by since Hannah had stumbled into Julio's House of Beauty. And during the intervening time, the famous Salon de Belleza had undergone a formidable transformation. Hannah's influence was evident everywhere. The stylish lounge where patrons sat and chatted while waiting their turn at the altar of beauty had become a lively center for artistic discussion, a veritable literary salon.

Now, not only the customary assortment of stylish ladies, manicured businessmen and politicians, along with the handful of dandified gangsters and movie stars, there appeared as well a daily assortment of shaggy poets, writers of all sorts, intellectuals, musicians and artists, most of whom demurred tonsorial blandishment. They came to bathe in another kind of beauty dispensed by the enchanting lady of the house.

It pleased Julio no end to observe how his Hannah had flourished into a remarkable and vivacious presence. Her body had become sumptuous. It was the mark of her sensuality, the flame he had ignited in her. Her voice had grown to a richness he was incapable of describing. Her throaty laughter rippled through the salon as if a breeze had set silver chimes in motion. Her parted lips, the color of warm amber, curved into a winning smile, settled on no one in particular, yet whoever caught sight of it believed themselves to be the center of her absorption. Indiscriminately, she cast her light.

Each day, Hannah presented the group with a topic to discuss, a poet's work to ponder, an artist's new exhibition, or a recent musical performance, or the latest art film to examine and tear apart or otherwise find praise for. Themes varied from the latest political and social theories of the day to the major world issues. No aspect of human life was omitted.

And most exciting about this interaction among the frequenters to Julio's Salon de Belleza was the way the two groups, those who had always come for the sake of their coiffeur and those new people to partake of spiritual and intellectual enjoyments, even though their worlds were so utterly different, nevertheless, the way they respected each other and combined their two utterly different areas of discussion, mixing the mundane with the arcane, low brow stuff with high brow stuff, all due to the charming manner in which his incomparable Hannah wove such colorful threads into a tapestry no other time and place had ever experienced—it was precisely this incredible performance of hers that provided Julio his supreme happiness.

And who would have guessed how easily that frumpy, reticent English schoolteacher could have possibly blossomed into this creature of sheer elegance and magnetism. Hannah herself often pondered this question. Somehow, she sensed this gift, which God had bequeathed to her, had lain dormant like a seed within her perhaps from eons ago in some other lifetime dormant until now when suddenly the numinous passion of love had descended upon her. Somehow, she sensed, this new Hannah was the result of her fervor over Julio, and his passion for her.

And of course to Julio it all seemed so natural. From the very first moment his eyes fell upon her, he knew a genius lived inside her, a gem of the highest order ready to be unveiled.

And of course, the good Rabbi Ytzhak was totally unaware of this uncanny transformation that had taken place in his daughter's life. It would have required a long stretch of his imagination to believe such a thing could possibly have happened, even more so than the switch that had happened to him from Ukraine revolutionary to Mexican rabbi, from rebel to servant, from raging idiot against the tormentors of humanity to comforter of mankind and beseecher of God. And even if the Rabbi had been aware, could he have seen how she had followed his genetic lead? Could he have fathomed a genetic likeness to himself in this variant performance of his daughter's? Most likely not.

The Rabbi's booming voice echoed in Miguel's eardrums, even now so many decades later.

"My daughter? My daughter? You wish to marry my daughter?"

His face had gone livid.

The Rabbi had been sitting in his library surrounded by the countless tomes that nourished his soul. He sat upright in his reading chair, his mind in repose preparing himself for the coming holy service that was his to conduct. Out of the corner of his eye he spotted Julio entering the room, a bouquet of flowers in his outstretched hand.

For an instant Ytzhak failed to recognize him.

"Yes?" He asked, somewhat bewildered. What had brought this young man into his study? Indeed, who in the world was he?

Julio stepped forward, nervous to the point of trembling.

"Sir," he stammered, "I've come to ask the hand of your daughter in marriage."

Immediately Ytzhak leaped to his feet. Now he knew! This brazen person! Now he knew who he was! A tangle of blood vessels, as if attacked by winds of fury spread across his forehead.

Ytzhak, with menacing rage sprang forward toward the young man. "My daughter? My daughter?" Miguel heard the words once more all these years later. "What have you done with my daughter? Marry? Marry? You wish to marry my daughter? You must be out of your mind!"

The Rabbi's short, chubby body danced around the bewildered Julio, his tightened fists explosively punching the air, his eyes beseeching an invisible presence hidden somewhere in the ceiling of the room as he repeated his angry words over and over, "Where is my daughter? What have you done to my daughter? You must be mad…" like the whining prayer of an absentminded supplicant.

Julio didn't know what to say. He had been prepared for resistance, yes. But such a venomous reaction he had not anticipated. The Rabbi's words tore into the glow in his heart, made ashes of his love.

It had been Hannah's idea. She had reckoned this a propitious time for approaching the old man. For was it not the eve of the Day of Atonement, when all pious souls petitioned forgiveness of their sins? She thought she had made a clever move. In her mind, and in her heart of hearts she felt it was the Rabbi who had sinned against her. Here was the perfect moment, the eve of Yom Kippur, for him to gain atonement. So she had thought.

Hannah listened to her father's ranting, her fists tightening with every word he spoke. Neither her beloved nor her father were aware of her hidden presence. As if on a Renaissance stage where the heroine waits breathlessly behind the proverbial arras the outcome of her fate, Hannah secretly stood behind the half-ajar door to the Rabbi's study, her ears burning. She heard his unrestrained anger, felt his rage. His sonorous voice penetrated the sternum of her chest sending a cascade of nerve signals into her brain, into her heart and from thence throughout her body. His rage amplified her own. Anger filled her heart. Why was he so adamant? Why so intolerant? For the first time in her life, she realized the truth about him. He was as much a bigot as those who had made him and his people the object of their scorn and, yes, their hate and persecution. Silently, she listened to his tirade barely able to contain herself.

"What right do you have to come into my house? Who do you think you are that you steal my daughter? Snatch her from her rightful place, turn her into a prostitute!"

Ytzhak's fierce screaming caused his eyes to bulge beyond belief.

"You are not of our blood! How dare you, I say! How dare you bring your foul blood into our midst! You unclean one!"

And Julio, never before accused like this, Julio, who prided himself on his punctilious cleanliness, until this moment as if a supplicant before the old Rabbi, now stiffened, every inch of his body a bright red. He had no idea the Rabbi was referring to the outer skin of his penis.

"Take your filth away from me. Leave my house. Now…Now…before I rip out your rotten liver with my bare hands, gouge out with my thumbs your putrid eyes. You are no more than a hateful beast in my presence. Go, I say! Go!"

Julio could not think how to respond to these verbal threats, so theatrical, so impossible to believe. Not one accustomed to boasting about himself, nevertheless, holding a reasonably fair opinion regarding his self-worth, Julio stood before the Rabbi neither crushed nor chagrined. Rather, he was completely dumbfounded. This interview that he had entered into with warm anticipation, prepared as he was to bare his heart, his soul, in making his modest request for the Rabbi's consent, this interview had turned into a nightmare. He felt his honorable intentions poisoned.

Having hoped for some kind of reconciliation between father and daughter offered in the form of the Rabbi's blessing, Julio now felt his love for Hannah tarnished. Ytzhak had tarnished their togetherness with his bitter words. And while the Rabbi raged invoking lightening and thunder on his head, Julio felt only sadness.

He sensed, by these accusations, something like remorse was expected of him. But he felt no remorse for his actions. His love for the Rabbi's daughter was as pure and unbounded as he assumed the Rabbi's love for his God. Why now tarnish it in this manner? He felt no anger toward the old man. Only sadness. Sadness for all three of them. For the Rabbi's pain. For Hannah's disappointment. For his own distress. This love they had, this exalted state they had discovered through each other, had done nothing but bring pain and a raging heart to the old man. Julio was now overcome by his awareness of the Rabbi's pain. Never had he ever wanted to be the cause of anyone else's unhappiness.

Julio stood and allowed the old man to scream at him. But Hannah was not so inclined. No, she could no longer bear hearing her beloved so furiously maligned. She leaped into the room – just like her father, her body churning with her own brand of anger, forcing herself between the two men.

"Stop!" She screamed in her father's face, on her tiptoes, her fingernails digging into his chest.

"You are no longer my father! I denounce you! Julio and I will be married with or without your blessing. Yes! We will be married."

The Rabbi raised his hand about to slap her cheek. He couldn't speak; he was totally outraged by his daughter's unexpected attack. A further outrage! His world was exploding in his face.

"Julio and I will be married," she repeated, "and in a church. Yes, a church! A priest…yes, a priest will sanctify our marriage. You…you could have performed our marriage…you could have sanctified our coming child…yes, we are having a child…and we will raise this child a Catholic. A Catholic, I tell you."

She spoke into his face with a calm, yet menacing demeanor fully intending to follow through with this cold-blooded threat.

Ytzhak's hand, frozen above his head, turned into a fist. And with it he began pounding his chest in the manner of thousands of years of mourners.

My God…my God…how you have deserted me…how has this come to me? My house disgraced…O God…on this night, this holiest of nights…how can I come to you?

Her words had turned him to utter despair.

Hannah focused on her fiancé, her face carved in stone She pulled his arm.

"Come, Julio. We shall go home."

But Julio was reluctant to move. He felt a need to comfort the Rabbi. He felt Yitzhak's pain as if it were his own.

"We cannot leave him like this," he murmured.

"Come," she repeated softly. "Come." And took his hand.

Slowly, Julio turned toward her, a catch in his throat, a tear sliding from the corner of his eye. Torn between his love for her and his sorrow for her father, he felt suspended as if over a precipice.

"This is so sad. I am so saddened. I wish…"

"There's nothing you could wish, nothing you could possibly say. We can only leave him now. Let him think about what he has done. Come."

So he relented even though he sensed that later he would regret abandoning the Rabbi, and together, their arms entangled, they slowly left the room, leaving the old man to his emptiness, a crumbled figure slouched in his reading chair, his vacant eyes staring at nothing, his fist pressing against an exhausted chest.

Miguel bent forward and stared into the blackening sea, the memory of that night vivid before his mind's eye. Hannah had insisted it was the Rabbi who had sinned, sinned against her and her lover, sinned against their child. Year in and year out, as time went on, she could never let go of this notion. Yet, despite his respect for her, he had quietly felt remorse, even more so particularly now, facing as he was his own dilemma over Manuela. A second blow coming from a different source.

"There is such a thing as fate, Hannah," Miguel spoke into the swirling sea. "If only you had not been so stubborn. If only we had made an attempt at compromise…you didn't have to become a Catholic, you know…"

Miguel's words caught his breath. Never before had he accused her like this. The words had been spoken in sorrow. They had come up from the depths. His own circumstance, he realized, had stimulated this deep sense of sorrow that really, now that he was willing to look at it, had never been fully laid to rest. And now it filled him anew. Filled him with remorse. The Rabbi. He had made the Rabbi suffer. And suddenly it came to him. Suddenly he snatched at a thought and made it the center of his mind. That night in the Rabbi's study—that night had marked the beginning of his time of exile. Yes, it suddenly became crystal clear to him. He and the Rabbi had formed an unholy secret alliance. Both had entered, together, the realm of nowhere.

The revelation burned in his head. It caused him to plunge his hands into the sea. With his cupped palms he poured the salty water over his head, felt it spill off his skull, stinging his eyes. His tongue tasted the salt, tasted the anguish of his memory. For years it had lain in the marrow of his bones; but tonight it gushed into his bloodstream like lava from a volcano.

This was the taste of all those years following the birth of their daughter, years of denying the cloud that had fallen into their lives, years of moodiness that came over Hannah sometime for days on end…moodiness mixed with stubbornness.

After that fateful night in the Rabbi's home, life in the Salon de Belleza took on a curious turn. Perhaps more from despair than real enthusiasm, Hannah threw herself into what became known among her new crowd of female friends as the "movement." Her vigorous intellectual interests shifted from social, artistic, and political inquiry to matters more relevant to an expectant mother. The curious turn took the form of a new cast of characters making their appearance. The shabby poets and longhaired musicians drifted away when mothers with their infants, and pregnant ladies with interior bodies in various stages of embryonic development began showing up. They came with pillows and blankets, plunked themselves down crossed legged on the floor, spreading diaper bags, bassinettes, feeding devices, exposing their nursing breasts while producing other kinds of paraphernalia, including lunch bags of food for themselves to devour.

    Meanwhile, the regular patrons pretended to ignore the show at their feet as much as they might. They felt perhaps as though a strange kind of circus, or maybe even a cult had invaded their house of beauty. Some of his best clients complained to Julio more than once. Others made excuses and canceled their regular appointments. The maestro was torn between devotion to his patrons and devotion to his wife. As always, he was eager to serve her, championing her causes. But when business took a downward turn, he became distraught, struggled within himself whether he should put his foot down. Things were getting out of hand. A new nursing program was being introduced to Mexico. The International Leche League had just come to town; and Hannah was playing a principal role in its outreach. Julio's Salon de Belleza was quickly becoming the league's headquarters.

    Miguel, looking back on those days, tasted his bitterness. Between Hannah's despondency over the rift with her father and her overexcited pursuits with Leche League affairs—it was now clearly evident to him how much her mood swings had damaged his own emotional states. Until now, he had had no idea how much his equilibrium had depended on hers, his happiness intertwined with hers. All of a sudden, at this late time of his life, he was seeing more clearly. He had once been an upbeat guy. How had he lost his cheerfulness? His mind shifted to his grave concerns for Manuela. And this thought added fuel to his burning despair.

Miguel stood in the swirling sea, tasting his bitterness. Something was erupting in him. By now, the night had become pitch black. With no moon to light up the sky, and the stars obscured by cloudbanks, Miguel felt totally alone. Not a soul was awake in the shantytown; all the people had long since gone to sleep. Alone in the silence, he stood by his rocky throne, the incoming tide rising to his knees, a bent and tired old geezer, unwilling to rouse himself and go home to bed, alone in the grip of his thoughts.

Gradually however, a strange sound came as if from inside his ears. A startling sound…he became aware…he thought he heard…a faint groan rise…slowly rising and increasing in volume.

And suddenly he realized the groan was coming from within him. Somewhere down in the depths of his groin, the groaning sound began a strange and haunting ascent, as though from a vast distance a thousand hounds were growling. The sound rose into his belly, and then burst into his heart. His throat trembled from its growing force, until finally it leaped into the darkness filling the sky like a powerful explosion. A groan that pierced the atmosphere, that sprang out into the stars; a noise so great one minor galaxy could not contain it. The groan vibrated across eons of time and space bouncing from galaxy to galaxy reaching into the farthest crannies of the universe, reverberating like the thunder of the ancient gods. Miguel roared anguish into the sea.

He stood, braced against the current, his feet glued to the sandy bottom, and filled the night with rage. Lights went on in many of the shanties. Toddlers, startled out of their sleep, cried, and begged to climb into bed with their mamas. Pappas with widened eyes stepped into the darkened night holding their underwear with one hand and lighted lamps with the other prepared to face the worse. What manner of beast had descended upon them?

Manuela leaped from her bed. Her naked body shivered from the cool night. She had heard the uncanny noise. Instinctively, she knew the sound had come from her grandfather. Quickly, she threw on some clothes, covering herself with a pair of jeans and a loose blouse. Javier was fast asleep in the same bed. She roused him with a shove of her bare foot. He stirred noisily, saw her frantic face and understood immediately that something was wrong. They had been lovers for some time, sneaking into her bed right under the old man's nose.

"What is that noise?" He whispered concerned they had been discovered.

"It's abuelito. He is not well. I can tell. We must find him. Hurry."

Manuela threw his clothes at him, and then put on her sandals. Javier dressed in a jiffy. The noise, she sensed, had come from the direction of the seashore. Without a moments hesitation she ran to the beach. She knew of abuelito's favorite spot. Certain she would find him there, she ran toward the rocky shoreline where the mountain marched into the sea. Javier followed nimble as a wily ram.

The sound of waves striking against the rocks dampened the splashing of their footsteps in the water. Miguel was completely unaware of their approach. A wind had come up. That and the cold water had chilled him to the bone. Yet his head burned with fever. He hugged himself, shivering uncontrollably. Then he felt her arms embracing his cold shoulders.

"Abuelito, you must come home. You will die out here. You are very sick. I can tell."

She pulled at him. He stood immovable. His feet had turned to stone buried in the sandy bottom. Manuela motioned to Javier to help her move the old man. Javier readily saw that it was hopeless to try and budge him. Instead, he lifted Miguel out of the water with a single swoop, as if he were pulling with his bare hands a massive Dorado out of the sea.

Miguel was too weak to offer any resistance. In fact he hardly registered the fact that it was Javier who was carrying him home. Manuela and Javier, holding up the old man between them, hurried up the slope of the beach, ignoring the looks of the village people who had come out to deal with the monster that had come into their world out of the night.

They lay him in his bed, covered his shaking body with blankets. Manuela dashed into the kitchen and fired up the stove to make hot water. Javier came to her his face full of concern. She had lit a candle. In the semi darkness of the room, their bodies loomed like shadows. Manuela bent forward into the cave of the stove and blew on the slight flame that weakly licked the kindling. She pointed to the water bucket.

"Get more water," she commanded. "We will need lots of water."

Javier nodded and dashed off with the bucket. One of the shantytown's two communal spigots was only a few steps away.

Lordy, lordy, he thought, *what will the barber think when he discovers we have been sleeping together right under his nose?*

This was a concern the teenager need not have bothered his head over. When he returned with the bucket of water, he heard the old man groaning. Manuela was with him. The barber was carrying on, as if delirious. The fire in the stove had gone out. Javier busied himself with re-igniting it. His thoughts ranged over the events of the night. They had made such beautiful love together. Their bodies, tightly entwined, were like a religious symbol to him. He loved this girl with all his heart. Nothing should come between them. The old barber dare not make a fuss. He, Javier, would just not allow it. Somehow, he thought, he would convince the old man to accept the fact that he and Manuela would be together until the end of eternity. But then, he thought, the old man seemed to be deathly ill. The issue of his granddaughter's love affair faded before this more pressing concern. Once more he saw himself plucking the old man out of the sea, and marveled at his feelings. He felt warmth toward the old man. He felt like a hero saving a drowning man. Not afraid of him as he had been these last eight years of his life, afraid of his penetrating eyes. He felt now more like a son to a father.

Manuela entered the kitchen.

"Quick, make the hot water. His body is icy cold, but his head is burning. I don't know what to do."

She was beside herself with worry.

"Go get Consuelo Diaz," he shot back. "She will know what to do."

"Of course! I didn't think of her. What's wrong with me?"

"Nothing is wrong with you," he spoke fervently. "Hurry, go get her!"

Manuela ran over to Consuelo's house and began to pound on the door. She didn't get a chance. Consuelo opened the door the same instant, as if by some uncanny means she knew what was happening. She held a basket in her hand. It contained her potions. She knew what to do. After all, wasn't she the curandera of the shantytown?

They raced back to the barber's house. Immediately, the curandera took charge. In her role as the healer her skinny, bony body seemed to transform itself into a more gentle, a softer presence, as if someone else had taken up residence inside her. She clucked and murmured secret magic words the while she surveyed the old man with her inner eye.

Manuela and Javier peered over her shoulder. She turned abruptly.

"Make hot water," she commanded.

"The water is on the stove," Javier spoke. The fire he had made was crackling and roaring inside the iron walls. There would soon be plenty of hot water. Javier stepped into the kitchen feeling proud of himself for being ready to assist the curandera. He held her in great respect, as did everyone else in this god-forsaken shantytown.

The hot towels brought to her, Consuelo shooed the children out of the room. Then she stripped off the blanket that was covering Miguel's suffering body, and removed his pants. For a brief moment, she eyed his now withered manliness that once had been Hannah's pride and joy. Consuelo observed him with a slight pang. Yes, she thought, here was once a man to be reckoned with! Then, with a sigh, remembering her duties, she swung into action, wrapped his legs with the hot towels, covered him again with the blanket, and began chanting in a soft pitched humming voice her magic incantations.

Consuelo, along with everyone else in the shantytown, often wondered about the barber's origins. He had always been a tight-mouthed cuss. There was not one item about his past available. Gossip and speculation relied solely on the strangeness of his actions since coming to the shantytown. He seemed so out of place among these simple fisher folk. Everyone had a different notion about who he really had been in the larger world. Rumors abounded. Often, he was eyed with suspicion. But, on the other hand, everyone appreciated his service as the town's barber. These crude looking fishing men, no matter how rough and coarse they may appear, their hair, pampered by the accomplished stylist, became like a crown of glory. The women sucked in their breath when their men returned from Miguel's barbershop. Their eyes sparkled; sap rose in their loins, prospects of magical nights flooded their minds. And Consuelo was no exception. Despite her bony torso and cold piercing stare, a heart of passion lived inside her skinny frame. Her love for her husband was such, she was willing to spend the money for a haircut at least twice a month!

The curandera bent over her patient. In his delirious state, he had begun a garbled struggle with some invisible force or mysterious being. Her ears perked up. She listened intently. Excitement made her body twitch. At long last she just might discover something juicy about this old geezer.

He was arguing with someone. This much she could make out; a phrase he repeated over and over. She wasn't certain if he was saying, *Don't do this anymore!* Or if perhaps he was saying, *Stop doing this to me! Stop, stop doing, doing.*

With only this small bit of evidence to go one, Consuelo convinced herself an evil spirit had entered the innocent man's psyche and was about to take possession of his soul. And for once there would be no argument from the barber. He had suddenly stopped mumbling and had fallen into a kind of trance as if he were entering a coma state. In fact, the curandera was certain, he was slipping into a coma.

Miguel had always prided himself for being the modern man, clucked his tongue at Consuelo's superstitious practices, called her beliefs nothing more than medieval gobbledygook, irrational, and without substance. How many times had he mocked her as she dashed past his barbershop toting her basket of magic on her way to an ailing villager? According to her, he carried on like a mad dog, scrambling out of his house, rebuking her sacred work. And she, with her jaws clamped, determined not to argue, would scurry past his door, her nose in the air.

But of course the curandera exaggerated. Neighbors, who paid close attention to feuds in general, and this feud in particular, could honestly count only two, possibly three, occasions when Miguel had actually accosted Consuelo outside his barbershop to give her a piece of his mind—and for good reason, some of the neighbors were inclined to admit. For wasn't it true that her influence over Miguel's granddaughter had grown considerably in recent years?

There had been times—earlier, not too long after Miguel and Manuela had arrived—when more polite disputation went on between them. In her innocence, Consuelo believed he only wanted to be set straight. She had thought it her duty as the healer of the community to help him become sane.

There wasn't a soul in the shantytown that distrusted her healing. Without a priest or a church, she was their sole spiritual resource. The people relied upon her—everyone, even Manuela—every one except Miguel. But such was no longer the case. Now it was quite evident that he needed her. Now she would show him how irrational her work was!

And when Manuela with Javier trailing behind, came into the room to see what the healer was up to, the curandera made her pronouncement.

"We must pray to the Santos Cuates," she spat out fiercely. "Your grandpapa is very ill. A bad spirit is battling for his soul. He is going off-balance."

The children fell to their knees. Consuelo, for her part, rummaged through her basket and produced a small brazier already smoldering with burning coals. Over these, she added some herbs, and sprinkled it with Perfume de Siete Machos. Then, while she wafted the smoke rising from the coals with repeated puffs that enveloped Miguel's head, she chanted secret prayers. While he, his mind in another place, continued to groan and mumble in his delirium, unaware that he was in the throes of a possession and a possible healing. Consuelo turned to the children and shooed them out of the room.

Manuela was nowhere feeling safe and calm. More had to be done; and when morning came, she roused Javier from his sleep asking him if he knew how to drive a car. Only two individuals in the whole of the shantytown owned an automobile, Miguel being one, the old pickup that he and Manuela had arrived in ten years before. Javier, having never driven a car, nevertheless claimed he was willing to try. Manuela peeked into her grandfather's room. Consuelo, still there sitting on the floor with her back resting on the bed, looked up, roused from a slight stupor.

"Any change?" Manuela whispered.

Consuelo shook her head, weary, but still working her magic. With no change in her grandfather's condition, Manuela became doubly convinced she needed to seek additional help. She could think of only one person whom she felt she could trust. The professor—the catedrático. The two teenagers took off in the pickup, lurching and swerving down the rutted dirt road that leads to San Carlos and then on to Guaymas. She remembered the way to the professor's house, yet still they made a few wrong turns, somehow managing the traffic without accident.

Escudero was about to leave his house for the library when there came a knock. His face went blank for a moment when he opened the door. And then he remembered who Manuela was.

"Please, can you help me?"

"What is the matter young lady?"

He was surprised to see her, to say the least, her face screwed up with fright, and the boy beside her looking the same. Although much of Javier's fear was the residue of all he had gone through making the pickup go where it was supposed to go.

Quickly, Manuela began outlining the facts. Before she could get more than a few sentences out, Escudero interrupted and pulled them inside. Her total agitation compelled him.

"Sit down," he commanded.

Dutifully, they sat down.

"Now, start from the beginning. What do you say has happened to your grandfather? Speak slowly, if you please."

Manuela filled him in with all that she knew, which wasn't very much. She had noticed her grandfather acting strangely in the last several weeks. She felt that his mood had something to do about her, but she really couldn't know for certain. And when he had glanced at the educational book she was reading (Manuela left out the fact that it's subject matter had to do with sex education) he positively had a fit; she thought he was going to have a stroke, or something. And then last night: how they found him alone in the sea—groaning and mumbling about things she couldn't understand, things that she was certain had nothing to do with her. She spoke about how they had to carry him home, how he was cold and hot and delirious, how they got the curandera next door to come have a look, how he seemed to be in some kind of mental state, possessed Consuelo called it.

"Oh, this is terrible!" Escudero grew as agitated as the girl. He was surprised by the power of his empathy for his friend. An old man himself, he could sense how maybe his own end might come at a time when he was alone in his house. And he was always alone in his house.

"But what can I do to help you? I am no physician, I don't know anything about the physical body."

"Yes, I know." Manuela bit her lip. Javier nodded. "You are the only one who knows anything about my abuelito. I know he has confided much in you."

"Not that much, my dear."

"But maybe enough…"

"What are you getting at?"

"He never speaks about his past…only to you has he revealed things. I know this because sometimes he talks in his sleep and your name enters the mixture of words—even when he mumbles my grandmother's name, Hannah, whom I never knew…"

"Get to the point, girl."

"I am getting to the point!"

Manuela, in this momentary irritation at their inability to easily communicate, was reminded of her grandfather's futile attempt at getting instruction for her from the professor, a man so difficult to understand.

"The point is this…please come with us and have a look at abuelito. At least do that. But more…you are a professor…you know how to find out things…maybe there is something you can find out…about abuelito's past…something that is causing this possession…some piece of fact that could remove the evil spirit that is gripping him…"

"What you ask is beyond me, Manuela. I have no ideas about possessions and evil spirits. This is not my field of expertise…"

"But you are a sociologist. You know about people. You know how to find out things."

"You mean, hunt down facts that might bring some rational sense into this psychic mess Miguel has gotten into?"

"Yes…yes…facts…"

Manuela was about to jump out of her skin, she was becoming so inflamed with this idea of capturing a fact or two that would eject the evil spirit from her grandfather's troubled psyche. Sometimes a simple fact, she was certain of it, a simple fact can make all the difference in the world.

"Okay. Possibly, I could do some exploratory investigation into Miguel's past. But to do this kind of research I need something to go on, a lead of some sort. All I know about his past centers around a period of a long time ago when he lived in Mexico City, and a little about when he came here with you years ago. I know the facts about how he and his wife got together. He spoke at length about their fairytale romance, about his difficulty with her father, a

Rabbi, and yes, a bit about Hannah and her involvement with the Leche League. And only vaguely did he hint at why you and he were living here in Sonora—he used the word hiding, but from what and why he didn't say. These are all the facts I know."

And now, just simply the prospect of conducting a real and most serious investigation began to intrigue the retired scholar. His creative juices were stirring.

The aged sociologist took courage from this youngster's ardent insistence. His knowledge of clinical psychology was slight indeed. Nevertheless, he convinced himself he knew a sufficient amount to postulate a theory. Miguel, in making him his confidant, must have been working up to pouring forth a revelation of some sort, a revelation about himself that needed airing. He must have repressed something that was eating him from the inside out. But time had caught up with him. The repression had turned into some kind of abscess, which now gave the appearance of a possession.

"So, now I must be a psychic surgeon and remove the cause of his possession."

"Yes!" Manuela jumped up, relieved to see him getting the point.

"Señor." Javier spoke for the first time.

"Yes?"

"Señor, do you know how to drive a car?"

And so it came about, that the retired professor of sociology, Eugenio Escudero—EhEh as he called himself—after driving the three of them to San Carlos and thence over the bumpy, dusty unpaved road to the shantytown with no name, after casting his eyes on the old barber Miguel Guzman lying in his bed in a comatose state, after bursting into tears when consulting with the curandera, Consuelo Diaz, and after a quick bite of delicious, mouth-watering tamales, prepared by the neighbor Maria Roybal whose whimpering, staggering presence seemed to fill the entire abode—after all this preliminary activity, EhEh booked a flight to Mexico City the following day, having at last, due to the intensity of the situation, squeezed out a single piece of information lodged in his vast mental bank, a remembered fact from one of the many facts Miguel had produced, and this one in a recent conversation, the name of one Elena Navarro purported to having been a close friend of the deceased Hannah Valladares.

He left in haste, toting a small carry-on bag stuffed with enough clothes to last a week, and a briefcase that had seen better days filled with blank legal pads. While in flight, EhEh made the first entries into what he termed his "Journal", intending to keep a complete record of his investigation, which he labeled simply:

"Notes on the Guzman Case."

Until a few weeks ago my principal informant regarding the story of his life had been Miguel Guzman himself. Unfortunately, he cannot proceed any further in this capacity simply because he has gone comatose. Not only has he passed out; he is in a deep coma. Temporarily in the good hands of Consuelo the curandera, the search for facts must begin in earnest. My mission is to uncover the truth regarding this man's life, the cause or causes that have brought him to his present misfortunate state.

I shall begin at the beginning, which is to say, how my involvement in this case came about. The barber Miguel came to my home in Guaymas several years ago. As is my habit, I frequent the local library. And this is where we came upon each other. Rather, I should say, it was Miguel who came upon me. I had never actually taken notice of him. He, on the other hand—as he later informed me—had become keenly aware of my presence in the reading room. Both of us being creatures of habit, it seemed we visited the bibliotheca at the same time of the day, although he came once or twice in a month while I came every day. For some unknown reason, he convinced himself that I was a sympathetic person and would be willing to hear his story. How he discovered my domicile, he omitted telling me.

I remember the night he knocked on my door. It was an unusually cool evening for Guaymas in February, perhaps as low as forty degrees. I had to find an old sweater to ward off the chill. Opening the door, I was surprised to see a stranger, yet someone whom I vaguely recognized. He quickly revealed to me our library connection and asked to speak with me about a matter of supreme importance [his words].

He was distraught to say the least. The major concern in his life, he told me, had to do with his granddaughter. He was her sole physical, mental, emotional support, he told me, in charge of her well being, and she was growing up too fast in his opinion and needed some academic guidance. In short, he wished that I become her tutor, if you will. But of course this preoccupation was merely the symptom of a more deeply disturbed nature. This much I discerned at the first meeting we had, the way he nervously twisted his hands and faltered in his speech. Although the tutoring of the granddaughter never really developed, Miguel continued coming to see me over the next several months, divulging to me some of the features of his life. In addition to his statements, I have endeavored to fill in gaps through a single brief interview just a day ago with the granddaughter, Manuela, whom I must say is a quite sensible young lady and easy to converse with, open to speaking her heart; contrary to Miguel who stammers easily whenever he is pressed for a detail, as if he mistrusts his memory, or is reluctant to reveal certain items of interest to me, even though he insists he has much to get off his chest. And Manuela's boyfriend, the charming Javier, like his sweetheart, finds it easy to confess to me what is in his heart. All these folks of the shanty fishing town outside San Carlos fascinate me, particularly the curandera Consuelo who, it seems, finds me sufficiently simpatico—enough at least to allow her to reveal to me a glimpse at one or two of her arcane secrets, secrets having to do with the way she constructs specific incantations. My mission is to bring back information that will assist her in this process of incantation making. My inclination to learn principles new to me of life has been whetted by this woman.

Since having been "discovered" by Miguel as it were, I have begun to see myself as the chronicler of his life, and once I have completed this present investigation, I have a feeling I will want to launch a full blown investigation into the lives of the "fisher folk," who live in the village, an unnamed shantytown to be exact, where Miguel resides. The sociologist in me is eager to dive in, as it were.

At first, I am tempted to write my findings using the fictional form as if I were writing a novel, having labored from time to time under the illusion of possessing the talent for bringing an artistic work into existence. The pop music of today has stimulated this inclination in me. But for now I shall resist making a discourse over this topic. Sometimes I have wondered why I chose sociology in opposition to literature as my academic focus. The two disciplines, after all, hold similar qualities in their approach to getting at something—something that we might call the "truth," written in small letters. I hesitate to write this word in capital letters, as if it were pointing to some hidden reality lying behind the mundane exterior of things. Yet there is something beyond what we ordinarily can see with our eyes, a "truth" we long to touch—a something that somehow gives us reason to embrace life with at least a modicum of affection, if not unmitigated joy.

And this brings me back to Miguel; for it would seem that in his early years as the proprietor of his house of beauty, he lived his life with the fullness of joy completely at his disposal. I find it extraordinary that he could have maintained in those days such a state of happiness, optimism if you will, despite all the misery in this sad world of ours, so openly available to any pair of eyes; while now, in contrast, his personal experience has brought him into the fold, as it were, and he now can be counted as one among those of us who know to what extent human misery abounds. Thus it is my intention to discover how this transformation came about. In this issue, I may find a way to help ease the poor man. He would do well to cultivate a stoic affection for life.

I am at the present moment (actually as I write this) in flight to Mexico City. I have the name of a possible informant, a woman called Elena Navarro. It was she who had introduced Hannah to the Leche League movement. This, I discovered from Miguel in an interview that occurred sometime, I'm not sure exactly when, before he succumbed to his grief. Manuela came to me with the news of his bout with a devil of some sort. She came the very first chance she had. She believed I might be able to help the situation. Her simple, straightforward manner touches me. I went with her to see the old barber. If I were a religious man I would pray for his recovery. As it is, I am laying my trust in Consuelo's abilities. It is my hope that if anyone can bring him out of his coma, it is she. If all goes well, I shall bring back a vital piece of information sufficient to help her bring him around. Now that circumstances have forced me to embark on this research, I must confess to experiencing a sensation of exhilaration, a somewhat ironic contrast in regard to Miguel's situation. It is as if the coma he suffers, due apparently to a deep-seated grief, has brought me out of my state of retired torpor.

The Guaymas Airport lies off of Garcia Lopez Boulevard, quite some distance from my home, therefore exposing me to the hazard of a maniacal taxi driver. My taxi got me to the airport just in time to make the 3 pm flight out of Guaymas, fifteen hours of zigzagging travel time, two stops, one in Phoenix, then to

Guadalajara, arriving in Mexico City 8 am next day, an exhausted retired sociologist questioning his sanity, wondering if he were not better off having remained at home, snoozing in his garden hammock, a turned over book settled on his chest, the birds in the cool of his tiny patio chirping away madly.

The next day, after a long rest in a modest hotel from morning to morning, intermixed with light meals, I set off in search of Elena Navarro, restored and raring to go. My question, whether she would still be alive, was happily answered through the efficacy of the telephone directory. She was in the book!

    Another crazy taxi ride got me to her apartment building. It's been years since I've visited Mexico City. Tumultuous cities never have appealed to me. The ride to Elena Navarro's had me wondering how long I would be in this noisy, choking city. So I was amazed to find the interior of her apartment twelve stories above the ground a sanctuary of serenity. Soft light filled her sitting room; a red parrot in an ornate cage greeted me with a single 'Hola.'

    A handsome dame with a pleasant face beneath a pure white swept-up pile of hair, what used to be called a bouffant, easily a grandmother, yet with a youthful bearing, outfitted in a baby-blue jogging suite, invited me to 'settle' [her word] into the comfortable easy chair next to a table laden with a tea service, cakes and finger sandwiches. She had already quickly positioned herself in a chaise lounge after letting me into her apartment even before her invitation for me to sit had finished crossing her lips. An empty cup of tea sat on a table beside her. Evidently, she had been sipping tea for some time before my arrival. "Would you mind pouring more tea for me?" So I jumped up before even having a chance to get 'settled' and did the honors. Was this a ploy, I wondered?

    As I stepped across the room, I noticed a faint hum off the street coming in from open French doors leading to a small balcony. Everything about her impressed me with the feeling of one who enjoyed [perhaps 'required' hits the mark more precisely?] an uncluttered, civilized life: comfortable modern furniture, comfortable modern art sensibly spaced on the walls, no glut of family photos, nothing garish [except the parrot, of course], and positively no bric-a-brac on shelves or in corner glass cases—so unsettling to the nerves, you know. She lived alone, she told me, for once in her life enjoying peace and quiet.

Elena, in the midst of her serenity didn't seem the right match as a friend to Hanna's volatile style. "Ah yes, Hannah. Of course I remember her, we were buddies for years." A dreamy look came into her eyes. And so began an engrossing afternoon. Sipping herbal tea that I could not recognize, munching on the lightest carrot cake imaginable, taking notes in between bites and gulps, a few hours quickly slipped by. Elena gushed information. It was as if she had been waiting for me, waiting patiently for years perhaps [I wondered about that], at last finally able to unburden a weight—or so it seemed. Elena spoke for two solid hours.

First they had become Leche League buddies "That was in 1964; we both had baby girls." Following their immersion into breastfeeding [her phrase], they moved on to broader women's issues. "We read Simone de Beauvoir in the 'barber shop'." And together ["A team…we were a team"] they joined the "movement without hesitation." Keeping to the pattern set by women all over the world, they took to the streets: marches, demonstrations, incessant meetings—babies on hips—long nights spent in writing speeches, essays, manifestos, the whole gamut of political action including neglect of spouses, family life a shambles, all this activism culminating in The Global Women's Project of 1975 that met in Mexico City. President Echiverria had invited the UN to hold the conference in his city. "We stood outside the building and protested. Betty Friedan was there, along with some three hundred of us. Hard core feminists we were. Echiverria wasn't going to pull a fast one on us. No indeed!" [After all this time, she can still get thoroughly agitated. I could now see where her temperament converged with Hannah's.] Their children, Dora [hers] and Rachael [Hannah's], dragged along to events, grew up crawling on filthy floors [Elena punctuated this remark by pointing to the spotless white carpeting of her sitting room] eating 'refreshment' food set out on long tables. The kids played between the grown-ups' feet with no idea they were being deprived. Later, when the girls were about eight, Rachael grew weary of this 'traipsing around' and took to staying with her dad at the "barber shop." And of course, her Dora just had to string along and stay with Hannah's Rachael hanging out at the beauty parlor. A wistful look crossed Elena's face.

And Julio? How did he fit in with this women's movement existence? Did you know him well? "Oh, him." Her eyes went up to heaven. "Sure, I knew him. Always gave me dirty looks. Know what I mean? Called me the instigator, with a capitol 'I'. Screamed bloody murder at me whenever he had the chance. Can you imagine?" This was all she had to say on the subject of Julio, at least for now. She was growing tired, ready to see me go. I realized I would require a second interview with Elena if I were to get more out of her. With this new picture of Julio emerging in my mind, I took my leave, expressing admiration once more for the quality of her 'refreshments'. We agreed to stay in touch, as the saying goes. And to demonstrate our willingness, we shook hands at the door. A smile, even, crossed her lips.

So, Julio had put up more resistance to his precious Hannah than he had given me to believe—or so it seemed. As I descended in the elevator, I pondered about what else Julio might have misled me. Elena had mentioned Hannah's visits to the Rabbi, and this piece of information intrigued me immensely. The rift between daughter and father had not been as clean as Julio imagined evidently. And how right that is! Everywhere we look in nature, we see the jagged lines. Just look at gorges, canyons—the two sides facing each other showing where they once had been attached, as if longing to reunite once again. And isn't this the fate each one of us endures, this inordinate longing to reunite—with what or with whom, difficult for us humans to pinpoint?

It took several visits to various synagogues before I found the right one. A young man led me into another kind of sanctuary, a dusty Rabbi's office, where a quiet gloom descended from two small windows high above. Another ancient one, the present Rabbi, greeted me with a squinty inquiring smile, his lips hardly visible beneath a massive gray beard. "Isaac Ytzhak." Another pair of eyes looking to heaven. "How could I forget him? He was my mentor, my beloved spiritual father." Then, looking at me, "What about him?" The Rabbi spoke with a clicking sound. Badly fitting false teeth, I imagined.

"He was an authentic God-man, if you ask me, not many like him in this world, believe me, a modern Moses, God spoke to him, and he spoke to God—Directly!" Eyes barreling into me, index finger pointing to the rafters. "—Nothing, nothing stood between them. His daughter? Oh yes, I remember her. She was something, I tell you. A schoolteacher gone amok. Married a católico. Had the gall to come here…here, I tell you. More than once, carrying an infant in her arms. Isaac would tremble. With rage? Oh no, nothing like that. He wasn't that kind. No, he would tremble and cry out to God, like Job he'd cry out. I couldn't bear it, so sad to see him tormented, wanting to take the little girl-child to his breast, unwilling to touch the catholic body. Oh, how he suffered his torment. A man full of love for his God, full of love for his demented child. And his grandchild…named after his precious wife…too much, I tell you…what shameful brazenness. The name? A chance for reconciliation, I suppose, calling the child Rachael. Could she really believe it would be that simple with a man of God such as poor Isaac? But I ask you, what are you trying to get at with these questions?"

When I explained Miguel's predicament [in this instance I used the name Julio], the Rabbi ordered me out. That name was never to be spoken in this house of worship.

His name is Rabbi Mendel. I wrote it down in my notes. He too, I have no doubt I will want to interview once more, if at all possible. More questions fill my mind regarding this daughter/father—father/daughter feud. Given Hannah is a full scale dyed-in-the wool feminist, there yet lingers a thread of dependence on the male figure it seems, some kind of need for recognition, despite the finality of her threat that night, as Julio [Miguel] had described to me, when he asked the old Rabbi for Hannah's hand in marriage, and upon being refused, she had burst into the Rabbi's study [neither of the men had been aware that she was hiding behind the door, listening] and declared she would become a catholic and raise their child a catholic—evidently an empty threat. It would seem that this 'dependency' was very much alive in her, yet not transferred, apparently, to her beloved Julio. Indeed, it would seem she led Julio around by the nose. But am I jumping to simple-minded conclusions too quickly? Notice, I put down, 'it would seem' more than once as a way of guarding myself against jumping too easily.

I go to sleep, mulling over Miguel's history. It suddenly occurs to me that I have yet to tackle the primary question, namely, the ostensible mystery. Why is he hiding in that obscure fishing village on the seacoast of Cortez? Talk about jumping. I've jumped right into the psychological mystery. My attempt to understand Hannah has sidetracked me. Well, I remind myself, turning over in my bed, what else did I have to go on, but the one contact, Elena Navarro?

Luckily for me, I had the impulse [a sixth sense?] to give to that young man at the synagogue the name of the hotel where I was staying. When I returned from breakfast the next morning [For my morning desayuno I found a wonderful little cantina down the street where I devoured a platter of huevos rancheros with two cups of the most divine coffee I've had in ages.] the clerk at the desk waived me over and handed me a slip of yellow memo paper with a name and telephone number written on it in a nearly indecipherable hand. It was a name I didn't recognize, but I phoned nevertheless. Michael Melcher, it said, who turned out to be the young man who met me at the door at the synagogue, the sexton he explained [shamus he called it, and then told me what that term meant]. He wished to have audience [his word] with me as soon as possible. I didn't know why he was whispering.

This time, the taxi driver wasn't racing fast enough.

Melcher was waiting for me. No sooner did I knock on the heavy door of the synagogue, it sprang open, and he popped out onto the sidewalk. In the bright morning sunlight, I could see he was older than I had gauged the previous time, more in the mid-forties range. He shoved a piece of paper into my hand. "Call this number. She wants to speak to you." The 'she' turned out to be his mother; this much I got out of him before he disappeared into the depths of the gray interior. The name Sadie Melcher and a telephone number were written on the tiny bit of paper.

A few minutes later, we were conversing over the phone. When can I see her? Right away. I am to meet her at a nearby plaza in ten minutes. She gives me exact directions, how to get to the plaza from my present location, on what side of the central fountain to sit, on which green bench. I hurry over; find the bench, sit and wait, in the meantime admiring the ornate colonial fountain. Pigeons approach me with expectant coos, their tiny heads bobbing as they totter about. The time stretches long past the ten minutes. I look at my watch impatiently; almost twenty minutes have gone by.

And then I see her coming. She is tiny and bent over, a cane in her fist. "Oi, Vai," her cheerful voice preceding her, "I forget how long it takes me these days. In my head I am still a young girl. No, don't get up Señor." She plunks down with a sigh, then opens a bag and proceeds to feed peanuts to her feathery friends. "I didn't expect you to be as old as the rest of us. We are at the edge of the plank, yes?" Not yet! I say to myself, and pull out my notebook. She has a twinkle in her eye.

Where do I come in? She squints up at me. We were girl friends as well as cousins, grew up together, lived in the same building. We are the same age, Hannah and I. Only, of course, she is long gone, died in '89, only fifty-four years old, God bless her. Too much tension she had. They call it stress these days. How many times I told her? Find peace, I said. She was all the time busy fighting something. This cause, that cause. You know what I mean? The barber? Yes, of course I knew him, not directly mind you. I only knew him through Hannah. We spoke of him when she came to the Rabbi's. Let me explain. After Tanta Rachael died, it was Hanna's turn to take care of her father; and after she left, under that cloud she made, I took over the task. Nevertheless, Hannah would come over more times than she needed to just in order to instruct me. How to make the kreplach just the way he liked; how to keep kosher for him, the great Rabbi, just the way he like it, a special way. She thought I was tamafate—you know, how you say it, feebleminded? Isaac was maybe a great God-man in his house of worship, but in his home he was like all the other chauvinist men. I don't include you, Señor. You are not a Jew. I don't know what your kind are like. I only know Jewish men close up. I'm not one to presume. From the way she talked about the barber I think your kind are different. [I assure her my kind are not any different; but, yes, there are exceptions; we cannot generalize. I waive my finger. I consider myself an exception, I tell her. And she nods in agreement.] How did Hannah talk about the barber? Well, to begin with, she talked about how sweet and caring, how tender he was in bed—this, it seemed was very important to her. Later, she changed her tune. But this was after the baby came, when she got caught up in the 'movement'—this is what she called her shenanigans. We were not such good friends then. I disapproved. But you know? A lifetime of growing up together, like sisters, you know, differences and disapprovals make no real division between sisters. We still talked our secrets to each other. And mine came out of my mouth just as much as hers. My man, after Michael came, turned into a drunk. It wasn't long before we split. I kicked him out. Anyway, I didn't need financial support. The Rabbi paid me well. And later, the Rabbi made me the most handsome gift ever. That was when he took Michael into the shul, made him the shamus. This he did for us just before he died. But don't think Michael's is a highfalutin position. Most of the time he works as the janitor. He only ushers during services. Hannah's secrets? Well, after the baby, she grew disenchanted with her Julio. She'd come over more frequently than she needed to, just to see how her father was doing. You know, she worried over him a great deal. She'd come over, and I'd spot her in the library softly caressing the Rabbi's armchair as if he were sitting in it. She'd ask all sorts of questions. Was he eating well? Was he getting enough rest? What about Julio? Oh, him. She told me with an exasperated tone—and more than once, mind you—how much he cared about beauty, about wanting to make everyone happy. According to her, this is all he ever thought about. According to her, he was the type who can't stand talking about serious matters, can't give a moment's thought about the masses being short-changed—that sort of thing. He was just too superficial for her taste, she said. I'm not sure what she meant by 'superficial.' A good provider, one who didn't get drunk all the time, sloppy and belligerent, who loved his daughter Rachael with a fervent passion—that was 'superficial?' So what kept them together? That's a good question. I often asked her the same question. It was the love making, she said. She was a very sensual woman. Their bodies were hot for each other, she said. It was a passion and a curse, she said. She would get very emotional when she talked about their passionate nights. This is something I cannot easily fathom. My man was a brute, pure and simple. I have no firsthand knowledge of tenderness. [She sighs.] I loved her, you know. And I miss her. There was a great deal about her that was lovable. Like what? Oh, her laughter for one thing. When she laughed it was like chimes ringing. [Julio said the very same thing.] He did? Well, we have something in common after all. And now I have to go. Time to make the Rabbi's lunch. [My dear, the Rabbi has been dead these many years. Why else do you have to go?] It's Michael I mean…I make his lunch now. Michael was smart I think never to have gotten married. Another time? I don't see why not. Oh yes, please call me. I have more to tell you.

And off she goes, hobbling along, scattering the last of her peanuts to her cooing feathered friends.

Naturally, it is impossible for me to resist observing a similarity emerging out of the lives of these two "sisters," the one flamboyantly beautiful, acutely intellectual, the avid feminist activist, twitching to 'wrestle the men to their knees' [Elena], yet lusty as all get out; the other 'sister' unassuming, subservient, ground down, literally bent over like a hairpin, 'exhausted from domestic enslavement' [Sadie's statement, by her own admission], presumably not lusty in the slightest. Both, despite their different performances, arriving at the same summation regarding the male instinct: 'chauvinist pigs.' Even the mild Julio, whose only ambition is to bring beauty and happiness to the world, cannot escape the contemptuous view these women embrace concerning the men. What is to be made of this? Will this be Manuela's destiny as well? Will she come to regard the charming young Javier similarly? And if such is the case, what's to become of our world? Will there be no progress? Is there no hope of moving beyond this implacable distance between the genders? Are the two types, almost separate species you might say, condemned to offer themselves only for the sake of biological obedience? This is a question never before explored by this sociologist whose own experience derives from a life-long adherence to bachelorhood. My eyes are being opened.

Only now has it occurred to me that you, Manuela will be (or might be) the most likely person (perhaps only person) to read these notes. Clearly, it behooves me to bear in mind your tender sensibilities. Recording the raw material—the style and mannerisms of my informants' statements—is about all I am able to accomplish in this hasty investigation. Insufficient time precludes anything that might resemble a formal report, adequately polished and in language more presentable for your consumption. What gets put down here will have to do. Yet, on the other hand, in seeking the truth, nothing must be omitted; each informant's statement must be considered a salient piece in this gathering mosaic. Embedded in all this muck is that kernel of truth, which yet remains to be uncovered in its powerful and bright lucidity capable of releasing poor Miguel from his anguish.

    Nevertheless, Manuela, (my young friend) I am totally conscious of what may be considered your meager hodgepodge of ideas regarding your grandmother. After all, she died several years before you were born. The picture you have, based solely on what your mom (herself no longer in this world—your grandfather knows the cause of her death and your father's, but he refused to tell me, and now he can't, at least for the present time—and I wonder, do you know the cause of their deaths?) allowed herself to tell you (completely unbeknownst to me, as you know—I expect you will fill me in, yes?) or that which your grandfather has divulged (which appears on the surface, in respect to these reports I am collecting, more a fantasy than an accurate representation)—their reports alone form the basis of how you picture her life, which is doubtless very different from the way these informants view grandma Hannah. You will, I hope, acknowledge how acutely aware I am. I can truly guess in no uncertain terms how these statements of her contemporaries (these facts, if you will, if indeed they can be designated as such) may be difficult for you to comprehend, may seem more like distortions. I encourage you to brace yourself. We must bravely proceed on this journey of discovery. You agree?

A phone conversation the next morning with Elena Navarro initiated by the informant.
    "Señor EhEh, buenos días."
    "Buenos días."
    "I couldn't sleep last night, thinking about you."
    "Oh…is that so?"
    "Believe me, it's not what you are imagining."
    "Madam, I am imagining nothing. And what were these thoughts, may I ask, that kept you awake through the night?"
    "To be quite frank, I worried over what your opinion of me might be…"
    "Oh…is that so?"
    "Señor EhEh, are you being provocative?"
    "Elena—may I call you Elena?"
    "Please do."

"It is much too early in the morning for me to even presume I am capable of provocation. I am an old man, and a bachelor to boot. So please, can we get on with what is giving you such concern?"

"It's that I never offered to take you to the barber shop. How uncharitable of me!"

"You mean Julio's Salon de Belleza? It still exists? But this is incredible!"

"Yes, it still exists. I'm not making this up. I'll come in an hour and take you there."

"Elena, that won't be necessary. Just give me the address."

"You'd never find it, my dear. The place is squirreled away in a tiny side street off the avenida, hardly noticeable to anyone but old-timers and aficionados. The entrance to the street appears like a narrow courtyard of a boutique. It was once simply a passageway, a short cut to another avenue. Besides, I've made an appointment for myself, haven't been there in years. It will be fun having my hair done at my old haunt."

"All right. I believe you. Yes, please come get me."

My attempt to sound calm actually caused my voice to quiver. I hung up wondering if she thought some kind of ardor was building up in me. I just had time to wash, get dressed, and grab a quick breakfast of coffee and fresh baked rolls—two with butter—at the cantina.

I waited outside the hotel, full of anticipation. Not in my wildest dreams could I have imagined this astonishing development. The Salon de Belleza still in existence! She arrived at precisely the time we had agreed upon. A huge, black Mercedes pulled up with her at the wheel. She was dressed in some kind of fluffy thing, and wore sunglasses, looking like an aged movie queen. And I? What was I looking like, I wondered?

While she steered through the traffic, she unburdened herself of personal history, again giving me the impression of someone having waited a long time for just such an opportunity. A widow, her husband, a wealthy industrialist who doted on her, never once complaining about her activities in the 'movement,' left her with a pile. She had no idea there was so much money in his possession. "I mean a lot!"

Did it concern her that she had so much wealth, ease and comfort, while her sisters struggled to make ends meet and still devote time to the cause? "Not in the least. And don't think me cold hearted. I gave plenty to this one and that one. And you know, we all have our special place. It's not up to one person to bring order to the world." I had to agree. Not since Jesus has there been a bona fide savior. "And beside, that was a long time ago. I left the 'movement' shortly after Edgar died."

Elena found a parking garage. There was no time for further explanations regarding this latest revelation. Why Elena had walked away from the 'movement' and under what circumstances, would have to wait. From the parking garage, a short walk took us to the epicenter of my avid quest.

As soon as we entered, a pleasant looking man, dressed casually in gray flannel slacks and a white knitted polo shirt, came forward and greeted us in a rather suave manner.

"Hola, Elena! Nice to see you! How many years has it been? But you look the same! Beautiful as ever."

"Hola, Alonzo. And you haven't forgotten how to flatter. And for once I'm on time for my appointment, thanks to my friend here."

"Si, on time. Wonders will never cease!"

He turned to me, and Elena formally introduced Alonzo Morales, whom I judged to be in his sixties. He had an athletic appearance, and presented himself in an open and friendly manner. As we shook hands, he glanced at the top of my head, noticing my baldpate and shaggy sides. Following this quick assessment, he looked into my eyes with a twinkle of his own. Obviously, he wasn't counting on adding me to his clientele. Here was a man, I felt, with whom I could easily become jolly. I had no misgivings anticipating a fruitful interview. Alonzo, with a wave of his hand, invited me to a brief visual tour of his establishment. Yes, it was immediately apparent that he was the proprietor.

Even though the hour was early, the place buzzed with coiffeur activity. I watched as an attendant escorted Elena to one of those complicated affairs resembling a dentist's chair. She disappeared, so to speak, into another world.

Alonzo gently took me by the elbow and steered me to a quiet nook. We sunk into two extraordinarily comfortable easy chairs made of the softest leather, so soft, a person just sank, sank and sank into it, causing me to wonder if I would ever be able to get out of it. An attendant came and placed a steaming coffee service for the two of us upon a black marble-top table at my side. Alonzo spoke while she poured.

"You wish to know something of me?"

"You have a sixth sense, Señor Alonzo."

"Not at all," he laughed. "Elena told me of your mission to make inquiries, but about what she did not say. Although, I must admit, she sounded quite mysterious, and so my appetite for juicy gossip has been stimulated."

He smiled. And so did I.

"So, what are we to talk about?"

When I spoke Julio's name, the man leaped from his chair as if he had been given an electric shock.

"Julio Valladares," he repeated in a hoarse whisper, slapping the palm of his hand against his forehead. Thoroughly agitated, he resumed sitting, but not relaxed as before, now on the edge of his seat, his torso bent forward leaning toward me.

"What about Julio? His name has not been mentioned since the massacre. We mourned for days, weeks, and then we just couldn't speak of him anymore, it was simply too painful to bring it up. His death was a great shock to all of us here at the salon, as you can imagine. We were all terribly distraught. I can't tell you how many tears were shed. I cried for days on end. My friend, my maestro, obliterated, gone from this earth, entirely."

Alonzo fell into silence apparently, from the look of sadness on his face, reliving those moments of mourning.

"You know something about the massacre?" He asked me.

I shook my head in the negative.

"I am taken totally by surprise hearing about this," I announced. "No one has mentioned this before."

"It's been ten years," he whispered hoarsely with a shake of his head.

When I assured him that Julio was very much alive, another shockwave passed through his body. Once again he leaped from his chair, and once again, in a hoarse whisper, he repeated my statement, "alive" but with a question mark in his voice, a completely incredulous question mark, I might add. Here was another of those persons who live out of their emotions. Such people have no control. Not enough for them to simply express their feelings by raising the eyebrows, or making a slight twist of the mouth. No, they have to register through paroxysms and convulsions, with contortions of the body, slapping of the forehead and other such dramatic explosions.

Again, he resumed sitting, waiting intently for explanations, droplets of salty emissions oozing out of the corner of his eyes. His emotional state touched me. Tears came to my eyes as well. Tears of joy and sadness, I might add, knowing I would be bringing bad news as well to his ears.

And so I quickly explained. Julio was alive, but alas not well, in fact deathly ill it would seem, under the care of an Indian woman, a curandera. No, I could not reveal where Julio was to be found. He must remain incognito at his present location, and for reasons that I myself did not know. Alonzo listened, his head tilted to one side as if, in this manner, he might glean something hidden inside my words. My mission, I told him, was to uncover a piece of information, something that may have occurred in Julio's life that is now buried, forgotten in the depths of his subconscious mind, which, once revealed might bring him out of his coma through magical incantations specially devised, that is to say, tailor-made by the healer Consuelo. Admittedly, the concepts behind these words were a bit more than the poor man could integrate into his mental system. I could tell by the look on his face.

"And now it's your turn to speak, Alonzo. What is this you mention about a massacre?"

A puzzled look came into his eyes. "But we were told that everyone had been killed." He paused.

"Continue, please. Who told you, everyone was killed? And whom do you mean by 'everyone'. Tell me everything you know." I spoke softly, gently, as if I were a counselor of some sort, urging him with professional probes.

And now it was my turn to be astonished. But I kept my calm, taking notes, writing as quickly as I could in order to put down the flood of words emitting from Alonzo's mouth—a non-stop outpouring, a diverse assemblage of subject matter, some of which, on the surface, seemed to have nothing to do with the issue of the massacre. It will take me hours to straighten out this messy discourse, I remember telling myself. As I wrote, part of my mind couldn't help asking: Was this the way Alonzo did his haircutting, in this hodgepodge fashion?

That strange day—it was March 21, 1994, thirteen years ago. It was a Monday. I clearly remember the date because it was the anniversary of my coming to the Salon, something Julio and I celebrated every year with a toast of Champaign in the back office, just him and me. We were compadres you know. Julio raced into the shop out of breath, a terrified look on his face. It was in the middle of the morning, just a half-hour before lunchtime. He whipped past everyone not saying a word, no greeting, nothing. Ordinarily, he greeted everyone personally, a smile here, a pat on the shoulder there, this was his way of sharing his happiness with our clientele, without exception. No, this time he made straight for the back room. I followed him into the office in time to see him stuffing papers into a briefcase. I watched him open the safe and take out a wad of cash. He turned to me and said, "From now on you are in charge." Gave me his big ring of keys, and ran out. Vanished…completely vanished, like a puff of smoke…right before my eyes. Never saw him again. Hannah was at the bottom of this. I felt certain about that. Oh, not directly, you know. By this time, she had been dead several years. But her presence was always around. She was always in his head. And ever since she died, he was not the same maestro who taught me everything I know. Such a powerful stylist. You have no idea how skilled an artist he was. To begin with, just look what he did for Hannah. You should have seen how she looked the day she walked into the shop. A mess, I tell you. And it was Hannah who turned his head. He was never the same after Hannah came into the picture. The massacre? It happened about five years after Julio vanished. In Los Angeles—actually Beverly Hills. At Rachael's Salon de Belleza. You don't know about Rachael's salon? Yes, she moved to Beverly Hills shortly after her mother died. Said she needed to strike out on her own. It was Hannah who kept a close watch on her, Hannah and that bitch Sadie, and after Hannah was out of the picture, Rachael made a run for it. But she actually didn't "strike out on her own." No sir. She took off with her cousin, the Russians. And they got married in Los Angeles. You don't know about the Russians? A branch of the family on her mother's side, the Rabbi's people. Came over from the old country the same time they all came. That was in the 30's I believe. A strange bunch those Russian Jews, the Zaslavskys. Gangsters. Every one of them turned to crime. Boris was his name. And his brother, a real shady character if ever there was one, Efim, they called him. All three high tailed it to U.S.A. Rachael? She learned everything from her father. Since she was about eight, she lived in the shop practically every minute of the day, except of course when she was at Sadie's. That was Hannah's cousin. Hannah dragged her over to Sadie's a few days every week, but most of the time Rachael went home with Julio after they had a meal in his favorite café down the alley. Rachael and another little girl named Dora—Elena's daughter come to think of it. They were pals; they both watched the hair cutters. Rachael especially watched Julio. She studied everything he did; in fact she eventually outdistanced Julio in many ways. You should see the way she could handle a pair of scissors. What a shame to be killed so young. The whole bunch massacred. Oh, how sad it makes me to speak of it. Even now, the pain is very much.

At this point, Alonzo dropped his eyes, his face grew somber, a gloomy look of mourning stole over him, a sharp contrast to the previous animated rush of words.

"Who told you everyone was killed?" I asked.

"The newspapers." He said, looking up. "The story was in all the newspapers, in some, the whole blasted story was on the front page. Come, I will show you."

The barber helped me out of the leather seat—it was like a one person sofa—and led me into the office, where he pulled open a drawer in a file cabinet and flipped through brown envelopes until he found the one containing the news clippings. He fanned them out on the office desk. I bent over to read.

The story—naturally—was presented in the most sensational manner imaginable. According to the report, the incident was apparently a planned assassination, taking place just moments before noontime. Only two individuals among the victims were actual customers. Julio's name was given the most prominence, obviously because of his Mexico City reputation. Witnesses claimed to have observed two men with hoods over their heads jumping out of an SUV in front of the salon, machine guns in their hands. They saw the two men partially entering the salon, standing just inside the door, blasting away with their guns, the noise was terrible, the sound of bullets ricocheting, screams coming from dying voices, the crash of glass shattering. The gunmen leaped back into the SUV, and the vehicle careened around the corner. It all happened within an instant, it seemed. Nothing could have stopped the mass killing. So far, at the time of the reporting, the police investigation had not come up with any answers to the many

questions being raised by the citizens of Beverley Hills, a town apparently where mayhem and disorder had been unthinkable before this incident. Anything resembling crime in their fair city—especially such unsavory stuff happening on the famous shopping street of Rodeo Drive—was an outrage, an abomination…and so forth. The people in Mexico City, reading this portion of the news item must have been amazed by the innocence of these Beverly Hills gringos. The massacre happened on Tuesday, May 18, 1996.
[That same year, I whispered to myself, the mysterious Miguel Guzman, with his granddaughter, Manuela, whose last name I now had reason to believe was Zaslavsky, thanks to Alonzo, when the two arrived at the small fishing village on the Sea of Cortez. Adding up the figures, it seems Julio lived in Beverly Hills with his daughter, Rachael, and family, for two years, presumably plying his trade as a barber at Rachael's Salon de Belleza, the similarity of name being no mere coincidence.]

Aside from these news clippings, Alonzo had nothing more he could contribute to the topic of the 'massacre'. The burning question in my mind now centered on the facts given me by this informant regarding Julio's breathless dash into the 'shop' and his immediate, hasty disappearance. What was that all about? There was yet much to be uncovered. But by now, it was lunchtime. Elena had long since finished having her coiffeur restored, and was seen waiting patiently in the lounge when we emerged from the back office. It was she who mentioned lunch, inviting Alonzo to join us. He demurred saying he had a business appointment, but agreed to a second interview "in a few days." He had much to think about, he said. He spoke obscurely. The news I had given him, he said, constituted an upheaval. "In a few days," I agreed.

Elena took me to an Indonesian restaurant. Ah… cosmopolitan, international Mexico City…a treat, she insisted, that I would enjoy, but I must say I was hankering instead for the simple life of Guaymas, wondering when I would be home again.

Elena took control over the business of ordering. Although hungry, I was unable to eat much. A growing sense of anger soured any zest I might have had. A picture persisted in my mind of Julio's life, a picture that took on too many dark contours. Everyone spoke of his innate upbeat spirit. But what was there to be happy about? Is there such a thing as an inborn will to happiness, a will so strongly embedded in one's fabric that one could easily overlook adverse factors? My mind dwelled on this annoying question as I dawdled over the plate in front of me. Elena interrupted my thoughts.

"Do you not care for this cuisine?" She asked.

"The food is fine. It's my mind that's not. To be truthful, I'm rather disturbed that you didn't tell me about the killings in Los Angeles. Surely, you knew about what took place?"

"Only vaguely," she shrugged. "And I really put all that out of my mind."

"It was in the papers—all over town."

"I stopped reading newspapers years ago. I stopped watching TV." Another shrug, as if to say, leave me alone.

And besides, she went on, long before that unfortunate 'occurrence', Hannah and her world was a thing of the past for her. About a year after Edgar died, she removed herself from the movement and cut off all connection with Hannah. Why? Because of Dora. Can you imagine my daughter going gaga over life in the beauty parlor? She confessed to me she wanted to become a hair stylist. Impossible! Edgar and I, we had aspirations for our daughter. Yes, I believed in equal opportunity for women. Yes, I was on the front line battling for our rights, believe me, I was in the thick of it. And Edgar, dear Edgar, he tolerated my activism, even though it caused him to become the butt of ridicule ['Joking around', he called it] among his friends and associates. But I knew better, even though he tried to hide it from me. His business involvements were suffering. But when it came to Dora and her future, I put my foot down, no more, even if it meant turning my back on the feminist cause. Dora was meant for higher things, a university education, and a good marriage with a well-connected family. And all that happened once I got her away from Hannah and Rachael and that horrible woman, Sadie, what a conniver she was forcing those two girls to play with that simpering son of hers, what a case. Oh yes, I knew about that, let me tell you, it was Dora who had the gumption to get on the phone and call me, she was beside herself with terror, the boy trying to get into their pants, I drove like a maniac to rescue her, took both of them away from that place, dropped Rachael off at the barber shop and never looked back.

Interview with Michael Melcher over coffee at a sidewalk café around the corner from his synagogue:

Sure, Rachael was in love with me. We played together since childhood days. Dora? No, I don't remember anyone by that name. What's she have to do with anything? When we were kids, Rachael's mom, from time to time, would bring her over to the rabbi's house where my mom worked. She was the rabbi's housekeeper, as you know. Hannah would come with Rachael when the rabbi was at the shul. Rachael was two years my senior, but we were equals, know what I mean? What did we do together? Well…well [an embarrassed look on his face] you know how it is with kids approaching their teens. Roaring hormones. We explored together, if you know what I mean. We would hide out in the rabbi's library, pretend to look at the books. This is where I always hung out anyway. I loved reading the stories about the rabbis of olden times. I even thought about how nice it would be to become a famous rabbi myself, although I had no idea how much work that meant. The rabbi encouraged me to read, particularly the Talmud and other important books that were full of interpretations, all too much for me to get a handle on. Once he told me point blank, he didn't believe I would get very far the way I neglected the serious stuff. Rachael? Well, other than 'explorations' we had very little to say to each other. She was obsessed with hair and hair styling, something that escaped my imagination. Sometimes we fought because she didn't appreciate the way I talked about her father, my mom had nasty things to say about him, and…well…I guess I repeated her words. My mom had this idea of getting Rachael back into the fold, so to speak—know what I mean? Even though she had been baptized a catholic, she never practiced that religion. My mom always talked about how the rabbi would take her in, so to speak, if Rachael and I were engaged. This was my mother's dream, to inveigle me into the rabbi's favor. Oh sure, I could have gone for that. I loved Rachael and truly wanted to marry her, but I was a kid then, what did I know? Rachael had brains and ambition, and anyway, after she was fifteen, I never saw her again, and by time she was twenty, she had taken up with that cousin of hers, the Russian.

My mom told me with a long sad face about the Russian, believing the news would break my heart, all her hopes dashed. But by then I was in a different place. I was eighteen, my face full of pimples, my grades at school a disaster. No, I never had another girlfriend.

And you had no idea why he raced into the shop a terrified look on his face? And still have no idea? Surely, you must have thought about that day once in a while after reading about the massacre. And how is it you didn't come to the conclusion he might be with his daughter?

    Such were my opening questions at my second meeting with Alonzo.

    It didn't occur to me that he might be in Los Angeles, since he despised the idea of going there. He never visited Rachael. Once a year, she came here to see him. As for why he took off the way he did, of course, I wondered. Look, all the time I knew Julio, his one burning ambition was to be the personal barber to someone important, as had been the case with his father and most of his ancestors, and that meant cutting the hair of the president of Mexico, no one less. But all those years, in which Hannah was active as a feminist, Julio was a political pariah. Yes, he had the best reputation in the city for being an extraordinary stylist. And everyone in this city is perfectly aware of how important one's image is in the eyes of the world, and the media makes this issue even more acute than ever. Julio would have been any politician's choice. But because of Hannah, he was overlooked. Did this bother him? Oh sure it did. But he never let on, not to Hannah or to anyone else, except me, we were compadres, you know. There were nights when we'd go off together, have a meal and a beer or two, sit in a corner and talk about his prospects and his sad situation. Did he ever blow his steam in public? No, I couldn't say he did. Oh, once maybe when that Navarro woman came in with Rachael in tow. She was furious over something having to do with her daughter, the little Dora—you know, she would have made a superb manicurist. She lashed into Julio for allowing Hannah her freedom to do anything she pleased, including taking her daughter to someone's house. Julio wouldn't stand for it. Ordinarily so polite and jolly with his clientele, when it came to someone speaking out against his Hannah he became a tiger. Lashed right back at the

Navarro woman. I don't remember all that he said, but it was enough, you better believe it. We never saw that woman again—until two days ago. Julio? Oh, well, after Hannah died—what a pity, so young, only in her fifties, runaway cancer in her lungs—I think it was the filthy air we breathed in those days, not until after the earthquake was anyone interested in doing anything about the air, and she was one of those, she still maintained her feminist position, but after the earthquake—what a terrible time it was, huge buildings crumbling like wounded dinosaurs, the suffocating air, you can't imagine—she turned to environmental issues, yes I know the lingo, Hannah taught me well, taught me a great deal actually, she was a true scholar and educator, look how she tackled her pregnancy for instance, bringing in all those experts to teach her and her new mother friends the modern way to give birth, feed babies—all that was amazing to me, right in the midst of our work, she taught me to see how serious life is, not just an opportunity to pamper and indulge, not just making people look pretty, Julio and I used to talk about this, he was very proud of her accomplishments. Julio? Yes. Well, after Hannah died, the political tide changed. But still, it took five more years before Julio's dream would come true. Finally, it was El Presidente Salinas, who summoned Julio. Almost a joke, you know, so little hair he had, bald at the top, a bit on the sides—like you, Señor EhEh. Do you know, when he was first getting started with his salon—when we were both young and innocent, Julio used to take walks in the Bosque past the presidential palace, dreaming about this day that never seemed to want to come. His family? A brother. He talked only about a brother living in Madrid, he was also a barber—to the current royal family no less. This bothered poor Julio, they were very competitive, you know. His mother and father? Died years ago, they were old to begin with when he was born. His father was barber to Poncho Villa, you know, and how long ago was that I ask you? And yes the day finally arrived. This is why I was so amazed to see him rush into the shop, that very same morning, with that horrified look on his face. I couldn't imagine what had happened. Had he nicked the presidential ear, or what? But he is alive. Thank God alive. You can ask him yourself what happened.

    I reminded Alonzo of Julio's comatose state, wondering the while I spoke if indeed Julio was yet counted among the living, my thoughts growing morbid of late considering the list in this family of departed ones. And then I questioned Alonzo almost holding my breath. A point that had been swelling my mind, and I felt he would be the one who could release the tension. I asked, "Do you believe Hannah loved Julio, truly, deeply? Not just their romantic obsession, mind you, but truly?"

[After a lengthy pause.] Absolutely, she loved him. And Julio was well aware. Yes, they had discussions, sometimes bitter discussions. In my presence, she never once said that she loved him, true. But she did love him, and he knew it. How? In our private moments he spoke about this to me. He had a complicated view, but I think he was correct in this. He said she demonstrated her love by never giving in to his wishes. He really didn't wish to change her ways. He saw deeply the beauty of her nature. She had to be what she had to be, and he loved her for what she was, even though at times he felt stretched beyond endurance. She showed her love, he said, by being totally herself, never bending to sooth his anxiety, never abandoning who she was for his sake. She showed her love in this way, because she knew that he loved her, loved her without conditions. Oh yes, he would plead with her, try to slow her down, try to get her to be reasonable—she was such a fighter in the trenches, the movement demanded so much of her, you know, sometimes she would go into a rage over the huge number of women who died from botched up, illegal abortions, I tell you it made me cry to think about it, many, many babies never having a chance, so many women turned into soil or ashes. And she would scoff at him, storm out for the day, and be back that night to meet him after closing, and they would go to eat somewhere, little Rachael holding their hands. A stormy love, yes, but a true love, you better believe it. And yes, I openly confess to you, Señor EhEh, in my own private way, I loved her too.

Of this confession, I told him, I had no doubt.

And now I must get back to work. This talk has taken longer than I imagined. You leave tomorrow you say. You will be seeing Julio? Well, please tell Julio for me this: tell him I am so thankful he is alive, even though not so alive, tell him to get well. Tell him he is still the boss. I never changed a thing, even though I believed him dead, but with no one to claim his estate, the best thing to do, I thought, was to do nothing, the business and the bank account still in his name. I kept good books, you know, all the expenses clearly laid out, all the profits in the bank still his, he has money, whatever he needs is there in the bank, my salary I increased, yes, but no more than is fair, I support a large family, he is well aware. Tell him…tell him…I have love for him.

Alonzo walked away, stifling a sob.

I am on the plane, Manuela, going over my scribbled notes, and sorting things in my mind. We have much to talk over.

One last piece of the puzzle came to me less than an hour before leaving the hotel. Elena Navarro rang me up. She apologized—rather too profusely I must say—for having walked out on me at the Indonesian restaurant, leaving me with the bill, no less. She had become so agitated from raking over the past. And she felt I had an attitude—a disdain aimed at her. Perhaps her revelations caused in my countenance an involuntarily contortion? A disapproving look? Nevertheless, I assured her nothing of the kind had crossed my mind. I prided myself, I told her, on being an impartial gatherer of information, not my place to judge, etc., etc. Mollified, she became solicitous and invited me to her apartment for dinner. But when I told her I was about to get on a plane, she grew sullen—I could tell by the way she breathed into the phone. And then she lightened up and expressed a desire to see me again upon my return to Mexico City. What made her believe I would be back? There was more to discover, she assured me. And then she dropped the bomb, and hung up leaving me flabbergasted. Elena told me that on her dying bed, Hannah, your grandmother, had whispered to her—yes, she, Elena, felt she must have a final moment of reconciliation with her old soldier friend [her words]. Julio almost denied her access to the hospital room, but in the end gave in. Dying of lung cancer, Hannah breathed hoarsely, clutching Elena by the wrist, and whispered, "Watch out for the Russians." Do you have any idea what she meant by this? Evidently, Hannah knew something—a secret that she took with her to her grave. Does this mean a return trip to El Ciudad is in order? Or would it be more propitious for me to go to Los Angeles for answers? We need to put our heads together. And while on the subject of Los Angeles, how is it you told me nothing of your life there? Be prepared, I will be asking you questions.

My place not to judge, I keep saying to myself. But I tell you, Manuela, so much drama packed into these revelations coming to me from all sides, penetrates my feelings, difficult for me to cast myself in the role of the disinterested observer. As the trained scientist, my job is to collect data about the attitudes, values, and behaviors of people of various groups, using observation, interviews, and review of documents. Sounds very abstract, doesn't it, and on the surface a relatively easy task. Certainly, I have observed, I have interviewed; but what to make of the information I have uncovered is another matter. My own emotions are too prevelantly embedded in any attempt at an evaluative study. When I look at Julio's life, a man raised in the catholic tradition—probably not very strictly—his operative religion, I would say, would be more appropriately described as tending toward hedonism, the pleasure principal strong in his makeup, his will to happiness along these lines disturbs my own stoic inclination. Emotions arise, exceeding the limits of my capacity. I am at a loss to see how striving for happiness can be a sustainable preoccupation, how doing your utmost to facilitate happiness in your fellows on this planet can possibly be attained, so many variables come to mind. And I ask, with even more perturbation, does spreading happiness among the populous represent a responsibility incumbent upon us in order that we may claim our humanity? As a scientist, I might ask what may be the statistical summation? What are the numbers? How many people in each of the various groups—Catholics, Jews, Protestants, and Atheists [don't forget the Atheists]—fall into this category? Is there some correlation we can discover that allows us to concur with a notion of obligation, we are obliged to support our fellow human beings in their search for happiness based on the statistics that a majority of individuals—if indeed a majority exists—have resorted to this quasi religious variant?

And what about Hannah? Her personality embedded in Judaism, she too converting the serious work of adhering to Yahweh's laws into a new formulation we can choose to call "social justice," what about her? Is it possible her inclination may be established as a subset of the will to happiness? Is it here where the beliefs of these two individuals, each from a different religious background, yet, nevertheless, from the same social experience, meaning the modern world—is it here where their lives converge? And if so, would this mean that her version of the happiness principle constitutes a new morality, affirming that no one may be happy unless everyone is happy? But maybe there is more to

Hannah's position. According to Sadie, she believed she walked a more serious path. For her, Julio's driving motive was on the level of superficiality. It is possible to conceive her motivation as a will toward meaningfulness. Striving for social justice meant something important to the meaning of her life, more meaningful, apparently, than how she construed Julio's sense of purpose? And what are the statistics for this point of view?

You see how abstract I have become, Manuela, just thinking about all this. All these thoughts keep rolling around in my head, backwards and forwards, arriving essentially at no concrete formulation. Is this my way of avoiding my emotions? Is this the reason I became a sociologist, so that I could safely observe and measure from a middle ground, distant from myself and from my subjects? This investigation you have propelled me into has struck me at my core. For some reason, it is causing me to examine my own feelings, and I am not happy about this.

The afternoon plane from Phoenix let down gracefully on the tarmac and taxied to the terminal. Among the arriving passengers, a somewhat thin, tallish man, bald headed and aged claimed his baggage, the carryon with which he began his journey insufficient to hold all the gifts he came home with. He left the building making a beeline for the taxi stand. He was eager to be in his own bed, had sat twenty hours in two terminals and three airplanes, and could think of nothing else.

The next day, morning arrived with brilliant sunlight pouring into EhEh's bedroom window awakening him to the sounds of wrens, sparrows and finches greeting the new day. Thoughts of his cheerful garden-paradise brought a smile to his face, happy to be home again. He stretched luxuriously in his comfortable bed, enjoying the cool morning. In an hour or two, the thermometer would rapidly rise. He would have to readjust to the hot desert air after the cooler temperatures of Mexico City. But thank God, the brutal heat of August was over. The arid winds from the south had ceased, and cooler air from the north had begun pouring in.

He remembered his promise to Manuela. He would come see her the minute he got back from the capitol. So, it's time to get moving, he murmured to himself, and rose out of bed stretching once more, this time in a standing position, then slipped into his house sandals. After a trip to the toilet, scratching his whiskers, he stepped into the kitchen and searched the old 70's refrigerator for what scraps might be at hand to make breakfast. There wasn't much. A small piece of cheese and a stale roll that he could soften by warming in his fry pan were just about it. He turned on the two-burner propane stove that sat next to the sink. At least he would have fresh coffee. He filled his dented metal percolator with water.

EhEh's house, a small four-room affair made of brick and covered in white stucco with bright blue painted trim around the windows and doors, was situated on a narrow calle near the center of Guaymas. It stood back from the street shaded by two huge mango trees. More mangos of lesser size and several lime trees filled the rear yard, with a small palm-thatched palapa positioned in the center of the garden, a colorful hammock hanging from corner to corner between two of the supporting poles where he loved to lie and read. In the front of the house, red bougainvillea climbed the trellises almost hiding the screened-in porch. EhEh had inherited this house from his grandmother, perfect for his needs in his retirement years. As soon as he could, he moved to Guaymas, happy to leave his teaching career at the university in Guadalajara behind him.

Finally, washed, shaved and dressed, he left the house, gripping the battered briefcase with the notes of his investigations tucked inside it. Miguel's old pickup stood on the side of the house. EhEh climbed in and started up the engine. Mixed feelings came over him as he tooled his way down the main drag of Guaymas. On the one hand, he was eager to share his findings with Manuela and the curandera. On the other hand, he was anxious about seeing Miguel, not sure of what his condition might be. It would be nice if he could stop at the Colmenar Restaurant and have a real breakfast. As quickly as the thought had come, he dismissed it, reminding himself he was duty bound to keep his promise. By time he reached San Carlos, the heat of the day announced itself. Through the resort town that hugged the sea, past the marina and the fishing boats, up over the hill he drove on toward the shantytown, leaving the paved highway, now bouncing along on the bumpy dirt road.

He stopped at the edge of the dune and climbed out of the truck. A handful of kids came running to greet him. "Dios!" He struck his forehead with the heel of his hand. He had forgotten the gifts! He saw the plastic bag full of trinkets sitting on the floor just inside his cottage door. "Mañana," he cried out loud as the excited children followed him to the barber's shack, shouting his name. Manuela sprang out of the house at the sound of the commotion, herself shouting "Hola!" more than once. EhEh was taken by surprise when she threw her arms around him with a big hug.

"Oh Señor EhEh, I thought you would never get back!"

"It's only been a week, young lady. So, how is he?"

A look of consternation crossed her face.

"He is awake. Consuelo has made a miracle happen. But, you know, he refuses to talk. Says nothing. Only stares. He lies in bed and stares. Only sits up when I bring him something to eat. He takes mostly soup, a bit of broth with some fish and vegetables in it. Once a day, that's all he will eat. I have been praying for him, and for you, Señor EhEh, praying that you bring good news, something that will help. Consuelo is convinced you will bring her the fact she needs in order to complete the healing. But please come inside. I'll go tell Consuelo you are here."

"That won't be necessary," EhEh smiled.

Consuelo had already bounced out of her house. All the men had long since gone to their fishing waters for the day; she had nothing to do but attend to her chores and her healing work.

"Señor EhEh, Hola! You bring news?"

"Hola, Consuelo. Yes. All in here," he patted his briefcase, hoping she could read his handwriting.

"Let us go inside," Manuela said, leading the way.

It was cooler inside, but not much.

"Do you wish to see him now?" Consuelo motioned to Miguel's bedroom with her jaw.

EhEh nervously nodded his head signifying he was willing. Consuelo opened the bedroom door and gave EhEh a gentle push. He stumbled across the threshold. The door closed behind him. Standing with his back pressed to the door, he studied Manuel's shriveled, whiskery face. The barber's eyes were open, but he seemed not to be looking at anything in particular. *Perhaps he only looks inward, but at what God only knows.*

"Miguel. It is me…EhEh…your friend."

There was no response. EhEh stepped closer to the bed.

"I've been to El Ciudad. I've seen friends of yours. I've brought news for you. News from Alonzo."

At the mention of Alonzo's name, Miguel's mouth gave a slight twitch. But other than that, there was no sign of acknowledgement. *So, you old fox, you do hear my voice!*

"Shall I tell you the news?"

Miguel did not stir. His blank eyes appeared to be staring at empty space. EhEh stood by the bed a while longer, completely at a loss. Then, muttering how sorry he was, he removed himself from the bedroom, his face drawn in sadness. It was no use. Back in the kitchen, he asked Conseulo who was sitting at the table, "What do you think is wrong?"

"The work is not finished," she looked up at him. "I was able only to bring him to consciousness with my administrations. He has sealed his mind shut as tight as an oyster. I need the special knife to pry him open. What have you brought from El Ciudad?"

"If you can read my handwriting, this will tell just about everything I have uncovered."

She took the notebook, and with help from EhEh, slowly deciphered the first few sentences. Meanwhile, Manuela got busy preparing some food. She would read the notes after they ate, she called back. EhEh now took notice for the first time that Manuela had tied her hair up in a bun on top of her head, like a married woman. He wondered what did this mean? And while he wondered, his eye took in another indisputable fact, one, however, that quickly sank below the surface of his awareness, hardly registered, nevertheless indisputably anchored. It was a fact destined to gain more credence as time wore on. What his eye took in was the detail of her waist having gotten a trifle thicker. In the whole of the fishing village, only the curandera knew what was happening to Manuela's body.

"Señor EhEh," her eyes were watering, "this is too much a strain on me. Your handwriting reminds me of the spider's path. I can do nothing with or without your assistance. Por favor, speak the main threads for me, eh?"

So, EhEh told the tale of his time in the city. Manuela bent her ear in their direction as she came with food, a steaming pot of frijoles laced with fried onions and green chilies, and a red napkin filled with warmed tortillas. They sat down to eat and to listen. Through the statements of his old associations Manuela heard a new version, that part of Miguel's life of which before she knew only what her grandfather had told her, bits and pieces casually uttered over the years that essentially hadn't been much.

Manuela's eyes grew wide, then glazed as she listened. A different picture of her grandmother was emerging. The heroic, political Hannah, it seemed, had not been much of a mother to the Rachel person, her own mom, whom Manuela could hardly remember. There was something like a gray cloud in her mind regarding her own childhood. Manuela's real and vital memory, she acknowledged to herself, properly began when she arrived at the shantytown. For her, vivid family memories dated mainly to times that stretched back into the Middle Ages – all those improbable tales with which her grandfather had filled her head.

Manuela slowly chewed her food, her interest in EhEh's talk waning as her thoughts turned to Javier, visualizing him at sea dragging in the nets with his papa. She could see Javier's gleaming brown shoulders bending forward over the gunwales, his curly head and neck straining as he pulled in the catch. All this she could see, and as well, even sense the taste of the salt water that splashed on his face, that she could feel on her own lips, so attached to his body was she.

Consuelo, meanwhile, took in EhEh's voice with intense concentration, and when he paused in his oration and swallowed a bite of the beans, she immediately jumped in, going straight to what was for her the heart of the matter.

"So, Señor EhEh, who are these Russians? Really, we know nothing about these gangsters, do we?"

EhEh nodded in agreement.

"We must delve into this more deeply," she went on. "I have a sense…" she held her forefinger to her nose… "These people have contaminated Miguel's mind. We must get to the bottom of this."

Consuelo, with penetrating eyes, stared into EhEh's, as if she were burning her idea into his brain. EhEh, on his part, looked startled and somewhat dismayed, for her intentions made it clear he would have to do more work in the field. He glanced at Manuela to assess her impressions. And what he noticed made him feel even more depressed. Manuela, her jaws absentmindedly grinding a mouthful of beans, seemed to be lost in some sort of reverie.

EhEh hesitated a moment before plunging into the subject of the Russians, casting a sad inner vision of his ailing friend in the next room, then resting his eyes on Manuela again, feeling a growing sense of the tragedy that was built into their lives, feeling its enormity enveloping him.

They hunched over their plates in silence, afloat in their separate mind swells. Stillness hovered over the wooden table that seemed to be floating in the soft kitchen light, while from out of doors came the shrill cries of the children at play beside the sparkling sea. By now, the morning sun had risen to its apex streaming noonday heat across the dunes. Not as stifling as in the hot month of August, EhEh thought, nevertheless plenty warm for September. He dabbed with his handkerchief the perspiration that had gathered on his brow, then cast a glance at Consuelo, then turned to Manuela.

"So, young lady," EhEh's sonorous voice filled the silence, "now that I know your full name, Ms Zaslavsky, I'm eager to hear more about your family."

Manuela, startled out of her reverie, stared at her investigator.

"I don't understand what you mean, Señor EhEh. Who is this Zas…Zas...?"

"Come, come. Surely you know your own name?"

"This…I can't even pronounce it…is not my name, never heard of it. Am I supposed to know this name?" She looked perplexed.

And so did the professor. What's come over her? So unlike the livened creature he was accustomed to. It seemed to him as if the spell that now enveloped old Miguel was spreading its influence into the granddaughter's mind. EhEh shook himself loose of this thought. He must scatter the gloom he was sensing. The air in this house seemed full of it.

"My name," she said as if in a trance, "is Manuela Guzman."

"Okay. Okay. I'll settle for that." EhEh smiled, sensing the need to humor her.

And now Consuelo finally came out of her stupor.

"Child," she commanded. "Tell the professor of your childhood in Los Angeles. This is what he wants to know. Tell us about your mother and father."

"Oh Consuelo, please, I can't remember a single thing. That was so long ago. I was only a baby. Please don't badger me."

Manuela's face was twisted in agony.

"Don't press her," EhEh urged. "She has no doubt suppressed hideous memories of the massacre. Stirring them up might unhinge her completely."

"Yes, so it seems. I agree, Señor EhEh. We are touching on a delicate place in her mind that we mustn't disturb just now."

She turned her attention to the young girl.

"Manuela, it is time for you to feed your grandfather. Go prepare his soup. In the meantime, Señor EhEh and I will make a field trip."

Señor EhEh cast a quizzical glance at the curandera. He was about to ask what she meant when suddenly the door to the outside burst open. A shaft of sunlight reached all the way into the back room where they sat. A young man's voice wafted in past the barbershop. It was Javier calling out Manuela's name. He strode into the room, in his hand a plastic bag smelling of fish, his body radiating excitement. Manuela leapt to embrace him. Suddenly, EhEh noticed, she was a different person. The two exchanged a quick kiss, which impressed the scholar-friend as having a calm quality more than of anything like passionate fervor. He now felt for the first time that he was beginning to understand the nature of their involvement with each other. His professional mind classified them as a happy, domestic couple.

Javier was full of himself with the news. It seemed that the men of the village were growing concerned over the lack of a barber. In just the short time since Miguel had succumbed to his mysterious illness, the fishermen had noticed the return of massive amounts of unruly hair. Their womenfolk had begun to treat them with indifference, some even openly complaining. No longer did they appear romantic in the eyes of their beloveds.

"So," his voice took on a conspiratorial tone, "the men have asked me to ask you, Manuela, if you will take his place."

"Take his place?"

"Yes. They are asking if you will cut their hair."

"Cut their hair?"

Javier shook his curly head in the affirmative.

"Yes, cut their hair."

"But I don't know how."

"That's exactly what I told them. But you know, they didn't believe me. They claim that you must know. They say you must know by instinct. After all, you are Miguel's granddaughter. You have his blood in your veins. They say you must just simply try. Your fingers will know what to do. They are certain of it. You see how desperate they are?"

He took in a deep breath, his hands grasping her shoulders, his eyes fervently seeking hers, as if he were imploring for the sake of harmony in the shantytown that she step up to the challenge. Manuela looked aside, her face registering disbelief.

"I don't know," she said.

"You could try," he said. "I'll help you."

"How? How can you help me?"

"I don't know. There must be something I can do." He ran his fingers through his hair. "I got it! I'll stand by your side while you snip. No one will dare complain if you cut too much here or not enough there."

He smiled, as if assured that his 'standing by' solved everything. But Manuela only shook her head in dismay.

Consuelo and EhEh exchanged glances. It seemed to EhEh that he and the curandera were simultaneously holding the same thought, namely, that the young couple had an issue to discuss that required privacy.

"About that field trip," EhEh muttered.

"Yes," Consuelo replied. "Come. Before the day grows any longer."

The two rose and left the house.

EhEh was full of curiosity. Out in the bright afternoon sunlight, he turned to Consuelo geared up to ask her what this so-called field trip was all about. But the curandera showed no signs of wanting conversation. Her body made a beeline for Miguel's pick-up, which was now to all intents and purposes EhEh's personal vehicle. He hastened to follow her. From the corner of his eye, he took in the fact that most, if not all, of the pangas had been beached, the fishermen finishing the day cleaning the catch they intended for themselves. Gulls and pelicans, white and brown against the blue sky, screeched back and forth over the tawny sand, colorful shells abandoned by former sea creatures rolled and tossed in the receding surf, the birds on the lookout for scraps of entrails. EhEh stopped in his tracks to admire the astonishing tumultuous commotion. For an instant, his mind felt young and fresh again.

Consuelo was already in the truck, honking the horn, causing the fishermen to look up and wave in EhEh's direction, who waved back. Then he strode to the truck, got in, started the engine and steered down the bumpy road toward Guaymas. He assumed the field trip would take place there. But Consuelo pointed in a different direction that led up into the mountains looming over the shantytown, an old, hardly visible dirt road that led from the edge of the sea into the high terrain where the copper mine had once been a thriving enterprise.

EhEh gave Consuelo a questioning look.

"That way," she shouted, her prominent larynx bobbing in her throat. She flapped her skinny arms. Her gray hair pinned to the top of her head sprung up with each movement of the truck. She was wearing her usual housedress of a faded flowery cloth over which was wrapped a threadbare, greasy kitchen apron.

What is this scrawny woman up to? He wondered. At this moment to EhEh she looked like a starved hen attempting to take flight.

He steered the truck up the dirt road in low gear avoiding the ruts and bumps as much as possible. They drove several miles winding around hills, going steadily deeper into the desert. Behind them, the sun dipped slowly from its noonday height toward the sea, lighting up with purple and orange tints the living rock of the several mountainsides in the distance. Small bushes and cactus plants, gray and deep green against the sandy terrain, stood vivid in the dramatic light. The atmosphere radiated wavering heat. EhEh wiped his brow with his handkerchief. He felt perspiration dripping from his armpits.

Consuelo, he noticed, showed no signs of sweating. She sat in silence, looking directly in front of her.

"Where are we going?" He ventured to ask.

"You'll see," she replied, and said no more.

Shortly after this brief exchange, the road came abruptly to an end. EhEh pressed the brake pedal and the truck lurched to a stop. Consuelo jumped out and started up a draw between two huge boulders. She paused before she would actually disappear around one of them and turned to look back.

"Are you coming?" She called.

It all had happened so quickly, EhEh hadn't had time to extricate his tall body from the cab.

"Wait! I'm coming!" He shouted, and plunged after her.

They walked about a half a mile up the gradual slope, EhEh stumbling over an occasional rock. The path narrowed, then turned to the left. Suddenly, they found themselves within a secret garden laced with several small ponds upon which floated lotus plants in bloom, an oasis in the dessert. Cabbage palms stood tall against the sky, their palm leaves, like Arabian fans, swaying from a gentle breeze, sending coolness to EhEh's brow. A variety of bushes grew everywhere, some covered with sprinklings of brilliant flowers the names of which he had no idea.

They paused here to rest. EhEh sat down on a large boulder that hung over one of the ponds, his eyes sinking into the beautiful colors and shades of green. Truly, he felt himself immersed in an enchanted place.

"This is a beautiful place," he murmured. "Thank you for bringing me here."

"We have further to go," she said almost whispering the words. Her voice had softened. She was obviously pleased to be showing EhEh her secret garden. She sat down beside him, slipping out of her sandals and lowering her feet into the cool water. "Take off your shoes and socks."

He did so, and then sighed a happy sigh as he put his feet into the water and felt the coolness. Suddenly, his mind went back to a similar experience of his youth. He could almost remember how it felt to him then, life, the real life of the body without its aches and pains. This simple walk up the hill had tired him more than he thought possible, especially his feet and legs. His seventy-six years—almost seventy-seven, he told himself—were showing his limitations. He wondered how many years had Consuelo seen so far. It was impossible to say how old she might be. One thing for sure, he noticed, she displayed the endurance of a young person.

"Okay," she interrupted his thoughts. "Enough of resting. Let's move on."

She rose, slipped on her sandals and trotted off up a steep incline. EhEh trundled after her. The path went alongside a ravine-filled stream that fed the ponds below, its mossy banks lush with ferns and spidery looking plants.

EhEh was puffing heavily; but after an almost impossible climb that was in actuality surprisingly brief, the path leveled out into an upper plain, and before them, a few hundred feet away, stood the most extraordinary tree EhEh had ever seen. It must have been over thirty feet tall, quite large by desert standards, and its round canopy almost as wide. It stood alone among the desert scrub, a place of shade and comfort to many small creatures and plants.

Totally amazed, EhEh watched as Consuelo stepped beneath the canopy's shade and bent over a small rodent of some kind that had emerged from among the roots of the tree as if offering a gesture of greeting. She held something in her palm, he couldn't say what, while the creature nibbled. Startled by this sight, he sucked in his breath. Only then did he truly realize she was indeed some kind of magical person. And this was a special tree; and she was its special friend. But even more remarkable, the tree sported two trunks, each as thick as a man's waist. And as he drew closer, as close as he dared not wishing to disturb the magical moment, EhEh saw the many thorns of these two pillars, spikes that extended several inches from the bark. He watched as the rodent licked Consuelo's hand, as if to give thanks, before disappearing into its sanctuary. Then Consuelo lowered herself to her knees, and murmured words of prayer in her native Náhuatl. One phrase was in Spanish, he recognized: 'Santos Cuates' the Holy Twins.

EhEh observed intently. He realized he was being given a view of something quite mystical and magical. He was seeing the work of a true curandera, a brujita, the term used for a "dear witch" – one who is a benign healer. He remembered this much from his reading in anthropology in his student years. He felt quite privileged to be present to this living example before his eyes. He was almost breathless with wonder, intent on taking in every gesture, every nuance of Consuelo's actions.

He watched as she, in silence, rose to her feet and began to pluck from the low hanging branches of the tree a number of brown bean-like seedpods, about two inches long. These, she stuffed into her apron pocket, and then quickly turned toward EhEh, brushing past him in silence as she began the walk back to the truck. As if a newly anointed disciple, he followed her silently down the steep ravine, making certain not to slip on any defying pebble.

They drove all the way to the shantytown without exchanging a word. As the pickup came to a stop on the dune overlooking the sea, a ruby, purple sky greeted them, an orange sun slowly slipping behind the horizon.

EhEh turned off the engine. Consuelo handed him three of the seedpods.

"Take one of the pods tonight before going to bed, chew each bean slowly, let your mouth fill with saliva. Take the second pod when you awaken, then the third after breakfast. Take them all no matter how you feel." She showed him how to extract the beans from their pod.

"What will this do to me?"

"You will see. These beans are food for the mind."

She spoke rather mysteriously, he thought. Nevertheless, he said he would do what she had prescribed. And, with a nod, she stepped out of the truck.

"See you tomorrow," she said. "Tomorrow, you will try again to talk to Miguel? Tell him details of your investigation. He will hear you and understand."

"And what will you do with the rest of the beans?" EhEh wanted to know.

"I make a potion with them. For Miguel, and for Manuela."

"More brain food?"

"Not for the brain. For the mind." She looked into his eyes. "Something stronger than the bean alone. Good night Señor EhEh."

She disappeared into the falling night.

He slept well, despite the many elaborate and florid dreams. There had been so many, it seemed, more than he could remember. But it was the last one that took him out of his sleep. In this dream, he saw a young child, but with a grown man's head, wearing short khaki pants and a white cotton shirt. He recognized the face. It was his own, the one he saw every day he shaved. The face showed a cranky expression, the very same he used to wear when he was the professor teaching at the university.

Even though he was lying in bed, he felt himself hovering in space, overlooking the scene before him. The child was on his way somewhere. He was walking, scrambling, jumping over and crawling under, moving through what seemed like a tropical jungle in full vivid color superimposed over a gray cityscape. Wild animals of all kinds glared out from open windows and doorways of houses. Automobiles and busses floated on black watery surfaces, somehow moving in both directions, upstream and downstream, driven by screeching monkeys. He couldn't hear them, but he saw their mouths making the sounds. Colorfully plumed birds, mostly parrots, flitted back and forth.

With his dreaming eyes, he followed the boy who pushed his way between grown men and women all of whom, without exception, wore the same cranky expression as the boy's. EhEh took these as normal expressions. But what startled him, indeed caused him to leap out of his dream, was the fact that all these people had the same face. They were all his face.

He woke puzzled, feeling oddly refreshed yet shaken by the dream experience. He felt as if his body and his head were two separate entities, the one dizzy, swirling in space; the other inert, totally relaxed yet feeling energized. It was the effect of the beans, he surmised. And now he was supposed to chew the second pod? He wasn't sure he wanted to do that. Did he trust the curandera, he wondered? He thought back to the day before, and saw once more the way she had communed with the rodent, the way she bowed before the curious tree, the way she had prayed to the Santos Cuates, the sacred twins whose lineage extended back into the misty past way before the time of the Spaniards, maybe even before the time of the Aztecs. He remembered what he had read in his student days.

This bean he was chewing – yes, he must have decided to trust her, because he saw that he had peeled open the pod and extracted the beans as if in a trance, seemingly under the control of her powerful bewitchment. Was he bewitched, he wondered? For a moment he felt alarmed at the thought. He felt as if he were losing his rational mind. He was sitting up in bed as he chewed and swallowed. Before very long, he began to feel dizzy, and his stomach churned and took a drastic nauseous turn. Suddenly, he was seized with the urge to vomit. He leapt out of bed and made a dash for the toilet, only to discover that his legs were like rubber, and he collapsed to the floor, lying on his side, green vomit pouring from his mouth.

He was disgusted with himself, but couldn't move. He lay there for some time, breathing heavily, only slightly alarmed by the intensity of his body's reaction.

For, to tell the truth, his mind felt free of a tightness, he recognized as the overall sensation he had felt almost all of his life. The tightness was gone, at least for now. He wasn't willing to make any permanent predictions concerning the state of his mind. He felt perspiration pouring from what seemed like every orifice of his skin.

Some huge alteration of his being was taking place. Of this, he was certain. But what it all meant, he had not a clue.

He only knew that he was beginning to feel giddy, and he burst into laughter. It felt good, whatever it was. It seemed like the affliction, if indeed that was what it was, had passed. Strength returned to his muscles. His head, feeling this new sensation of lightness, once more became a thinking machine. He was able to get himself up from the floor, clean himself, clean the mess he had made, get shaved and washed and dressed, his stomach eager for food. What a relief, he thought.

A huge breakfast was on his mind. He would go to the Colmenar and have his favorite huevos rancheros, tortillas and beans and two cups of thick, strong coffee.

Suddenly, he remembered the child in the dream, and he decided that somehow he must change the expression on that child's face, and the meaning and purpose of the dream crashed into his awareness. Years, all those years, he had spent cultivating a cranky mood. Would he ever be able to rid himself of this attitude, he wondered? And with the thought, he felt a cranky expression draw itself across his lips.

He was out in the morning sunlight. His previous good mood reasserted itself as he took into his nostrils the cool morning air. He could smell the deep odors of earth and mango-bark that were giving off their scent while there was time before strong sunbeams stifled the fresh odors.

EhEh got into the pickup and started driving toward the Colmenar, when suddenly it occurred to him to do a bit of research. He steered to another part of town to the home of an old acquaintance who was an amateur botanist, an old man by the strange Nahuatl name of Zeltzin, which was rather ironic, as Zeltzin himself was always prone to point out; for the Nahuatl word meant 'delicate' and he was anything but delicate. In fact he was a huge man with thick arms and legs and fingers, his head and neck a single stump on his beefy shoulders, but with gentleness in his face that matched his love for plants.

Zeltzin lived in that part of town that was a cluster of adobe brick hovels piled one on top of the other up steep inclines overlooking the port city. EhEh's truck chugged up the steep winding narrow streets until he lost himself and had to make enquiries. Everyone knew Zeltzin. But not everyone gave the same directions, so complicated was this rabbit warren of domiciles. Eventually, he found his way to Zeltzin's house.

"Aha, Señor EhEh, hola! What brings you to my humble abode pray tell? Many years since we have crossed paths."

"Hola, Zeltzin. Yes, it has been a long time. May I come in?"

"But of course, old friend. I make you tea? It's much too early for tequila." He stepped back to allow EhEh room to enter.

"I'm sorry to say, Zeltzin, I have no time for tea and conversation. My visit has to do with saving an old man from his affliction. I need your expert botanist opinion. Can you tell me what this is?" He extracted the last seedpod from his pocket and pressed it into the botanist's beefy hand.

The two men stood side by side, the one tall and skinny and practically bald, the other the shape of a hairy gorilla, their heads bent over the object in question. Morning light poured through the single window into the dusty front room of Zeltzin's tiny house. He was a bachelor and spent little effort on tidiness. Dust laden books sat on several dust-covered tables that stood between two well-worn upholstered chairs, one covered in gray corduroy, the other in a faded plaid pattern that was once ubiquitous among stylish middle class homes of the 50's. It was Zeltzin's backyard garden that got all his attention.

Zeltzin gave the seedpod a quick glance, then handed it back to EhEh.

"You want to know what this is, my friend? Well it's a simple problem you have handed me. So simple, I am almost disappointed."

"Yes...yes?" EhEh prompted impatiently.

"This is a seedpod from a common tree," he pronounced its Latin name, which EhEh immediately forgot. "These trees abound in our Sonoran deserts. Nothing unusual."

"There are beans inside," EhEh said, pointing to the pod.

"I know that, my friend."

"Are these beans medicinal?"

"Who gave you these beans? A bruja, I bet. From where else would you get such a ridiculous idea? Medicinal? No, my friend. These beans are not medicinal. They are poisonous. Not extremely toxic, I admit, but if you eat enough of them, you will be in trouble for certain."

"I was with the woman, yes, a curandera, when she plucked a handful of these pods from a tree, a big one, maybe thirty feet tall, very unusual with two trunks coming out of the ground."

"Not unusual, my friend. There are many like that, even with more trunks. And they are very old."

"How old? Is that important to know?"

"Only if you are a superstitious bruja. Some can be as old as fifteen hundred years."

"Really? I wonder how old this one is."

"She gave you this seedpod?"

EhEh nodded.

"To take…to eat?"

"She gave me three of them."

"And you've eaten two?"

EhEh nodded again.

"Well, my friend, aren't you the proud one. Listen to me. Go to the nearest herb shop and buy a purgative and take it. Do it right away."

EhEh looked down at his shoes.

"So, my friend," Zeltzin chuckled, "it is you, eh? You are the old man with the affliction, no?"

"I don't know about that," EhEh said, feeling uneasy.

Zeltzin ushered him to the door with a fond pat on the back.

"Go, my friend. Hurry. Take good care of yourself. Take the purgative. Come back when you feel better. We will have a nice cup of tea and some interesting talk, yes? I must caution you not to be so suggestible to old wives tales. Stay away from their lore, Señor Sociologist."

EhEh, somewhat miffed by Zeltzin's slur, found himself out in the street full of bafflement. He had to decide. Medicine? Or poison? Which was it to be? Heed the botanist, or heed the curandera?

He drove down the hill, mulling over the question, when suddenly a voice whispered in his head: *Take the medicine.* Was the voice referring to the beans or to the herbs, he wondered? The voice spoke again, this time more insistently. Who was speaking to him? Consuelo? Zeltzin? Himself? Maybe it was the boy from the dream?

"Get a hold of yourself," he muttered aloud.

At the bottom of the hill, now on the main drag, surrounded by other cars and pedestrians, everyone busy with the challenges of the day, the merchants with their doors wide open, the shoppers with their plastic, netted shopping bags scurrying across the traffic-filled intersections, full of purpose striding into establishments that sold furniture, appliances, electronics, but mainly into the large and complex downtown mercado with its innumerable produce stalls and meat stands, its rows of wares, from hand woven blankets to hand carved leather goods, toys and clothing, while outside on the street corners the food vendors were cranking up their portable grills already filling the atmosphere with inviting smells, EhEh felt a bit more himself amidst these familiar, rational activities.

The crowd of people downtown gave him the impression it was Saturday, the town's big shopping day. Was it Saturday? Had he lost a day somewhere? What had happened to Friday? Just the thought that he might have lost a day made his stomach feel a bit queasy again.

"Old man," he said aloud to himself. "Settle down. You are acting like a scared kid."

Then he thought of the boy in his dream, and decided to be brave like him. He was convinced the boy had been brave. He decided he would continue the regimen set forth by Consuelo, his mentor in things magical. And with this idea firmly established in his head, he drove to the restaurant, and, once inside and settled at a table, he was already feeling stronger and fully resolved, and ordered his favorite huge breakfast.

An hour later, heading toward San Carlos, he slipped the remaining two beans into his mouth. The breakfast he had eaten with gusto sat well in his belly. He decided it was the second dose that had been the cause of his jitteriness. And now he mused over what the last set of beans would do to him. He slowly chewed, filling his mouth with saliva as Consuelo had instructed, feeling confident everything would be fine. But the more he chewed and swallowed, the more his vision became blurry. The road before him began to shimmer. Then it rose and curled upon itself becoming something like a roller coaster. He wanted to stop the truck and pull over to the side of the road, but there was no side. The roadway was floating in midair. So he did the next best thing and stopped in the middle of the pavement, hoping no other vehicles would crash into him. But to tell the truth, at this point, he wasn't at all certain he was on an actual road. He could be anywhere. He laughed with giddiness, as he found himself actually nowhere, no longer in the pickup. Why this amused him he couldn't say. But, if not in the pickup, where the devil was he, he wondered? He remembered the boy in the dream, and suddenly he was there, running alongside the boy, running into the jungle and weaving between the trees and ducking under hanging vines, vivid shapes and colors penetrating his brain, changing form with kaleidoscopic speed. He yelled to the boy, "Who are you? What's your name?" The boy laughed and said he was EhEh, only he used his proper name, Eugenio. EhEh laughed at the sound of his name. For some reason unbeknownst to him, it tickled his funny bone to hear the boy say he was Eugenio. "We have the same name. Isn't that a kick?" EhEh laughed, and the boy laughed with him. Then the boy leaped up, grabbed one of the hanging vines and swung himself into a low branch of a tree. "Can you do this?" He yelled. And EhEh laughed. "Of course I can you silly bumpkin!" And up he flew without even the aid of a vine. Screaming and laughing, they flew from tree branch to tree branch like a couple of monkeys, flitting through specks of sparkling sunlight that penetrated the dense forest. They were having a grand time. When, suddenly, everything stopped, and EhEh found himself sitting in the pickup that was parked at the edge of the road miraculously intact.

    Sweat trickled down his armpits. The morning coolness had turned into late morning heat. The day was destined to be a very hot one. He sat motionless for a while, feeling his body vibrating. The sensation caused him to feel powerfully energetic and alive, thankful the poison had not destroyed his mind. Surely, he thought, if the beans could do this to him, they must be poisonous. Then he wondered what affect Consuelo's concoction would have on Miguel and Manuela.

"The fishing village!" He slapped the steering wheel with the palm of his hand. He should have been there by now. Or perhaps yesterday, he mused. Had he really lost a day? He started the engine and pulled back onto the road driving as fast as he sensibly could in the swift, heavy traffic. It must be Saturday, he mumbled to himself.

The children came running to the truck. "Damn!" He had forgotten the presents again! EhEh walked briskly toward the barber's shack, explaining as he walked among the clamoring kids that he would bring them their gifts, he promised he would bring them the very next time he came. He was sure they would be pleased. He had gotten them all baseball caps of the favored Mexican ball team. Before leaving for the capitol, he had counted every child's head in the village, both the boys and the girls, everyone treated equally. And with the caps, all adjustable to fit each and every head size, he had gotten them as well four professional bats and a dozen baseballs. When they heard this, they screamed with delight and shouted like frenzied fans, "Beisbol! Beisbol!"

A group of men, hunkered down outside Miguel's house, greeted the tall professor with happy faces. EhEh stepped inside, amazed to see one of the fishermen ensconced in the barber chair. Standing behind him, snipping away at his locks, stood Manuela, her face screwed up with concentration, Javier, as promised, a few feet behind her. The boy smiled at EhEh, proud of his accomplishment.

Javier had prevailed. A new era had dawned. EhEh imagined a sign hanging outside over the door to the shack: Haircuts by Miguel and Manuela. But of course, there was no need for a sign in this tiny shantytown. And maybe, alas, no need for Miguel's name on the signboard. EhEh sighed, wondering if his friend's condition had altered from Consuelo's new ministrations.

He stepped into the back room expecting to see her there. But the room was empty. He felt confused. Maybe she was in the bedroom with Miguel, he thought, and decided to take a peek. Passing the kitchen table, he saw his notebook lying there half under a plate with specks of dried food on it, and wondered if Manuela had read his report. He still had much to discuss with her. Then, he stood before the bedroom door, and pressed his ear to the rough wooden boards. No sound came from within the room. He pressed the latch and slowly pushed open the door, his eyes peering into the dim room. She wasn't there. Miguel's body, just barely visible, lay flat on the bed, his chest rising and falling with peaceful, even breaths, and with each breath a feeble snore issued from his nostrils.

He walked back to the front of the house and entered the barbershop. He asked after the curandera. Javier and Manuela looked at each other with quizzical expressions, and then shook their heads, as if to say they had no idea where she might be, then suggested that he go next door and look for her there. But the fisherman, with his hair half cut, spoke up and said they weren't home, she had gone somewhere, no one knew where, with her husband, Diaz, in his panga, maybe to Guaymas

EhEh felt at loose ends. Consuelo gone somewhere, no idea when she would return. Manuela engrossed in hair, with all the men waiting outside, no idea when she would be available for a talk. There seemed nothing for him to do here. He decided to go home. And the first thing he would do, he told himself, would be to load the package of baseball caps along with the bats and balls into the back of the pickup. Before anything else, he would do that. Everyone – the men waiting outside the barbershop, the fishermen on the beach repairing their nets, a few of the women hauling water to their hovels, the kids playing in the sunlight – everyone followed him with their eyes as he made his way to Miguel's pickup.

Driving home, his thoughts turned to his own affairs. His finances were in a shambles. He had spent a great deal of his cash rushing off to the capitol. If he were forced to do any more traveling, he would have to dip into his savings, which he was loath to do. And his pension check was not due to arrive for another two weeks. This investigation in Miguel's behalf was proving to be an expensive affair.

But maybe there was a way out. He thought of Alonzo and all the money Alonzo claimed he had stashed away in Miguel's – actually Julio's – bank account. Money, he had said, available to his boss and mentor, any time he needed it. Well, this was the time, EhEh said aloud.

He turned the pickup around, made a u-turn right in the middle of the one and only main street in the San Carlos, and headed back to the village. Luckily, he hadn't gone too far from the shantytown. He drove back to fetch his notebook, which had, somewhere in its pages, Alonzo's telephone number.

One of the few luxuries EhEh afforded himself was his own telephone, although he seldom put it to good use. For him it had been emblematic of his professional status. At any time, one of his former students or colleagues might need to speak with him over academic matters. He felt he had to be available. And occasionally, the phone did ring, put into just that kind of service.

As he parked the truck at the edge of the dune and climbed out, he noticed how everyone stopped what they were doing and looked up to watch him clamber over the sand to Miguel's. He had been gone maybe no more than twenty minutes. Yet it seemed as if the villagers regarded him as a total stranger invading their privacy, the way they stared. It made him feel a bit self-conscious. He realized, even though they showed friendly feelings towards him, they still, nevertheless, saw him as an outsider, and maybe even a figure of the official world, a threat to their illegal status, below the surface of their awareness, of course. He doubted if they consciously believed he was truly a threat. EhEh pondered this issue with the swiftness of his professional intellect. Nevertheless, he failed to acknowledge the one irrefutable fact, namely, that although he had as much Mexican blood in his veins as they did, he looked like a European straight from the old country, while they looked precisely like the indigenous people they were. They were steered by suspicious feelings embedded deeply in their collective memory. EhEh, so thoroughly embracing his democratic instincts, easily forgot this distinction.

Once more, they all stared at him again as he trudged back to the truck, the notebook in his hand. He couldn't wait to get home to call Alonzo Morales. It was still not too late in the day. He hoped to find Alonzo at the beauty parlor. This was his only hope. He had no other phone number.

"Bueno?" A woman answered. There was no question, by the sound of her voice, that she played the role of the receptionist to its fullest extent, although, EhEh noticed, she had failed to mention the name of the establishment, rather unprofessional, he thought.

"I wish to speak to Señor Morales, please."

"May I say who is calling? He's terribly busy at the moment."

"My name is Eugenio Escudero. Tell him EhEh is calling. From Guaymas. Tell him, please. The matter is urgent."

"From Guaymas? Does he know you, Señor…?"

"Escudero. EhEh…tell him EhEh. Yes…yes, he knows me. We spoke just a few days ago in his Salon."

"One moment please."

EhEh drummed his fingers impatiently on the top of the side table where the phone sat next to his easy chair in the front room. He had his shoes off. The cool cement floor felt good. A fan, hanging from the ceiling, slowly whirled, creating a facsimile of coolness in the otherwise quiet room. EhEh loved his home. He was happy to be back. This was where he felt his best. He waited, staring at the photo of his grandmother that hung on the opposite wall. He nodded in gratitude to her, grateful that she had held on to this house and had passed it on to him at her demise. It was a gift for which he would never stop being grateful.

At last the phone came alive with the woman's voice.

"Maestro Alonzo will be with you in a moment. He is just finishing up with a client."

"Thank you," EhEh murmured into the speaker.

He threw another glance toward his grandmother, then relaxed deeper into the easy chair, and waited.

"EhEh," Alonzo's voice came across the wires cheerfully. "What can I do for you? How is our friend Julio?"

"He is out of his coma, I'm happy to report. However, he does not communicate. He stares into the void without relief. But we have hopes. His healer has hopes."

"And you need some cash, is that so?"

EhEh was taken aback.

"Well…yes…as a matter of fact this is why I am calling. I need to do more investigation in the field. I suspect I will have to go to Los Angeles."

"Well, there is no cash, my friend."

"But you said…don't you remember?"

"Yes, I remember what I said. Listen, EhEh, do you take me for a fool? I was on to you right from the start. What a likely story you fed me. Julio alive…what a load of bunk! I didn't for once believe you."

"But…but…"

"But nothing. You imagine I can't smell an extortion trick when I see one?"

"Smell? See? What are you talking about? This is no extortion trick. I'm a respectable retired professor of sociology. I have a reputation… And what about Elena? Do you believe she is part of a scheme as well? After all, she is the one who introduced me to you."

"Elena? Of course not. I don't know how you got to her in the first place or what you may have told her. But she's not terribly clever, you know. She can easily be hoodwinked."

"I got to her because Julio told me her name. How else would I know about her?"

"I'm sorry, Professor EhEh, I am not willing to believe you, nor will I help you with cash." He said 'cash' sardonically. "I must go back to work now. You are lucky I don't turn you over to the police. If you bother me again, I will do so."

And with that, he hung up, leaving EhEh flabbergasted. He was utterly astonished that someone would disbelieve him. Aside from disputed theories that passed back and forth between himself and his colleagues, he had never before had his veracity so ignominiously questioned. He burned with anger and shame.

This thing was becoming a fiasco. The more he thought about it the more livid he became. He had to talk to someone about this. But who? And then he thought of Elena. He was certain she would understand his dismay, would take his side, maybe even come up with a suggestion. He flipped the pages of his notebook in search of her number.

His ear to the receiver, he listened to the buzzing of the ring, his fingers busy again on the tabletop.

"Bueno?" Came Elena's cheerful voice.

"Hola, Elena. This is me, EhEh. Do you have a minute?"

"Where are you? Are you here in the city?"

"No. I'm at home in Guaymas. Listen, I have something terrible to report. Alonzo does not believe me. He thinks I am scheming to extort money from him. He even threatened to turn me over to the police. Can you believe such a thing?"

His voice was quavering, his chest heaving.

"Hold on, EhEh. Calm yourself. Tell me the details. Slowly. And what about Julio? What is his condition?"

He felt relived. Evidently, she was still on his side. So, he told her everything of the events since his arrival home. He spoke of the curandera, of the seedpods, of Manuela, of the haircutting, of Javier. He went on and on rehearsing every aspect of the situation, even down to mentioning Zeltzin the botanist and the baseball caps for the kids. And Elena listened, as if she had nothing better to do with her time. He could hear her sipping her herbal tea as he spoke. And finally, he brought up the subject of the Russians and his probable need to go to Los Angeles, and the sorry condition of his finances.

"And that is why I phoned Alonzo. When I saw him in his salon, he said he had money for Julio. But now he tells me he never believed my account of Julio's coma. He doesn't believe that Julio is alive."

"Your story, you mean," Elena interrupted.

"So, you don't believe me either?"

"I didn't say that. I mean this is the way Alonzo sees it. To him, you are telling an unlikely story."

"But you believe me, yes?"

"I would like to. Are you intending to ask me for money?"

"No! No! Absolutely not!"

"Well then, what do you want?"

"I have savings. I can dip into them. But I can't just go to Los Angeles on a wild goose chase. I can't just be throwing money away. Maybe you can tell me more about the Russians. Where do they figure in all this?"

"Really," she replied, a hint of sadness in her voice, "I don't know anything about the Russians, only what Hannah said when she breathed her last."

"But you led me to think you had gobs of information on this topic."

"I know, EhEh. I'm sorry. It was just a ruse."

"A ruse?"

"Yes. I've taken a shine to you, EhEh. I wanted to entice you back to the city. When you said you were on the verge of flying out, I felt cheated and wanted to somehow pull you back. Is that so wrong that I have feelings for you?"

EhEh couldn't believe his ears. Out of his simple, quiet, easygoing retirement a kind of madness had entered his life. He was getting deeper and deeper into something he couldn't comprehend.

And all this was happening to him because of a casual conversation that took place in the Guaymas public library a few years prior.

"Are you there, EhEh?"

"Yes…yes, I'm here."

"I just thought of something. That cousin of Hanna's, the Melcher woman."

"Sadie Melcher?"

"Yes, that's the one. She may still be alive."

"She is. I spoke with her when I was in the city."

"And you didn't ask her about the Russians?"

"I think she mentioned them. I'll have to check my notes. I know that her son, Michael, mentioned them. But it didn't click in my head the way it does now. I must admit I'm not a professional crime detective."

"Well, she is the one who can give you information. I'm sure of that. What a busybody she is. Do you have her number?"

"I believe so. I'll have to check my notes."

"Speak to her, then call me back. We'll put our heads together. Goodbye for now, dear man." And she hung up.

Oh my God, he thought, she's still gunning after me.

But despite this misgiving, he was satisfied that at least in her he still had an ally and not a disbeliever. He set the receiver back on its cradle, got up from his easy chair and went to the bathroom to relieve himself. Then he made some coffee, settled back in his chair, and, in a calmer mood, searched his notes for Sadie Melcher's phone number. But when he came to the section devoted to his interviews with Alonzo, his ears began to burn. *Talk about lies! Alonzo even cried pretending his love for Julio! Oh, what a sham!*

EhEh brooded over Alonzo's strange change of heart. When they talked in the city the previous week, the barber never questioned EhEh's veracity, never once doubted the news he gave of Julio being alive. Why now this mistrust? Why call him an extortionist? Apparently, Alonzo meant to set a trap when he mentioned there was money for Julio. But why? What could have been his motive? His thoughts went back to the previous week and the sequence of interviews. When he had told Elena about Julio and his granddaughter living near Guaymas under a different name, and that he was desperately ill, actually in a coma, she had shown no disbelief, didn't even seemed surprised. He remembered, she claimed not to have known very much about the massacre in Los

Angeles, didn't read the newspapers anymore. Her interest in Julio was altogether practically zero. Evidently, she had no reason to wonder if Julio was dead or alive. With the words, 'dead or alive,' his thoughts shifted back to the Russians, and suddenly it dawned on him. Alonzo, he realized, believed that he, EhEh, must be in cahoots with the Russians. Else how would he have come up with that idiotic idea of extortion? Alonzo had pegged him as one of the gangsters. As absurd as it sounded, he was now convinced this was what Alonzo believed him to be. A gangster! *Alonzo believes I'm a gangster! I've got to get to the bottom of this!*

With trembling fingers, he dialed Sadie's number.

"Hallooa?" Her singsong voice gave the impression of an aged opera singer.

"Señora Melcher?" He said courteously. "This is Señor EhEh speaking."

"Ach, mein Gott! Señor EhEh! I vas just speaking about you yesterday!"

This is too much, he thought. And what kind of an impact had he made on her?

"Is that so?" He tried to sound nonchalant.

"Yes. Over lunch with my boy, Michael. You remember him?"

"Yes, of course I remember him. What were you saying about me?"

"Vell, to begin with, what a nice man you are. But more to the point, we talked about you and the Russians." Her voice sounded conspiratorial.

Oh, oh, here it comes. They think I'm one of the gang.

"What about me and the Russians?" An irritated edge came into his voice.

"Vell, Michael vundered to me over lunch. You know, he comes home everyday from the shul to have his lunch. So, we talked about your interest in us and in Hannah. And Michael looked at me full of surprise. 'You know,' he said, 'we must have been fools to think he' – meaning you Señor EhEh – 'could help us.' You see, both Michael and me…well, we had this idea, maybe you could of helped us. That's why Michael called you to tell you I wanted to see you. And after we talked, you said we would talk again. But you never came back. Never called. Not until now. And oh, my prayers have been answered. You are calling me back. Thank you, Señor EhEh."

"Señora Melcher...Sadie...please let me interrupt for a moment. I'm not at all certain I understand what you are telling me. What has any of this to do with the Russians?"

"Those crooks," she spat into the phone. "You see they wanted the Rabbi's money. Money that belonged to Hannah. Money that belonged to Rachael after Hannah died. And the Rabbi always told me he would leave money for me and Michael as well. But when the Rabbi died, there was no money to be found. When I asked Hannah, she looked at me wide-eyed and said, 'There is no money. My father gave all his money to the Russians.' I tell you, Señor EhEh, I couldn't believe my ears. Something was fishy about all this. The Rabbi was always kind to us. He always told me how much he appreciated the way I took care of him. He always promised he would protect me. Señor EhEh," she began to cry, "can you help us?"

EhEh, hearing all this, felt himself slipping deeper into a hole not totally, but somewhat, he had to admit, of his own making. First Manuela, her plea for help to which, in his sympathetic innocence, full of empathy for the suffering of his friend, albeit a purely casual friendship, not at all an old established childhood tie (the type of friendship he never actually knew) but simply a mild connection—to which he nevertheless responded as one fellow human being might ordinarily respond to another person's plight given the proper circumstances, that is to say, with the willingness, in fact, he had to admit, with something more like eagerness, almost with enthusiasm, the kind of enthusiasm he once associated with those he had always deemed impossibly afflicted with the disease he called savioritis that now apparently afflicted him. Would he ever be able to climb out? Such were the thoughts that raced through his mind with lightening speed. In fact, he felt as though a bolt of lightening had struck him upon hearing Sadie's cry for help.
He felt her emotion burning up the insulated wires of his heart.

All his life he had managed to live free of responsibilities other than to himself. And now in his old age he sensed himself losing his grip. He felt himself lost in a situation as though a huge octopus—an octopus of responsibilities were insidiously wrapping its tentacles around his legs, dragging him into an abyss he felt powerless to resist. His throat felt stuck, he couldn't speak.

"Can you help us?" Sadie repeated into his ear.

"I...I don't know," he croaked. "You will have to tell me how I can help you."

"Señor EhEh, we thought...Michael and me...we thought you might know, or could find out, where these Russian rascals are hiding. You know what I mean? You know how to move in the big world. You could find them maybe, and make them give back the Rabbi's money to the proper people. Maybe you could..."

"Listen, Sadie," his throat quivered, "I might be able to find them. In fact, I have been working on this task. You see, I am trying to help Miguel...I mean Julio...get well. And I have reason to believe that the Russians may know something that will help me in this effort. This is why I phoned you. I need more information about them. They are cousins, correct?"

"Not on my side. Hannah was my cousin from her mother's side. From Rachael's side. Rachael and my mother were sisters. The first Rachael, I mean. Not Hannah's child. The Russians come from her father's side. From the Rabbi's side. We know next to nothing about them."

"Tell me what you know."

"Does this mean you will help us?"

"I'll...I'll try. But I can't promise anything, mind you."

"Oh, Señor, if only you will try, that is all we are asking. Just that you try."

"I'll do my best." He felt his throat tightening. "Tell me what you know."

"Vell, like I said. Very little. I only remember Hannah saying once that one of the brothers was taking a shine to her Rachael. I think he was the Boris one. Hannah wasn't happy about this Boris in Rachael's life. And then Hannah, bless her poor heart, died from us. And the next thing we know, Rachael goes off with this Boris creature to California. And the money goes with them I'm guessing. Maybe you could find him in California?"

"He may be dead, Sadie. Along with Rachael, he may have been killed in the massacre."

"Massacre? What massacre? You say Rachael is dead? ...Killed in a massacre?" She began to sound hysterical.

"You didn't know about the massacre?"

"No. This is impossible to understand. When did this happen?"

"My God, Sadie, it happened ten years ago. How come you were never informed?" He now suddenly realized how insulated this Melcher family's life must be. Never seeing a newspaper, never watching the television, living in their own tiny world.

"I didn't know. Who is left to tell us of these things? I can't believe it."

"I wish I weren't the one to have to tell you, Sadie, but it is true. Rachael is dead. She's been dead for ten long years. She was murdered, killed in cold blood."

"Oi vey es mir."

She sounded like her body had caved in. He could feel the pain in her voice. Her voice gurgled as if a knife had been plunged into her throat. She began to sob. The news had penetrated her to the core, and he felt her sorrow.

"She was like my own baby," the poor woman moaned.

EhEh could see in his mind's eye her frail body, her shoulders bent forward from years of toil. He could see her moaning as old women moan pounding their chests, huddled at the graveside of a departed loved one, and his heart went out to her. Somehow, he must make things better for her. Somehow…he said to himself...

"Sadie," he spoke softly. "I'll find him, this Boris guy, dead or alive. Or if not him, I'll find his brother. I'll get to the truth. Somehow…" his voice wavered, as if it were an entity separate from himself, and it knew how impossible a task that might be.

"I can't talk about this anymore, Señor EhEh. Please forgive me, but I must hang up now. I can't think of anything but my poor Rachael. Ten years. I have ten years of mourning staring at me. Goodbye, Señor…"

Softly, she hung up. EhEh listened to the silence that clung to the inside of the phone like a ghost unwilling to depart, as if, by straining his ears he might hear her tears falling into the microphone, and then slowly returned the receiver to its cradle. He sat for a long time alone in his house. He thought about this family he had come to know, about their tragic lives, once so full of hope and high expectation, and he felt he understood his reasons as a young man for avoiding the complications of an emotional life. He thought about how he had made a kind of abstraction for himself as his way of being, taking up the life of a dispassionate scientist, just so he would not have to feel the pain these new friends were submerged in, the pain all humans have been condemned to experience since time immemorial, that he had attempted to avoid but was now caught up in. How ironic, he thought, despite his attempt to escape, his humanity had caught up with him. He sat until the evening shadows crept across the floor of his living room embracing him in its gloom. Then with a heavy sigh he took himself to bed, his stomach empty.

In the morning, the insistent ring of his telephone awakened him. His eyes opened to slanting brilliant sunlight that burst through his bedroom window like an explosion. Grumbling, he left his bed and went to the phone in the other room, barefooted, clutching his pajama pants so they wouldn't slip and cause him to stumble.

"Yes?" He roared into the phone.

"You never called me back."

For an instant, he had no idea who was speaking to him. Then he recognized it was the sound of Elena's voice.

"I'm sorry, Elena. I didn't have the heart to speak to anyone after…"

"After talking with Sadie?"

"Correct. I tell you it was so very sad. You see she never knew that Rachael had been killed. All these years, she had no idea of what had happened there in Beverley Hills. And I was the one who had to tell her. I tell you, she was devastated. And so was I. I still am… how you say? Bummed out."

"Oh, you poor darling man. And Sadie. What a shock for her. She practically raised the poor child when she was at her youngest."

After that, neither spoke for a moment, both engaged in their own thoughts.

"So now?" Elena broke the silence.

"So now," EhEh repeated the words without any self-consciousness. "So now, I must go to Los Angeles and find out what I can find out. I have Miguel…I mean Julio…to think about. I must find out whatever I can that might help him come out of his depression. Consuelo, with her magic, has pulled him out of his coma. But he is still very much depressed…so much so that he refuses to talk…refuses to acknowledge that he comprehends whatever you might be saying to him. He shows no signs of life, even though he breathes and takes in nourishment, a little bit of soup that Manuela prepares for him. He just sits in his bed and stares at nothing, just stares into the void."

"Consuelo?"

"Yes, the curandera who lives next door to Miguel and his granddaughter. And what I discover may be helpful as well to Sadie in some way."

"Oh, you poor man. I can tell by your voice, you feel discouraged. So, this Miguel is actually Julio?"

"If he's telling me the truth. And I do believe him. And I want to help him."

"You don't have much hope you will learn anything that might make a difference. I can tell, you really didn't ask for this problem to fall in your lap, did you?"

"No, you are correct. I was living a simple, uncomplicated life before this…this task fell to me to carry out. But now it is my task. And I will carry it out."

"But you said you have no money. How will you get to Los Angeles?"

"I didn't say I have no money. I said I would have to dip into my savings. I can do that. And I will."

"Listen, my friend. I have an idea."

"What idea?"

"Never you mind. Give me an hour. I'll phone you back. Get yourself washed and dressed and make yourself a good breakfast."

She hung up. How did she know he was in his pajamas? He scratched his behind with one hand while with the other he returned the receiver to its cradle half believing Elena had some kind of clairvoyant aptitude.

He went to wash up and took note as he stepped into the shower of how starved he was, his spirits rising now that he had determined he would go to Los Angeles.

And to her credit, Elena was back ringing EhEh's phone exactly within the hour. He had just finished eating.

"Bueno?" He answered, this time in a cheerful mood.

"EhEh, listen carefully. Oh, excuse me, dear man. I know you listen carefully. After all, you are an educator, a professor."

"What are you babbling about, Elena? Get to the point, will you?"

"Listen. My friend. Go to your airport and book a flight. Your ticket is there waiting for you."

"But how…?"

"Never you mind," she broke in. "It's all arranged. Go, and don't ask any silly questions."

And with that, she hung up.

For an instant, the old EhEh felt alarmed. Another tentacle had attached itself, a commitment that would lead him down some unknowable, unforeseeable path was staring him in the face. Elena was putting him in an embarrassing situation. But then the new, just barely emerging EhEh, felt a stirring of excitement welling up from hidden depths. He felt positively giddy as he shrugged, and said to himself: *What the hell…in for a penny, in for a pound…*he remembered this English idiom from his student days when he spent a year in England on a graduate exchange program; it always tickled his fancy, mainly because he didn't quite fathom its original use until the end of his stay. Most people used it as a gambling expression, whereas originally it was in reference to receiving punishment. In the old days, it mattered naught whether you stole a penny or a pound – whatever amount, you got the same severe punishment. It was the phrase itself that caused him this giddiness he was now experiencing as he flipped the ignition key and the pickup roared into action. He was in all the way now.

EhEh pulled up at the top of the dunes overlooking the sea, and climbed out of the pickup. This time, he was on top of his game. The baseball caps and other paraphernalia were in the truck bed behind the cab. The kids came over, not with as much anticipation as previously. However, their enthusiasm went sky high when they saw EhEh unpack the red baseball caps. He showed them how to adjust the strap at the back of the cap so it would fit snugly on any size head. Everyone roared with appreciation. EhEh felt he had hit a home run. Each cap had the favored ball club's emblem, the stylized M of the Diablos Rojos del México across the front.

There was a spring to his gait as he strode across the dunes to Miguel's shack. He was hoping he would find Consuelo in the house, and his hope was rewarded. She came out of the back room to greet him, a broad grin on her long, narrow face. To EhEh, she looked like the proverbial cat that had swallowed the canary.

"I'm back," he said, as if the fact of his presence were not enough. And then he added, "You look positively triumphant, Consuelo. Some change has occurred?"

"You bet your boots. Come, I'll show you."

She led him into Miguel's room where, from the open window, a pleasant breeze from the sea ruffled the thin muslin curtains. The room was full of cheery light. Some transformation had taken place. EhEh was totally amazed. He stepped into the room, half expecting to see a restored Miguel sitting up in bed smiling at him. But the surprised look on his face was nothing short of absolute mystification. The bed was empty.

"Where is he?" He exclaimed, turning to the curandera. "What has happened? I've been gone only half a day, and something momentous has happened. Tell me!"

"I went to Guaymas," she said complacently, "to see an old friend. He is an ancient brujo, and in fact my teacher in the art of soul retrieval. We put our heads together and came up with a plan using one of his most guarded secrets. So, I cannot tell you what we did. I cannot even tell you his name, so don't ask."

"You haven't told me where he is, what has happened to him? Have you made him disappear? Is this the magic you and your brujo conjured up?"

"No...no," she laughed. "Miguel has not disappeared. He is down at the sea in his favorite spot, visiting his Hannah. Javier and Manuela carried him there. At his request, mind you. No fuerza... And what have you been up to?"

EhEh reported to her whom he now regarded as his spiritual mentor the conversations he had had with the people in El Cuidad. He spoke about his anger toward Alonzo for believing him, EhEh, to be one of the gangsters, which wasn't exactly true, Alonzo had called him an extortionist, but it was EhEh who made the inappropriate conclusion that linked his name with the Russians. EhEh knew that his exaggerated assertion was not scientifically sound. Nevertheless, he preferred exercising his new taste for the dramatic that had been unleashed by his conversation with Sadie. And when he spoke about his talk with Sadie, his emotions went full blast into play. Her sadness over the news of Rachael underscored his feelings about the whole family he now felt so closely linked to. Once again, he pictured Miguel as Julio dashing into his beauty salon in a terrified state, as Alonzo had described.

Suddenly it occurred to him that what Alonzo had reported may not have been true. Suddenly he harbored suspicions about Alonzo. All this he shared with Consuelo, wondering the while as he spoke, if it weren't something the curandera had done or said that had unlocked something in him. Something had been let loose...something that now seemed to promise becoming a constant volcanic eruption. For by the end of his lengthy account, tears were streaming down his cheeks.

They were still standing in Miguel's bedroom. Consuelo, seeing EhEh in such a state, grabbed him by his upper arms and pulled him to her bosom. She was almost as tall as he. EhEh had only to tilt his head a trifle and it rested on her bony shoulder, and as she patted him softly on his back, as if she were burping him, he let loose with heavy sobbing.

"There...there..." She murmured. "It's all right now. You'll be fine now."

After a bit of more sobbing, he pulled himself back and stared at her.

"What's all right now?" He wanted to know.

"This energy...your emotion...it was all bottled up in you for so long. Once we pulled the plug, all this feeling, all these sobs had to come out."

"Who? Who is this we you are talking about?" He felt baffled by her assertion.

"All of us. Each one of us played our part in your healing."

"Healing? What are you talking about? It's not me who has been sick. It's been Miguel."

"My friend, you must understand. In the end, it is all of us who have been sick. And when one of us is healed, all of us are healed. It is the law of nature."

Such laws of nature EhEh had never heard before. His education at all the universities he ever attended never addressed this natural law. He wasn't at all certain he had the mental equipment that would aid him in understanding Consuelo's cosmology.

"I don't understand," he said.

"Never mind. In time you will. I assure you. You see, EhEh, how simple it is to become one of my students?"

"Yes," he said. And pulling himself together, he offered her a smile. "I've stepped into the invisible blades of a helicopter. It's slicing away pieces of my mind. Ordinarily, I would be alarmed. But you know? I don't even care anymore about preserving my mind. I'm going to Los Angeles."

The young people had just returned and had overheard EhEh's last statement.

"You are going to Los Angeles," they both said in unison, making it a fact.

"What have you done with Miguel?" EhEh asked, a proprietary lilt to his voice.

"We left him at the tide pool," Manuela spoke for the two.

"Are you sure that's a good idea?"

"He'll be alright. He wanted to be alone so he could talk in private, he said."

Consuelo turned to EhEh. "When do you leave for Los Angeles?"

"As soon as possible. First, I want to have a talk with Miguel. I'm hoping he will be willing to answer some questions."

Consuelo became thoughtful.

"He may not be ready for that. We can't push him too fast." Then she added, "Come, children. Let us make a fiesta meal. We'll pool together our food. Let us get Maria Roybal to help."

By time they were ready to eat, the sun had become an orange ball slowly sinking into the darkening sea, now a deep purple. Javier and EhEh had gone to fetch Miguel while there was still a sky bright enough to turn the bottom side of puffy clouds into shades of ruby red. And when they returned the old barber noticed it was EhEh who had helped carry him, and he greeted him with a broad smile and announced with a sweet demeanor that he was happy to see his friend. He was curious to know what had brought the scholar from Guaymas to visit him. By the way he talked it was evident he had no idea the role EhEh had been playing in Miguel's personal drama. EhEh felt it unwise to immediately jump into the burning questions. The old barber was so cheerful, raking over old wounds was obviously not a good idea. Instead, EhEh focused on the night of fiesta before them.

"We are celebrating. I've come to join in the fiesta."

"Yes," replied Miguel. "Isn't it marvelous? I was so against this when I first suspected. They were too much together all the time. I worried so much for her welfare. But now I am happy about it all. Aren't they wonderful?"

"What in the world are you taking about?" EhEh was beginning to wonder if the old barber had lost some of his marbles after all.

"The kids. Manuela and Javier. Just look at him. He's a grown up giant now!"

EhEh had momentarily forgotten that Javier was there standing right beside him.

"Isn't he a fine strapping boy?"

EhEh nodded. "Sí…Sí."

"And you know why I am so happy, Señor EhEh?"

EhEh shook his head in the negative.

"I am happy because I am soon to be a great-grandfather!"

The dinner party proved to be a huge success. Due to the combined efforts of the three culinary artists, Manuela, Consuelo, and Maria, the top of the small kitchen table in Miguel's back room had practically disappeared under the pile of delicious odors. There was a huge platter of steaming tamales stuffed with green chilies and bits of unidentifiable meats, and beside it another huge platter of rolled up fried tortillas with spicy shrimps and fresh green onions inside, and a bowl of salsa to dip the fried tortillas in. And there was a bowl of pisole, and a bowl of stewed beans, and dishes of steamed rice mixed with a medley of vegetables at both ends of the table. There were small dishes of olives, pickles, marinated onions and other assorted delicacies and spicy sauces.

And Diaz came to the party, Consuelo's elusive husband as tall and skinny as she, as did Maria's man, the shy Roybal. And others came, men and women of the village. They dipped in and out of the shack and sampled the cuisine, congratulating the soon-to-become-great-grandfather with fond pats on the back, the men, now that it was officially recognized, congratulating the young Javier in celebration of his new manly status, some of the woman measuring Manuela's slightly swelling belly with the palms of their hands, announcing with exclamations of female insight predictions of gender and size, everyone overjoyed to see the barber obviously on the road to recovery sitting at the table, stuffing his mouth that was grinning from ear to ear, all so jolly, especially the wives the hair of whose husbands had been rather butchered under the erratic scissors of Manuela's novice hand, they especially sidled up to the old barber and planted respectful kisses on one or both of his proud greasy cheeks, the man, now after ten years of cutting their hair, no longer looked upon as the foreigner.

EhEh refrained from asking the many burning questions that were on the tip of his tongue. It was indeed a time only for celebration; definitely not an occasion for soul searching into the past; and the festive mood persisted deep into the night. Nevertheless, he was impatient to get on with his research. For although it seemed to be the case that Miguel, from Consuelo's magic, was on the road to recovery, EhEh strongly believed that all pockets of this vast mystery, the history that had provoked the illness in the first place, must be turned out—just so no relapse might occur. What was needed, he firmly believe, was a total cleansing. But, in all honesty, he had to admit, it was more his scientific instincts that required this satisfaction, for it seemed that all of them, Manuela especially, were content now to let the sleeping dogs lie, but he was determined to discuss the matter with Consuelo just as soon as things settled down. That night if at all possible. Or at best the very next morning. Not wishing to upset the apple cart, he wanted her concordance before questioning Miguel—and Manuela as well. Yes, Manuela, he couldn't completely believe she remembered nothing. True, she was only a six-year old at the time. And surely she must have been severely traumatized. But still he couldn't but help feel there was something she knew but refused to reveal.

So, he waited with all due patience, meanwhile taking part in the joyous celebration by stuffing himself with the very tasty dishes, laughing at the jokes that flew back and forth among the witty ones, drinking more than his share of the ruby wine that didn't seem to run out, bottle after bottle.

And in the morning, he found himself awakened by the screech of gulls as they skimmed over the dancing water vigorously in search for breakfast. His body felt stiff. His throat parched. He had curled up in the cab of the truck, somehow packing his long legs and torso between the doors, his head on the armrest of the passenger's door, his feet jammed against the door of the driver's side, his knees hanging over the seat curled around the gearshift. He opened his eyes to the brilliant light, and immediately clamped them shut.

Consuelo was dead set against EhEh interviewing the two Guzmans. EhEh outlined the questions he was most interested in getting some answers to. The way he talked, she interjected, it sounded like he saw them as two suspects in a criminal case.

"Not on your life," she said. And her voice indicated she was unmovable.

They were walking along the beach, their bare feet sloshing in the surf. To a casual observer they offered a view of an old couple enjoying a day on the strand. Consuelo held a seashell in one hand, her sandals in the other. EhEh had his shoes, their strings attached, dangling around his neck, his trousers rolled half way up his shins. A slight, warm breeze rustled his meager endowment of hair, his head bent forward in the direction of her voice. He studiously listened.

"His condition is very delicate," she was saying. "He could easily swing back into his depression. We do not want him to have to dwell on old sad memories. A thin scab is only now forming. And Manuela is happy over her coming motherhood. Why burden her with the ordeal of dredging up the past?"

She went on with a pithy discourse regarding the role of the shaman, and the sacred responsibility one assumes in this arcane work. Following this, she launched into the fundamentals of her calling, allowing him insights into the manner and means by which one prepares the arduous task of discipleship through association with a master, glancing at him from time to time to observe the effect of her words. Was he getting the picture? Did he see that in order to grow and achieve mastery one must listen carefully and dutifully follow the direction of the teacher?

EhEh listened and nodded demonstrating with serious fleeting looks in her direction, that, despite his professional status and his advanced age and experience, he was totally willing to place his trust in her. This was the look he tried to convey. Was she seeing his trust?

This was something quite new in his life, being led by someone other than himself. He felt excitement. He thought back to that day when he observed her in that magic place where the little rodent, a wild creature had taken food from her opened hand. It took his breath away to think of it, that he was stepping into this elusive and wondrous side of life in which the mind could experience something that his earlier learning had only alluded to, namely, the touch of the numinous. She, the *brujita*, could teach him how to open these doors into the mystery, and he felt grateful that Consuelo had chosen to be his mentor.

"You said you were going to Los Angeles. Here is your assignment. Go there and do all the snooping you so desire. And when you do, sharpen your senses. Catch every nuance expressed in the faces and body movements of those you interrogate. Investigate, investigate, and investigate. Come back with something tangible. Then, if I feel they are ready, I will allow you to question them. As for now, they need to be coddled."

"I understand," he said, but he was miffed nevertheless. He sensed this would not be the last time his desires would run contrary to that of his spiritual mentor. In subtle ways she was teaching him a new understanding of life. This he recognized and appreciated, but her ways were difficult for him to easily comprehend. He envisioned the process would be a struggle, and reminded himself to be forbearing. Nevertheless, he felt miffed.

The next afternoon, a US Airways DeHaveland-8 lifted off from the Guaymas Airport bound for Phoenix, Arizona, the first leg toward Los Angeles. At the tail end of the craft, among a swarm of giggling teen-agers—offspring of Guaymas elite society—sat an elderly gentleman dressed in his best white guayabera shirt and black slacks. A pair of metal spectacles rested halfway down his nose. His balding white head angled over a notebook, a ballpoint in his hand, the man seemingly oblivious to the back-and-forth ruckus swirling around him like a cloud of airborne grackles.

It was Señor EhEh.

With no advanced notice for a proper reservation, he had to take whatever seat was available. When he stepped up to the ticket counter that afternoon, he was amazed and delighted by the airline's efficient communications system. He had only to say his name and show his passport to the young lady on the other side who typed it into a keyboard, and a set of tickets to Los Angeles popped out of the machine, the modern equivalent of magic. EhEh had gone to his bank before heading to the airport to extract 20,000 pesos from his savings account, converting the money to U.S. dollars, just in case something went awry in Elena's plan. But the modern equivalent worked. Elena had caused all this to happen. How she had accomplished this trick, he had no idea. Evidently, wealthy people had the ability to make the world move according to their every whim. Quickly, he wiped the thought away. That was a nasty slur, he mumbled under his breath. He reminded himself of how grateful he ought to be to his benefactress. Because of her, his meager savings would remain intact.

"Lo siento, Señor Escudero," the young lady interrupted his thoughts, "your 1st class ticket cannot be honored. We have only one last seat available. It's in the back of the aircraft. Your flight may be a bit noisy."

EhEh murmured that he would put up with noise, whatever that meant, all he wanted to do was to get to Los Angeles in reasonable comfort. She smiled back at him with cheerful reassurance, "Rest easy, Señor, our service is impeccable; you will very definitely arrive at your destination intact." EhEh smiled in return, accepted his ticket, and moved on to the security screening area, making note that the word, 'intact' was becoming a theme for the day. He took it to be a good omen.

On his way, side-stepping the mob of passengers scurrying this way and that, everyone anxious not to miss their flight, EhEh made a mental, sociological note regarding the young lady at the ticket counter. She had the slender and vibrant face of a typical Guaymas young woman. On his weekly food expeditions to the Mercado, he encountered gobs of such youngsters. In contrast to their overstuffed and haggard mommas and aunts who wobbled among the meat and vegetable stalls filling their net bags with ingredients for supper, these young females stood out in their spangled tight jeans and colorful tank tops like happy-go-lucky birds of a tropical rainforest flittering about from one ropa stall to the next.

But this one, despite her hygienic appearance in the white tailored US Airway blouse with the company's insignia embroidered on the cloth above her left breast, she somehow came across as a variation of a modern Hollywood vamp. It was the super-bright lip shade she wore in combination with the makeup, pinkish-tan stuff, on her cheeks that gave him this impression. Not to mention the fanciful mousse job—her hair looked like the twisted blades of a crashed helicopter. It was a hairdo he had never before seen in Guaymas. Examining his thoughts, he recognized with a grin that he was exercising, in anticipation of his arrival in Los Angeles, the investigative acumen Consuelo had advised.

EhEh sat scrunched in his seat thirty-five thousand feet above the ground, looking down though the small window of the droning aircraft. He could see puffs of white clouds beneath him, with patches of Mexican rural countryside peeking back at him, a mingling of scattered fields under cultivation with stretches of white desert sprinkled with bits of green and black dots that he assumed were rocks and trees.

The vibrating plane groaned onwards, its belly filled with human bodies as though it were a mythological creature that had devoured them all and was working hard at digesting its food. I am in the belly of the beast, he murmured to himself somewhat giddy for it reminded him of childhood fairytales, and he felt indeed that he was being taken to the land of make believe where anything could happen. A sense of foreboding steeled upon him.

His notebook rested on the little table he had unfolded from the seat in front of him. He turned back to it and absorbed himself in organizing his thoughts. The Los Angeles phase had begun, he didn't know what to expect, only that his inquiries were going forward, and there was no turning back. He began by addressing himself to the person who had, in the first place, brought him to this unlooked-for turn of events in a life that hitherto had been totally unadventurous.

My dear Manuela:

I'm speeding to Los Angeles, jammed in the back of a plane packed with people your own age. They are on their way to visit Disney Land, a destination, I gather, favored by young people. I must admit it is difficult for me to imagine you among them, free of the milieu in which you are immersed, free of family responsibilities, free to explore the many possibilities that beckon a youthful soul.

Your life has taken a different turn, not one wholly of your own making to be sure. I can relate to that. The web of fate gets woven in mysterious ways both for you and me. You had no part in the shape and scope of the small number of choices life has given you. Your grandfather swept you away from the home you once knew, where something horrible happened that your soul has suppressed. For whatever reason, Miguel brought you to this remote shantytown that has become the only world you know, and here you have made a destiny for yourself that is swelling you toward motherhood. And because of that, Consuelo has constrained me from burdening your spirit with difficult questions. You mental state is too delicate she insists. Well, I'm not sure I agree. Be that as it may, I comply with the dictates of my teacher. Yes, Consuelo has become the mystery school I have stumbled into. In that regard, you and I, I believe, are fellow students.

And speaking of mystery, indeed, I have been plunged into a whirlpool of mystery. What lies ahead in Los Angeles, will either clarify the past with facts that you once felt so strongly would be the instrument of Miguel's healing, or drown me in a morass of total bafflement, or even worse. You see I have a sense of foreboding over what I might uncover. Even though facts are now unnecessary it seems, for it seems that indeed Consuelo has performed a miracle, answers for any of the questions that haunt me may prove the eclipse of that very same miracle, unhinge the whole thing, including myself. Will any wisdom come of this? At some level I think I am questioning my own sanity. For it seems that I am now the only person in this affair who cares about finding out the truth. You seem perfectly happy with Miguel by your side, out of his depression, besotted with the thought of a great-grandchild brightening his waning years, with Javier by your side, the proud papa now officially acknowledged as your bed partner, with Consuelo by your side, taking your temperature every five minutes. Why can I not leave well enough alone? Why can't I just simply go back in peace to my bungalow in Guaymas, loll in my hammock, and study my books? Why do I need to know? Know what, you ask? For one thing, are you a Zaslavsky or not? And if so, which one is your father, Boris or Efim? And what exactly happened in that Salon of Beauty on Rodeo Drive? What was the massacre all about? And how was it that Julio was reported killed when he claims to be Miguel the barber living in this shantytown. Is he truly one and the same person? And how did he ever find this unknown place at the edge of the sea? I even question if you are truly his granddaughter. And then there is the question of the life in El ciudad. What was it that terrified him so much that he disappeared over night? This is just a small sampling of the issues I am enthralled by. Yes, enthralled is the right word. I feel truly I have stumbled into a fairytale, or perhaps rather a nightmare that I cannot awaken from until my feet are firmly back on terra firma.

EhEh had written himself into a tizzy by the time the plane touched ground in Phoenix. He felt peckish and hoped there would be time enough between flights to grab a bite. He came upon a news kiosk on his way to a food arcade and decided to buy an American newspaper so he could brush up on his English. With his carryon strapped over his shoulder, a bag of sandwiches poked into his briefcase, and the newspaper wedged under his arm, he boarded the plane happy to discover he had a 1st class seat waiting for him.

Seated by the window was a man dressed in a business suit who looked up from his reading and smiled as EhEh took his seat.

"Business in LA," he said, pointing to the report, an open file on his laptop screen. The man was more interested in talking. He closed his computer and commenced to speak about the nature of his work completely assured that his neighbor would be as fascinated with the topic as he was, particularly because of the way EhEh paid such close attention to his words. And EhEh was very pleased to get out of his head for a while. He listened with growing interest about the ins and outs of network computing programs designed for the feverishly active business world.

"Business to business programming. Very lucrative. What line are you in?"

EhEh replied that he was a retired university professor of sociology, just simply on a vacation. He thought of possibly visiting Disney World while in Los Angeles.

"Really?" The businessman said, his eyebrows rising. "A study you are making, eh? From Mexico?" He inquired observing EhEh's attire.

"Yes," EhEh smiled. "Right on both counts."

They conversed all the way to LAX, sipping wine delivered by an obliging flight attendant. EhEh spoke of his year in London as a graduate student many years ago, and his love for the English language, happy to have a chance to practice after so long a time, making only an occasional trip to the U.S. to attend professional conferences, mainly at the University of New Mexico where he had also been employed as an exchange professor for a single year back in the late 70s. The businessman said he was still a toddler in the late 70s and chuckled over that, then went on to talk about his schooling in computer science at the University of Arizona in Phoenix and the firm he now worked for, joining right after getting his degree, working his way up the ladder, now in marketing. Then he talked about his wife and two children and the joys of suburban life. It was a rather dull conversation, but satisfying to EhEh for its pleasant effect of freeing his mind a while from the morbidity that had seized him like an angry ghost. That had been a most dreadful plane ride, he decided. Dull reality can be so very soothing. At the terminal, they parted with a handshake both happy to have made the acquaintance, content they had fulfilled the standard social obligation, and were now free to go their separate ways.

EhEh, his body stiff from hours of sitting, stood hesitantly in the baggage claim area surrounded by hurrying travelers sweeping past. He wasn't sure about his next move. He had failed to consider where he would stay. At length, he nudged himself forward in the direction of the exit that would take him to the taxi stands, his mind focused on finding a hotel, at which moment his eye fell upon the most astonishing sign he had ever seen. It was at eye level, held by two well-manicured hands that belonged to a young man dressed in a chauffeur's black uniform.

The sign read: Mr. Eduardo Escudero.

He stepped up close to the sign ignoring the man who held it, as one would examine a notice nailed to a telephone pole. Like a nearsighted buffoon, he peered at his name. What the hell was this, he wanted to know, then jumped back startled by the man's voice. They had been standing practically toe-to-toe.

"Are you Mr. Escudero by any chance?"

"As a matter of fact, I am. Please explain the meaning of this."

EhEh's voice exceeded normal volume by a notch or two. The young man smiled in reply happy to explain. He told EhEh his own name in soothing tones, the company he worked for, the name of the hotel he was assigned to take his passenger to, everything in order, this was the normal world, nothing unusual, no mistake.

He offered to take EhEh's carryon saying, "Follow me, please." EhEh grunted, handed over his bag, and followed the young man, somewhat alarmed that a hidden hand was meddling in his affairs, yet somewhat relieved that he evidently had a roof over his head, at least for the night.

The chauffeur guided EhEh to a cream colored stretch limo. It was parked just outside the exit door in a spot reserved for celebrities, he was told. EhEh sank into the soft leather seat, and ruminated over this surprising turn of events. The driver was so far forward EhEh could hardly see him. It seemed as though he were being transported to his night's rest in a magic machine. Not a decibel of sound from the traffic whizzing by penetrated the limo that was sealed off from the world like the vault of a bank. They drove through the streets of a city that never seemed to sleep. The time was a little past ten at night.

It was not too difficult for EhEh to figure out whose hidden hand had arranged all this. Elena's, of course. The mystery part was not so easily deciphered however. What was she trying to accomplish with her largesse? He could imagine only one glaring motive. He squirmed in his seat at the thought.

The limo pulled up in front of the Beverly Wilshire Hotel situated on Wilshire Boulevard in the heart of Beverly Hills, just steps from the renowned Rodeo Drive with its many exclusive shops, he would soon discover. A bellhop popped out of the building, took EhEh's bag, and escorted the elderly gentleman to the front desk, where it was disclosed that he had already been registered. The bellhop gently steered EhEh to the elevators and up they went to the 12th floor where he was safely deposited in a suite of three rooms. He was shown the major features of the sitting room, the huge plasma TV that took up half a wall, the island bar outfitted with a sink and a refrigerator stocked with all kinds of hard and soft drinks. His attendant deftly slid the sliding glass door that led to the balcony outside. With a sweep of his arm he invited the guest, treated like a national treasure, to step outside for a moment and take pleasure in the broad view the suite offered of the glittering city nightscape. Finally, the door to his bedroom was opened and the bellhop laid EhEh's bag on a stand built for that purpose. EhEh fumbled in his pockets for a suitable tip. Alone at last and totally exhausted, EhEh slipped out of his shoes, tumbled into a bed he registered as fit for a king, and closed his eyes, wondering for the briefest moment before drifting off what the function of the third room was in this luxurious suite.

Morning light stole in through elegant sheer drapery, as silently as a stalking cat, and brought EhEh to his senses. He awakened with a feeling of profound rejuvenation. Not an ache in his body, from head to toe. His hand patted the comfortable bed affectionately as he rose to meet the day. And after an invigorating wash-up in a shower stall he could only describe as amazing—it was as large as his entire bathroom at home, and full of gadgets he never knew existed—he donned clean clothes, brown cotton slacks and a blue polo shirt, then stepped to the door, bracing himself for what awaited him on the other side. His sixth sense already whispered to him he would find Elena in the sitting room. And his hunch proved correct, or rather partially correct, for he found her actually sitting outside on the balcony at a glass-top table that was loaded with breakfast goodies.

"Good morning, professor," she said with a cheery voice, imitating a starry eyed student. "I trust you slept well?"

"I should have known you'd be here the minute the plane tickets were in my hand."

"Oh, don't sound so disgruntled. Sit down and have some breakfast."

At the sight of the food—a large platter under a glass dome full of sparkling scrambled eggs and a variety of grilled meats, a basket of scrumptious looking rolls, scones and fancy fruited danish, a small barrel of whipped butter, and a silver thermos of coffee—EhEh felt his stomach growl. He was famished.

They ate and talked leisurely. Elena pointed to the marvelous view of the Hollywood Hills that stretched before them. She mentioned with warm praise the famous Rodeo Drive, every bit as splendid as the Polanco in El Ciudad. And, turning to the issue of climate, she observed how this was the best season, mid September, to be visiting Southern California. EhEh reminded her he hadn't come here for a vacation. He had serious work to do. She shouldn't harbor any misconceptions.

"I hope you understand," he said.

"Of course I understand, dear man. That's why I'm here. I've come to help you."

This brought a raised eyebrow to EhEh's otherwise non-committal countenance.

"You don't need to look so dubious, my friend. I can help you in many ways."

"Yes?" He said not without a trace of sarcasm.

"Yes indeed. Look, let's not beat around the bush. For one thing, I have a car downstairs in the garage, a nice rental convertible to be exact. You will need quick transportation to get around. And as for that, as your driver, I can get you anywhere. I know this town very well." She gestured with an outstretched sweeping arm. "I went to school here at UCLA, just a few miles from where we are sitting. You see my father had this idea that a good education in the U.S. would land me a good marriage. Not an original idea to be sure, but an accurate one. And it paid off. Beside my good looks, it was my education and of course papa's bank account that got me Edgar Navarro, and Navarro got me very rich."

There she was doing it again, throwing her money in his face. He was convinced now more than ever that she was gunning after him. But why? What did she see in him?

"And one more thing," she went on, "Hannah, you recall, was my friend. And Rachael was almost like a second daughter to me. And when Hannah told me on her deathbed to watch out for the Russians, I somehow sensed that a day would come when I would want to know what she meant. And that day has arrived. And it is you, EhEh, who has brought me to this point. Over the years, other considerations distracted me. Hannah and the movement, all that feminist stuff, went out of my mind a long time ago. Had you never looked me up, the memory of Hannah in the hospital would have eventually slipped totally into oblivion. It was you who made me aware so vividly of poor Rachael's fate when you told me how hard the news had struck poor Sadie. I've had nightmares about her murder ever since."

Elena's speech gave EhEh the feeling he might have found an ally in her. For one thing, her attitude toward Sadie had softened. She too had experienced some empathy for Sadie. He felt he could confide in her. He told her, in conciliatory tones, of the state of affairs at home. He spoke of his bafflement over the disinterest the principal figures—those very people whose same blood as Rachael's ran through their veins, her own father and daughter—how remote they were from wanting to know the truth. He reminded Elena of Manuela's pregnancy and her convenient lack of memory. He was quite certain she was purposely suppressing something. Then he turned to Consuelo and her sudden triumph in Miguel's healing, how she mysteriously overcame his self-imposed silence, turning him almost into a joyful nitwit as if he had been given a lobotomy. He spoke about his wanting to ask the old man all sorts of questions, that, had he been given sufficient answers, would have in all probability made this journey to Los Angeles unnecessary. And then the final straw, Consuelo's insistence that he, EhEh, not probe any further into the collective Guzman psyche lest the old man sink back. They had to be protected from the truth and not forced to talk. But he avoided mentioning anything about Consuelo's impact on his own psyche.

"Typical, isn't it?" He said overcome with frustration. "I'm the only one who cares to know what really happened."

"But in that, you are not alone, dear man," Elena replied, a trace of triumph in her voice.

"Yes, I can see that."

EhEh felt a sense of relief that she indeed had come to Los Angeles to be helpful. Yet, on the other hand, he felt cautious. He sensed she harbored an ulterior motive, one that filled him with dread. He sat back sipping the last of his coffee, and scrutinized the person before him.

She was a handsome woman he had to admit. Slim and well proportioned, she knew how to dress sensibly as well as stylishly, wearing a simple, obviously expensive brown blouse, lighter in color than the dark brown of her slacks. And he noticed she had changed the look of her narrow face with a new hairdo, cut in what he knew was once called a Dutch boy. She had dyed it a dark brown with cunning streaks of gray. A strand of colored gems hung around her neck. She looked considerably younger than her 60 plus years, the skin of her chin still snug against the bone.

He liked what he saw. His thoughts of her as predator softened if only slightly. A bachelor all his life, having had only a rare physical encounter with the opposite sex that always resulted in disaster, he felt himself a dismal failure when it came to relations with women. It would never have occurred to him in this late time of his life that any woman might take an interest in him. She had said she had feelings toward him. Those were her words, he recalled. What exactly did she mean by them? She had some kind of energy about her that seemed to breathe the way he imagined a wild animal breathed, a kind of dangerous passion that could spring out at you at any moment. It was unsettling.

She smiled at him. And he smiled back, amazed at himself that he felt warmed by her smile.

"So," she said, "what is your first move?"

Just then, a knock at the door brought a young man into the suite who was dressed in what gave the impression of a modified butler's outfit. Unobtrusively, he removed the breakfast dishes. The pause gave EhEh time to think about his first move. His mind fell back on the one place he comfortably knew.

"The library," he said. "I want to read the actual news reports of the massacre. I presume there is a library in Beverly Hills. They would have archives, I believe."

"Good," she said. "I know where it is. I'll take you there."

They sat side by side at a table in the reading room pouring over three issues of the L.A. Times. In the first issue the incident that happened so many years ago occupied a portion of the front page. They read the initial story and then the two brief follow-ups relegated to secondary pages, passing the documents back and forth.

The incident had occurred close to noontime on Tuesday, May 18, 1999, the day before the news report. An ordinary weekday on Rodeo Drive, shoppers calmly strolling from store to store, patrons of sidewalk cafes chatting and enjoying their lunch, when suddenly the peaceful setting shattered like broken glass. Witnesses saw two masked men with machineguns smashing open the glass door of a salon-boutique with a burst from their guns, then stepping inside, spraying the interior for what seemed like an eternity, as if time had stood still. One man, whose name was mentioned, said the guns had blasted away for about thirty seconds. The two gunmen dashed into a car parked at the curb. The vehicle shot around the corner before anyone actually registered what had happened. The same male witness said he thought it was a white SUV, no idea what make.

The report continued with details of the subsequent investigation. Here, EhEh paid close attention. Police officers arrived at the crime scene within five minutes. The paper gave the name of the investigating officer, a Sergeant Barientos. EhEh wrote down his name wondering if the Sergeant spoke Spanish. Four bodies were described as having been found sprawled on the floor in pools of blood, three men and a woman. Only the woman and one of the men were identified. Rachael Valladares, the proprietress of the establishment, and Julio Valladares, presumably a relative of the female victim. The remaining two victims apparently had no identifying papers on their persons, according to the police. EhEh wrote in his notebook this mystifying piece of information. Also, he took down the address of Rachael's Salon de Belleza.

The police were not able to make any headway with the case, as the second and third reports indicated. These subsequent news items centered mainly on the public's indignation. A quoted statement by one Beverly Hills citizen complained about the authority's inadequacies when it came to protecting the public from such outrageous outbreaks. The absurd complaint, EhEh surmised, was quoted obviously for its comedy value, the whole affair treated as some kind of unfortunate anomaly in the busy lives of the Beverly Hills populous, as if the media and the authorities were intent on minimizing alarm in the minds of the county's upscale citizenry.

    EhEh pointed to the newsprint and expressed his assessment of what appeared to be some sort of cover-up, and Elena agreed, showing disgust. She vented her jaundiced feelings on the subject of governments and authority in general for a good long minute before catching her breath.

    "You know," she continued, "when I came here in the 60s the campus scene was rife with anarchic sentiments. Opposition to the establishment and the war in Vietnam, the beats and the hippies, the pot and the acid—everything was out in the open then. The authorities couldn't hide the facts. The whole scene pulled me in. I got radicalized. And then I went home and got married, played the dutiful daughter, hooked up with a businessman. A bit of depression set in. But then I met Hannah and I was in heaven again."

    "But after a few years, you dropped all that."

    "I know. It might not make sense to you, but I began to see the downside of Hannah's life. The impact her commitment to the movement had had on her husband and daughter. Left to herself, Rachael began living a wild existence cavorting with dangerous people. I got a whiff of how she was carrying on, and I became afraid of the same outcome happening to my daughter. I guess you might say my middle class programming won out over youthful idealism. Or I just got tired of the never-ending struggle. Or I just simply slipped back to what was easy. I don't know."

    "Probably a combination of all that," EhEh sought to console her. "Those were exciting times. I was not engaged. I watched from the sidelines. All of that a fascinating study for me—the feminist movement, the pop culture, the activism—I observed as a sociologist. I wasn't a participant like you. You have nothing to be sorry for. You did your share. You couldn't ask anymore of yourself"

"Of course, I would like to think you are right. But I do wonder about how different Dora's life might have been had I stayed involved, not slipped back. Because of me, she's living the same kind of boring life I endured caring for Edgar's needs, hosting his silly parties, attending those silly affairs he dragged me to—all just for the sake of his business. No, that's not true. Dora isn't bored in the least. Maybe that's what hurts. Her husband is a successful plastic surgeon, a sportsman and a travel buff. They go all over the world mindlessly indulging their pleasures, as if that alone were their only purpose, the only meaning of life."

"And what does the meaning of life suppose to look like? That's been my perennial question." EhEh murmured, turning inward.

"I don't know," she said, and looked down at her hands as if the lines in her palms had the power to unravel this ancient riddle. "I wonder what Rachael would have said about the meaning of life," she whispered.

"Yes, poor Rachael." EhEh sighed. "To die so young. Was it a meaningless life that got extinguished?"

His voice trailed off, his mind cast back to the young woman lying on the floor drenched in her own blood, and he shuddered. His imagination fruitlessly searched for a sense of what her life might have been like before it's violent ending.

A blanket of silence lay over them, the whole reading room a vault of stillness, dust particles floating in shafts of illumination emanating from the tall, narrow windowpanes, the sun high in the sky. It was close to noontime just as when the massacre had happened back then only a few blocks away from where they sat. Except for them, no one else was in the reading room.

EhEh stood up abruptly and laid a hand on Elena's shoulder.

"Let's get out of here."

She placed her hand over his. Her touch sent a penetrating shock through his nervous system.

"Where to?" She asked.

EhEh cleared his throat.

"I want to find this policeman, Sergeant Barientos."

"Well, we don't have far to go," said Elena, getting up and gathering the newspapers. "The police department is just a few doors down the street."

They paused for a moment before the imposing, stylized art deco edifice. Its flanking wings formed a courtyard before the main entrance that was set back from the sidewalk. The building gave the appearance of a small, exclusive college. EhEh, accustomed to institutional structures, felt at home. He strolled confidently down the concrete pathway that led to the front door, Elena by his side.

Inside, a woman police officer at the desk asked them to state their business. EhEh responded in his best English accent that he hoped he might have a meeting with Sergeant Barientos, if the officer were in his office. The uniformed woman, who was of medium height and wore her shiny black hair swept back to a short ponytail, enquired of EhEh of what purpose he wished to speak with Sergeant Barientos. EhEh explained as briefly as possible. There were so many intricate threads to pull together.

"One moment," she said. "I'll see if he is in."

His story apparently made sense to the young officer. EhEh felt relieved, and waited patiently while the officer typed the Sgt's name into the keyboard of her computer.

"I'm sorry," she said after a while, "Sergeant Barientos is not in our active data base."

"But that's impossible," EhEh blurted. "His name appears in the newspaper as the investigating officer."

"That may well be," she said. "But he does not appear in our data base. It's possible he may be retired. Would you like me to check?"

"Yes, please do."

EhEh felt impatience creeping into his body. The officer performed some rapid finger work with the keyboard. The three waited for the computer screen to change. EhEh glanced at Elena, then back at the officer who stared at the screen he couldn't see.

Finally, she spoke.

"Yes, here it is," she said cheerfully. "It shows Sergeant Barientos on the retired list as of January, 2001."

"Can you tell me where he lives? It's very important that I speak with him."

"I'm sorry, sir, we don't give out that information. If you want to talk with him, you will have to find him on your own."

EhEh felt a bit annoyed. The woman cop was being very polite to the elderly couple; this was true. Nevertheless, as always, it was the bureaucratic crap that got his gall. She seemed positively delighted to deny his request.

"Anything else I can help you with?" She asked, eyeing them standing mute before her, like a couple of bewildered cows.

"Is it possible I may see the police report? You have it on file?"

"Of course we have a file."

The expression on her face seemed to say, 'Whaddya think, booby?" she pointed to a glass door leading into another room. "Just inquire in there," she said. "It's the public records room. All files are open to the public."

They turned away, thanking the young lady.

It didn't take long, reading the terse report, to realize there was nothing more here than what had been published in the news account. The journalist covering the case just simply copied the report, EhEh guessed.

"We're stymied," EhEh whispered.

"Let's have lunch," Elena replied. "I'm starving."

They ate at a sidewalk French bistro. A grilled fish from the morning's catch done with a white wine sauce, and alongside beautifully steamed fresh thin asparagus spears laced with butter. EhEh enjoyed his meal, Elena was happy to observe. She had no reason not to like this man.

"So where do we go from here?" She asked over coffee, no desert, thank you, EhEh shook his finger.

"I very much want to find this Sergeant Barientos, but I have no idea where to begin. Any suggestions?"

She shook her head. "Outside of the phone book, no."

"There's probably a whole page of Barientos, if not more. But that's our only recourse for now. Agree?"

"Sure," she said agreeably. "We can do that tonight at the hotel. Why not look for the shop while we still have the afternoon? You wrote the address?"

EhEh nodded enthusiastically. He was beginning to appreciate Elena's brains.

"I wish I had copied the police report. There was a statement in it I would like to recall. Maybe we should go back."

"No need to, my dear man," she smiled with a glint in her eye. "I have a copy of it in my digital."

"You're kidding!" EhEh beamed. "Fast with the camera are you? To think, I hadn't noticed you with a camera in your hand. Let's see the shot."

Elena produced her camera, saying she photographed the report when he had gone to the bathroom. She turned on the camera and located the image of the police report, handing it to EhEh who looked at the tiny screen with a single glance and then handed it back to her.

"How am I expected to read this?"

Elena showed him how to use the zoom feature, and passed the camera back to him.

"Ah," he said full of amazement. "Yes…yes, there's the sentence I'm looking for. It vaguely struck me when I first read it in the library. Now it seems it may be significant."

"Which sentence is that?"

"The witness saw the gunmen shooting open the glass door. That must mean the door was probably locked. Why would the door be locked in the middle of the business day?"

He stared at Elena, as if he were a prosecuting attorney in a court of law grilling a defendant.

"You have a point," she said.

"Yes, I agree, Elena, let's go find this the shop. The building ought still to be there."

EhEh felt enthusiastic as they walked to the lot where the convertible was parked. It was only a few blocks over to Rodeo Drive, where they would have to find another place to drop off the car. EhEh suggested they simply go back to the hotel and park there. Everything was really within walking distance in this small downtown.

"It's like a village," he remarked.

"That's what they call it," she grinned. "The Village."

EhEh nodded with a professorial air, proving to himself it is possible sociologists knew how to size things up.

They strolled along the glamorous avenue, their eyes wandering to the numbers on storefronts. EhEh noticed their reflection in the store windows. They looked like any of the other casually dressed, well fed couples on this busy street, happy faces milling around, examining merchandize in the windows, stepping in and out of establishments packed with treasures from around the world.

This was a world of which EhEh knew very little, a world he generally held in disdain. Yet here he was. In the reflecting windows he appeared as an integral part of the scene. Something to marvel at, he thought. One day nestled in his modest home in Guaymas. The next day, literally out of the sky into a whole different milieu. Not without a bit of irony, he asked himself if he were the same man, walking alongside this handsome woman on an avenue designed strictly for gratifying any fantasy money could buy. He was here on serious business, yes, operating a bit like the sociologist he actually was, attempting to unravel the knot in Miguel's psyche. But right now, just for this afternoon, he could imagine himself another person, a person with a girlfriend, strolling along the edge of a forbidden paradise, among the other consumers.

They were approaching Santa Monica Boulevard where the fancier shops of Rodeo Drive thinned out. Finally, they came to the storefront they sought. Not surprisingly, the business conducted inside was the same as before, a beauty parlor; only the name had been changed. EhEh and Elena looked at each other and then stepped inside. It was an ordinary beauty salon with the ubiquitous fragrance beauty parlors around the world give off, as far as EhEh could tell, nothing at all like Julio's Salon in El Ciudad. On one side, a customer was having her nails manicured, on the other, a woman was seated facing a mirror watching her hair being trimmed. The two beauticians both young and skimpily dressed looked up when EhEh and Elena stepped in. A counter that served as a reception desk separated the investigators from the rest of the space. The older one, doing the nails, spoke briskly.

"We're booked for the rest of the day."

EhEh explained that they were hoping to get some information about the previous proprietress.

"Oh, oh, here we go again. Listen Mr., I told the last guy, we don't know anything about her. All I know is she moved to Santa Barbara. And that was two years ago. My partner and I," she nodded toward the one cutting hair, who, EhEh noticed, displayed a flowery tattoo that ran up her calf, "we took over the lease, and that's all. We don't have anything to do with her financial obligations."

EhEh apologized for causing them any embarrassment, explained he was not in any way attempting to collect on someone's bad debts, he was actually enquiring about a person who owned the business for a number of years until 1996.

"You gotta be kidding. Ninety-six? You're talking about maybe half a dozen operators since then."

Elena spoke up.

"Is there anyone nearby, a neighbor perhaps, who might have been here then?"

"Oh sure," she said, this time smiling. "Just go next door at Adriana's, the Everything Shop. She's been on this street since before the Ark."

EhEh thanked the woman.

Next door they found an oddball store full of unusual items eccentrically arranged in subdued light. Curiously shaped cubistic styled chairs next to tables holding brass and silver art deco objects. On some counters there were oil lamps made of hand carved alabaster sitting alongside abstract leather-sculptured items. There was a display case containing one-of-a-kind jewelry pieces made of metal and glass. On one wall stood a rack of long silk dresses in a variety of colors and designs. And crowded in between were all sorts of other items that EhEh couldn't identify.

They found Adriana standing in front of the dress rack barely discernable, herself wearing one of them, blending in with the costumes behind her.

"Good afternoon," she said, her voice in the dim light giving her presence more substance.

EhEh repeated her greeting, then went on to state his business, mentioning Rachael's name and asking if she, Adriana had been acquainted with her, emphasizing that he was speaking as a friend of the deceased woman's family in Mexico and that reasons too complicated to go into at this point in time brought him here on behalf of the family's interest to discover certain matters important to the family, and would she by any chance have a moment or two to assist him and his friend here in their inquiry?

After which, EhEh took in a deep breath. And so did the woman.

"You want to know about Rachael Valladares?"

"That's correct."

"After all these years?"

"You knew her?"

"Yes, I knew her."

Adriana let out a deep sigh, which led EhEh to think there may have been more than just a neighborly acquaintance between the two women.

"Do you have a few minutes?" Elena gently asked.

The woman seemed to have some trouble deciding. Finally, she moved toward them and said, "Come this way," leading them through a beaded curtained doorway into a back room where she invited them to sit down. There were two upholstered chairs with a table between. Across from them a large old-fashioned desk and a modern leather swivel chair took up the remaining space, on the floor lay a Persian rug. Adriana sat down at her desk, and swiveled in her chair to face them.

She was probably in her fifties, EhEh guessed, a bit plumpish with an ample chest and large rounded shoulders, bright red finger nails, long dangling earrings, a mound of rusty brown hair. Her face was smooth, her skin clear, a bit of fuzz on her chin, no lipstick.

"What do you want to know?"

EhEh hesitated, marshalling his thoughts. Elena leaned forward.

"Ms Adriana," she said, "Rachel Valladares had a daughter who is now sixteen years old. She is living with a man who is taking care of her, who claims to be her grandfather. We've read the local newspaper reports, and the Beverly Hills police file regarding the mass killing that took place next door ten years ago. Both report that a man by the name of Julio Valladares was among the victims, along with Rachael. After making inquiries in Mexico City, we know that Julio was Rachael's father. So, there's a bit of mix-up here. We want to find out if we can, who is the man taking care of the girl. Is he indeed the grandfather he claims to be?"

Elena paused. EhEh regarded her with growing respect for her acumen.

"You see," Elena continued, "we have located family members who have an interest in the welfare of this child, of whom they have only now, because of our involvement, become aware of her existence and her situation."

Elena glanced over to EhEh hoping she would find an encouraging sign from him for the spin she was putting on the facts, fabricating as she went along, making up this extenuated fib.

EhEh nodded approval.

Adriana, on her part, took in this speech with a convulsive heave of her chest, her face expressing fear.

"She was kidnapped. I knew she was kidnapped. I said this to the cop. He practically called me a liar. He claimed there was no evidence of a child in this case."

"Was that Sergeant Barientos?" EhEh interjected.

"No. This was someone else. I'm not aware of a Barientos. This was a different cop. I can't recall his name. He questioned me the day of the killing. He said he was from the FBI. And he wasn't very nice."

All three sat in silence for a while, absorbed in their thoughts.

"Madam Adriana," EhEh finally spoke, his voice registering hope.

"Just call me Adriana, please."

"Adriana then. Can you tell us the girl's name?"

"You don't know her name?"

"Well, we know the name she presently uses. We merely want to verify her real name."

The proprietress bit her lip. EhEh could see she was becoming agitated. He feared he was losing momentum.

"We want to make sure our client is indeed the same person you are describing as having been kidnapped, so we could go forward with our task."

"Stop. Please stop, Mr. Escudero, I'm feeling overwhelmed. After all these years out of the blue you barge in here and dredge up these old memories. It's intensely painful. Rachael was a dear friend. I can't talk anymore about this, not right now." She began to cry.

"Adriana," Elena intervened. "Let's do stop here. It's getting late, and anyway you will no doubt want to close up your shop soon. Let's give it a rest. Can we talk another time?"

Adriana reached for a tissue from a box on her desk, and looked appreciatively at Elena as she blew her nose.

"Okay, another time maybe," she said. "Give me some space. I need some space to think."

Elena rummaged through her purse for pen and paper, wrote down her name and cell phone number, handing it to the woman.

"We are staying at the Beverly Wilshire Hotel. The room is in my name. Call us when you are ready to talk more. We really need your help, you know."

EhEh and Elena walked back to the hotel comparing notes.

"She's very much afraid of something. I wonder exactly what it is?" This from EhEh's lips.

"More like she's terrified, I would say." Elena's response.

"Terrified is getting to be a theme. First Julio running into his salon, back from his hair-cutting session with El Presidente, terrified out of his wits. Now this Adriana. What is it that terrifies them?"

"Death, violent death. What else?"

"She knows something. I'd bet on it."

"Yes, just like Julio knew something. Something that terrified him."

"Well, we have one new piece of the puzzle," remarked EhEh, "Barientos was the chief investigator only just long enough to get his name in the papers. What does it signify when the FBI takes over?"

"More things to find out," she said.

Back in their suite, Elena proposed they order from room service. She reached for the menu that was conveniently placed at the bar.

"What's your choice?" She asked.

EhEh glanced around for the phone book, eager to start the search for Barientos.

"Please, you order for me. I'll take whatever."

Elena gave him a mischievous smile.

"You're developing confidence in me perhaps?"

"Sort of," he grinned.

EhEh ate quickly making phone calls between bites. Elena watched him. He didn't seem to notice what he was eating. She gathered this was the bachelor's habitual way of dealing with food, pouring over his books while he ate, always the eminent scholar. Then her thoughts turned to Barientos, wondering why EhEh thought Barientos would know anything different than what had been reported in the files.

The phone book did not cover the entire metropolitan area. EhEh quickly ran out of possibilities.

"We need more directories," he said. "We'll have to go the library."

"Maybe they have some at the front desk. Shall we go find out?"

"How about in the morning? I'm wiped out. It would help if we could get Barientos' first name. Wouldn't that police woman grant us this small piece of information?"

EhEh's sarcasm didn't go unnoticed.

"Yes, and why not?" she stretched. "Well, we've gotten a fair amount accomplished today, wouldn't you say? Let's relax a bit. It's too early to go to bed."

He picked up the phone intending to call room service to come fetch the remains of their meal.

"Don't bother," she said. "They can get cleared away in morning. Come, EhEh, let's sit on the sofa and watch something entertaining on the plasma."

EhEh felt a wave of caution. He stayed put at the dinner table. Her voice had that same intonation she displayed when he first met her in El Ciudad. Was she attempting to lure him? It occurred to him, all of a sudden, that they were having their first night together in this suite. He felt a bit trapped. One thing had the potential of leading to another.

"Come on," she chortled. "You don't need to be a worrisome wonk all your life. I'm not going to bite you."

She patted the cushions. Challenged this way, he felt he had no choice. He got up and plunked himself beside her. They watched the first half of an HBO movie, the only one that seemed halfway worth seeing described on the selection screen as a romantic adventure story, in other words a movie about sex and violence.

Elena curled up close to him, her breast pressing his arm. The soft, warm touch made him slightly delirious. Nothing like this had happened to his old self in a long, long time. There was no other place to put his arm except around her shoulder, which he did. It was a maneuver that caused her to rest her head on his chest. He took in the fragrance of her hair, and felt a flow of excitement that brought him to the brink of enjoying himself. Should he just let go of his inhibitions? After all, they were not youngsters. What harm would it do? Enjoy it for what it is, he told himself, and attempted to switch some of his focus back to what was happening on the plasma screen that covered half the wall. It was definitely not the kind of cinema he had been accustomed to back in his academic days. In fact, the movie was becoming much too violent, the sexuality totally blatant. Elena gave a grunt of disgust, grabbed the remote, and shut the damn thing off. What a relief.

"That's all I can take," she said.

She took him by the hand.

"Come handsome, let's go to bed. Show 'em how two civilized old-timers make out."

EhEh gulped at the sudden shift from the plasma screen to real life. He felt as if she had jammed a thermometer in his mouth and was taking his temperature. His body understood what she meant. It felt hot. He swallowed hard.

"I'm not sure I recollect the process," he muttered.

"I'll help you remember, dear man."

She pulled him toward her, and kissed him tenderly.

He awakened with a start. He was in his own bed. How did he get here? He had no memory of leaving Elena's bedroom. What he remembered made his body glow again. It had been glorious. He was so pleased with himself. My God, I'm having an affair. He felt charmed by her. What a sweet, tender lady!

EhEh rose from his bed and went for a shower, not too surprised to hear himself humming as he lathered up.

Dressed in his customary uniform of brown cotton trousers and polo shirt, this time an orange one, he stepped into the sitting room to find her already consuming her breakfast. She was wearing her blue jogging costume; a few beads of sweat still clung to her forehead. She looked vibrant.

"Morning, champ," she called out. "My, you are the handsome one this morning."

He stepped up to her and smacked her cheek with a kiss.

"I'm a gigolo now, thank you."

"Is that so bad?"

"It could be, I suppose. Right now, it doesn't feel so bad. I'm a hungry bear, and the food is here on the table waiting for me. I have to tell you, Elena, this kind of life can become addictive."

Elena's massive warm smile gave him the feeling she actually liked him. *She likes me.* He was willing to believe in this notion. A new world had opened to him. When did it start? With lightening speed, he recounted the steps that had brought him to last night, to this morning, to now. Incredible.

Once again they stood before the information counter at the police station. It was a different officer this time, a middle aged man with a potbelly. EhEh took this as a hopeful sign. The officer looked up and EhEh began his prepared speech.

"Sir, we are attempting to locate Sergeant Barientos. I know he is retired. And I know you cannot divulge his address. All we are asking for is his first name. Knowing his first name might help us find him."

"Who did you say?"

"Sgt Barientos," EhEh repeated more loudly.

As the words came out of EhEh's mouth, a man in a crumpled blue gabardine suit walking past obviously overheard the name and stopped.

"Barientos? Did I hear Sergeant Barientos' name?"

The man had a jolly looking face, his steel gray hair badly in need of a cut. It came down halfway over his ears and curled around the back of his neck. His tie, a solid dark blue affair, hung lose, the top collar of his shirt unbuttoned. He was a large man, a bit on the plump side. In other words, he looked the typical plain-clothes policeman that he was.

"Yes you certainly heard his name," EhEh offered his hand. "My name is Eugenio Escudero. I'm trying to locate Sergeant Barientos. I've come all the way from Mexico to find him. And this is my associate, Elena Navarro."

They took turns shaking hands.

"You are a Mexican Federal policeman?"

"Good Lord no!" EhEh spat out, and handed the man one of his cards that indicated the social status he preferred to be known by.

The policeman glanced at the card and said, "Follow me please."

He led them through a door and down the hall, past a row of glass offices that were as small as cubicles. Uniformed men and women sat in each space in front of a computer screen. They went down a short flight of stairs and through another hallway coming to a stop in front of a paneled door. He opened it and invited them to step inside.

He seated himself behind a metal desk, leaned back in his swivel chair, demonstrating with a casual sweep of his hand the magnanimity of his hospitality: two wooden chairs that faced his institutional sized desk.

Now that everyone was seated, the plainclothesman cupped his hands behind his neck, leaned back even further in his chair, and commenced to speak.

"I'm Lieutenant Moore, Homicide Division. Sergeant Barientos worked for me. As you know, he is retired. We are friends. We stay in touch."

The Lieutenant then lunged forward, his smiling face suddenly altered into something approaching a snarl.

"Why are you looking for him?" He wanted to know.

EhEh, startled by this Norte Americano's sudden aggressive manner, jumped out of the chair and blurted, "I'm an honest Mexican citizen. I have good reason to believe that Sgt. Barientos can clear up a matter of deep concern to me and others of my friends."

"Wait a minute, Mr. Escudero. Let's start over. Please sit down and tell me your story."

The Lieutenant spoke in a less threatening manner. EhEh sat down and began by saying that it was a long and complicated story he had to tell, it might take as much as an hour to cover all the points. The Lieutenant interjected that he was prepared to spend the time. EhEh fumbled for a moment, wondering where to begin.

"I'm here because of a massacre that took place at a beauty parlor on Rodeo Drive. It happened about ten years ago. I read yesterday in the official report that Sergeant Barientos was the investigating officer. The report also states that one of the victims was Julio Valladares."

And from there he went on to speak of the Julio Valladares he knew, not mentioning the name Miguel Guzman, explaining all the ins and outs of that topic, rambling from his discoveries in El Ciudad to the ministrations of the good curandera, not mentioning the actual location where that kind healer made her residence, bringing in the secondary considerations of the granddaughter's condition, winding up with his own relationship to the matter pointing to his initial status as mere casual acquaintance to his present self-described acknowledgement as an intensely interested friend of the family, now optimistic of dispelling all the dark clouds that surround this worthy group. And in the telling, EhEh recognized he was growing weary of having to hear himself repeat this story over and over again. And finally, the most delicate aspect of the story, the question of the grandfather's identity, was the Valladares he knew the same Valladares identified as one of the massacre victims. But that would be impossible, and therefore their reason, his and his friend the good lady sitting beside him, for coming to Los Angeles in search of…" his voice faltered for a moment, "…of the truth."

"That is to say, we are hoping to clear up this matter once and for all."

The Lieutenant listened intently, occasionally putting pen to paper, making notes. Mr. Escudero was good at organizing his thoughts. It was a pleasure to have a scholar as a witness. When the Mexican closed his mouth for the final time, Lieutenant Moore remained silent for a while, regarding the man and woman in front of him, looking up at the ceiling, then down at his notes, as if he were pondering what to make of this unusual, damn near unlikely tale. In his time, he had heard any number of unlikely tales, mostly pure bullshit. But this one, he believed, had a ring of authenticity to it. He was deciding how he wanted to play his cards.

"I'm not certain we are discussing the same Valladares, Mr. Escudero. There's no record of a child in this case. So, you think Sgt Barientos might help you? Joe is his first name, this is what you came to find out, right? All these years later, you think he can tell you something to take home with you to cure your friend, is that it? And you read the official report, and you don't believe it is complete, is that so? You believe Joe knows something he failed to include in his notes, you really think so?"

All this with body language laden with ironic insinuation.

"Listen, my friend, you don't mind if I get cozy with you? Our Joe Barientos was a cracker-jack detective, if something was to be uncovered you can bet your bottom dollar Joe would uncover it, that was not the problem, the problem was, he didn't have time to do his work properly, only one day, we sat in this office, this very same room, and discussed the turn of events, not every day we get a mass murder in our quiet town, one so violent and cruel as this, no siree, not every day."

"Yes, I understand," EhEh dove in. "Your local newspaper made a point about this very thing."

"The whole mess was ripped out of our hands, FBI took over, just like that…no-ifs-ands-or-buts," Lieutenant Moore continued, ignoring the elderly man seated before him, his policeman's eyes on the ceiling, his hands clasped behind his head.

"But why?" Elena leaned forward with her query.

"Why?" Lieutenant Moore glared at her. "I'll tell you why, drugs, plain and simple. They claimed this was the work of a drug cartel. The FBI jammed themselves into our precinct, told us hands off, claimed it a narco war, from over the border, spilled over to our side of the Rio Grande from your side, Mr. Escudero, yes, don't look surprised, the drug scene is every where, even here in quiet Beverly Hills, a big business, gigantic, in their eyes that made this a Federal case, an FBI affair. The FBI took over, hook, line and sinker."

"So," EhEh asked, "are saying you don't think this was a drug related massacre?"

"I'm not saying it was, I'm not saying it wasn't," his eyes rolled back to the ceiling, "but I'll tell you this, whatever the FBI found was never disclosed, the case went to ground, nothing came of their investigation, except…"

"Except?"

"Look," he lowered his gaze, his eyes, like a pair of windshield wipers, boring into their eyes, first to the one then to the other, "Let me put it this way, all kinds of strange bed-fellows in this drug business, people in high places sucked in, big money, big pay-offs, secret deals, even between government officials, yes, even between governments, a lot of people who shouldn't be, looking the other way."

And at this point the policeman granted them his brand of a cheerful grin, stirring his unruly hair with a meaty paw.

"You're shocked? You get my drift? Yes, a cover-up. Everything shoved under the rug. Just like that."

"But how do you know for sure?"

"Look, my friends. A local precinct investigates, makes its analysis, and if necessary, calls in the Feds, not the other way around, you see?" He wagged his pudgy finger. "But I'm not here to argue points with you, Mr. Escudero. You've come into my precinct, raked up this old frustration for me, and Joe too, he never was happy over the situation, I'm feeling burned all over again, and your story, I'm counting on it being a true story, adds a dimension to this affair, might just blow something wide open, you never know, so I'm thinking, why don't we help each other? How can I help you? Well, I can put you in touch with Joe. That's what you want, a conversation with the investigating officer…right? It couldn't hurt, your story gives this a new angle, gives Joe something to chew over, he gets bored sitting in that assisted living place."

Out of breath, the plainclothesman pulled out a pad and wrote an address.

"Here's where Joe hangs out these days, if you want to call it a hangout. And here's my card. Keep in touch. Daily reports. I want to hear everything that happens. Who knows? You might get into a tight spot, might need a cop to save your skin, never know, right? You can call me anytime, day or night."

This last statement made EhEh edgy. He hadn't counted on having a menacing situation to deal with.

They headed for Santa Monica taking I-10 West. The traffic was brutal even though this was not rush hour time. Elena raised the convertible top so they could hear each other talk.

"The way you look," she began. "I would say you are a man who is thinking very hard."

"This Lieutenant made it all much too easy for us. And the last thing he said about saving our skins, what do you suppose he was pointing to?"

"He has a hidden motive, you think?"

"I don't know. It's quite possible he thinks he can use us to flush out someone, a remnant of the drug gang still hanging around."

"But this happened ten years ago."

"That's true. However, the gangs are more vicious today than ever. Almost every day there's a report in the papers about mass executions, decapitations, whole towns taken over by killers armed like military war units. Such is the daily fare for those living in the border towns, a horrible reality that makes me shudder. This massacre that happened ten years ago is still an unresolved issue for the authorities, and it may be for the cartel people as well."

"Another reason why I don't read the papers. When you speak like this, you frighten me. If you are right, then it must mean money is the issue."

"Correct. A lot of money not accounted for. Money missing. Until now not a clue. And then we show up. Very interesting, eh?"

"My God, EhEh, what have we gotten into? We must be very careful. A good thing you didn't give Miguel's name."

"Or Manuela's, or Consuelo's. I'm surprised the good lieutenant didn't probe us for more details. There's something cagey going on. He decided to take our story at its face value. Why do you suppose?"

"As you say, to use us like meat, bait for the killers? You really think so?"

"That, or something else. And I can't think of what that might be."

"Oh my God, EhEh. I just thought of something. You gave him your business card. Maybe that wasn't a good thing to do."

"It's an old card, from my university days in Guadalajara. He'd have to do a lot of digging to find me in Guaymas. I doubt if there's anyone still there on the faculty who would remember me."

"I hope so. You dear man, I can see you didn't count on this."

"No indeed." He gave her a rueful smile. "I merely thought I was helping a casual friend when this all began. And now here I am. Here we are, I should say, sticking our necks out. And why have you gotten yourself into this mess? You didn't have to come here."

"There's our exit. Let's make a stop. I need to use the bathroom."

"I could use a coffee as well."

They stopped at the nearest establishment, a Denny's. EhEh took a booth and ordered two coffees, while Elena headed for the lady's. While he waited for her return, he mulled over what indeed was her motive for coming to Los Angeles. It couldn't have been just simply to get him into bed with her. Her husband had left her with tons of money. Had he been involved in the drug racket? In the higher echelons far removed from the dirty business of street killings? Was Elena somehow implicated? He didn't want to believe this. She was too nice a person. He wanted to push the thought out of his head.

"So why are you here?" He plunged in as soon as she was seated.

"In Los Angeles?"

"Yes."

"Why shouldn't I be? Hannah was my friend. She was more than a friend. We were sisters in the good battle. I've only now come to realize how much we loved each other, gained strength from each other. And when she spoke to me at her death bed, warned me about the Russians, I felt as though she had given me a charge to fulfill, but I didn't know what to do with the revelation. And eventually, my link with her slipped into a misty past. But then you came and resurrected this past for me. And when it was made clear to me that Rachael had been killed, murdered in her own salon, I felt I had to come meet you here. It was you who provided the opportunity. And right now," she began to sob, "I can see her there in that shop, sprawled on the floor machined gunned to death," tears gushed from her eyes, "Oh, it's horrible. Horrible."

EhEh's throat choked up. He also could visualize the dead bodies on the floor of the salon. A sensation of deep sorrow filled his body, a sorrow he had never before experienced, a sorrow that began in his gut and burned its way up into his chest, filling his neck and head with a pain that startled his intellect. His life had been dedicated to mental activity, speculative thoughts, the business of the intellectual scholar, far removed from the visceral reality of life. And now, because of Miguel, he realized, he had come face to face with his authentic humanity, right there in his belly where before the only sensations he had felt had been that of hunger and a full stomach there now roiled raw fright and sorrow.

He lay his hand over hers, offering human empathy. He needed it as much as she. Elena put her other hand over his. He felt her warmth, and all thoughts of paranoiac suspicion went out of his head.

"Let's get out of here," he mumbled, shoving away his unfinished coffee.

"I'm ready." She answered. "I want to meet this Sergeant Barientos. I want to find out why this happened to Rachael."

Back in the convertible, Elena checked the GPS on top of the dashboard, got her bearings, and swung out into traffic. EhEh marveled at her knowledge of the city. She must have been quite a student, he thought, one of the wild ones, and chuckled to himself.

They had only driven a few blocks when EhEh heard the sound.

"Do you hear something?" EhEh asked.

"What?"

"I'm not sure, sounds like a cartoon jingle. Can't you hear it? It's coming from somewhere in this car. But the radio is not on."

"Oh my gosh! It's my cell phone. Quick, it's in my purse. Find it."

EhEh fumbled through Elena's bag while she pulled over to the curb. Passing cars honked and sped past. Elena took the phone, pressed the key to receive the call.

"Bueno!" She shouted. "Yes…Hello…yes? Adriana? Is that you? Yes…Very well. Good. Señor Escudero and I are very pleased. Come by around 7 tonight. We can have dinner in our suite. Just come right up. Suite 1214. We should be back by then. See you at 7."

She snapped the case shut, and handed the phone back to the professor, deftly slipping back into the traffic pattern. She could be a racecar driver, he mused. EhEh held the phone in his hand for a moment, marveling at this piece of technology that till now was not part of his once prosaic existence, then slipped it into her bag.

"The woman from the Everything Shop wants to see us," she said.

"So I gathered. Good news."

EhEh felt elated, another odd sensation. He had schooled himself to feel only slight amusement when, for example, in the past he had discovered a new theory born from hours of diligent effort. There had been several occasions when his name had been selected for high praise and academic prizes, and his response had been hardly more than a chortle of delight. But now, this sensation he felt was like the lifting of a weight, as though his body were literally rising. The earlier sense of foreboding had momentarily evaporated, and he turned his thoughts to the coming interview with the retired policeman, full of anticipation. No telling what might unfold.

At this very moment, another phone conversation was taking place.

"Joe, Marty here. Yeah, I'm doin' okay. And you? Listen, two people, a man and a woman, are on their way to see you. They've come all the way from Mexico. No, I'm not kidding. Yeah from Mexico. Listen, remember the drug war massacre on Rodeo ten years ago? Right, that one. Was there another one? Still the wise guy, aren't you. Listen, they've got questions about an identity issue, at least that's what they claim, God knows what they're really looking for. No, I don't know who they really are. I've got a business card, probably a phony, the guy pretends to be a retired university professor, can you beat that? I'm putting out a description, we got a good snap of them from our surveillance camera, maybe something will come up. Listen, play them along. You know how. Find out what you can. Call me back. Names? His card reads Eugenio Escudero. She goes by Elena Navarro. My best guess? I'm guessing they're either cops or crooks. Yeah, yeah, smart ass, one and the same. Call me after you talk. Okay? I'll call you if anything comes up. Yeah, I gotcha…bye."

The retirement home was situated on a cliff overlooking the Pacific Ocean, in every way resembling a five-star resort. EhEh wondered how a retired police sergeant afforded such opulence. He couldn't help make the contrast of this exclusive beachfront property on the Pacific Ocean to Miguel's unofficial shantytown on the Sea of Cortez, both enjoying healthy sea-side air, yet at opposing ends of the social scale with the drug wars somewhere between them.

They were immediately taken to Barientos' suite, as if the staff knew whom they were and what they had come for, and found him sitting in an easy chair by the sliding glass door that led to a small patio. The sergeant's bulky body filled the chair almost to overflowing. His head, totally bald and as shiny as a steel ball, appeared minute in comparison. His bright blue eyes sparkled, reflecting the sunlight coming in through the glass. It was about high noon. A light blanket covered his legs. EhEh noticed immediately, there were no feet showing below the fringes of the blanket. And Barientos noticed EhEh's swift glance.

"That's right. Diabetes got them. It happens to the best of us. No need to feel sorry for me. Sit down."

The retired policeman pointed to two chairs, obviously arranged for this interview.

"They're putting a new battery in my motorized. Anyway, I like sitting by this window. Seeing the ocean soothes me. So, Señor Escudero – yes, I know who you are, and you too Señora Navarro, Marty gave me a heads up. You're interested in the event of ten years ago, right? Well, may I ask why?"

"You speak Spanish Sergeant Barientos?"

"You can call me Joe. No, I don't. My people have been here since the days of Spanish rule, but we long ago lost the language. You'll have to stay with English, I'm afraid."

Once again, EhEh patiently made his long explanation, omitting any incriminating names, emphasizing the mission of healing the sick man, their having been sent by the curandera to ferret out any facts that could help clear the old man's head, and the need to resolve the issue of possible mistaken identity regarding both the old man and the granddaughter.

"What we want to discover from you, if possible," EhEh concluded, "is your eye-witness impressions of the scene where the massacre happened."

"Whoa…wait minute. We can talk about that. But first, I have a few questions of my own. You want to make sure this girl you have down in Mexico is the child of the deceased woman Rachael Valladares, is that correct? And why is that important? You say she is in her grandfather's custody who claims to be the man we identified as the deceased Julio Valladares slain along with the woman. In other words, who is the real Julio Valladares, the sick one or the dead one? Is that correct? And why is that important to you? I know you say you are a dear friend of the family, blah, blah, blah. Don't get me wrong, I'm not unsympathetic. But I tell you, Escudero, your story smells a bit like rotten fish. To begin with there was no child in this case. There's something you're not telling me. What are you hiding?"

EhEh cast a glum look at the sergeant. He was unaccustomed to being called a prevaricator.

"You are right, Sergeant Barientos," Elena leaned forward with an earnest look on her face. "We also want to locate the two Russian brothers, cousins to the family, who came with Rachael to Los Angeles."

EhEh wondered why she was bringing this up.

"Ah, now we're getting somewhere," Barientos chortled. "Tell me more."

"We believe – or at least I believe the Russians kept money that didn't belong to them. There was an inheritance from Rachael's mother, my friend Hannah who was the wife of Julio Valladares, money that came from her father, Rabbi Ytzhak…"

"Okay," Barientos broke in, "It's a bit complicated, but I'm following you. So this is how I'm reading you. If this girl in Mexico is who you think she is, then this money belongs to her. Is that correct?"

"Yes," Elena smiled, happy to be understood. "My friend Hannah, on her death bed, told me about the Russians, and…"

"And you think the money still exists? First, we have a child who didn't exist when the killings occurred, and now we have a fortune in cash that probably doesn't exist either." Barientos let out a gaffaw. "You think these Russian brothers are running around somewhere here in L.A. with a suitcase full of money after all these years? It must have been a fortune, if the money still exists. What kind of racket was the Rabbi doing? Do Rabbis have such fortunes? Now tell me how do these Russians figure in? Who are they again?"

"They belong to the Rabbi's side of the family," EhEh chimed in. "Do you think they are the remaining two victims in the beauty parlor who were not identified?"

"It's a possibility. Can't rule anything out. What are their names? Do you have their names?"

EhEh hesitated, glanced over to Elena. He wasn't sure he wanted to divulge this information. The sergeant, of course, being the astute cop that he was, sensed EhEh's reluctance.

"Look," he said, "if we're going to be helpful to each other, we have to have some trust. Don't you think so? Why are you holding back?"

EhEh spread out his hands in a placating manner.

"We hear all sorts of tales about drug cartels and police officials working hand in hand, not only in our country but in other countries also. And…well…"

"We're not that kind of cops, me and Marty. Yes, I know, you no doubt heard him talk about a cover up, the FBI taking over the case and then nothing coming out of it. That sort of thing happens more often than we would like to believe. And you could easily think Marty and me are likewise part of the scheme, two more rogue cops in the mix. Well take it from me we aren't. You'll just have to trust us."

At this precise moment in the conversation, a knock at the door filled the empty space that had resulted from EhEh's doubts.

The knock was not a request for entry, but more an announcement of an impending action, for the door immediately swung open, and two burly men entered, one of them pushing the mechanized wheelchair into the suite.

"Excuse us," the one said, full of cheerfulness. "It's time for lunch, sergeant." And without further ado, they manhandled the heavyweight-retired cop into his mobility, each giving him a friendly pat on the back like a couple of old buddies, and then left the room.

"Well my friend," Barientos laughed, "they came at the right time for you. The names of these Russians will have to wait. This is a tough match. Come. I invite you to have lunch with me in our fabulous dinning hall. The food is excellent here, as you can well imagine. The chef once worked at the White House, back in the Nixon days."

He moved a toggle switch. The machine headed for the door.

"Mind opening it for me? I can do it myself, but its cumbersome."

EhEh and Elena exchanged glances. The sociologist opened the door, and they followed Sergeant Barientos toward the dinning hall.

"What's your opinion?" EhEh asked her in a low voice, falling back so the sergeant wouldn't overhear.

"I think we should tell him their names. What harm can it do? And it may help. Not directly perhaps, but in a round about way. At least it will show that we are being cooperative. Make any further questions easier for them to answer maybe."

"I agree." He took her hand and gave it an affectionate squeeze.

Elena looked up at him and smiled.

"You have a handsome face," she said.

"You think so?"

"Even when you look grim."

They entered the dinning hall. EhEh took in a whiff of the pleasant odors and was surprised by the growl in his belly. He realized he was starving, and was happy to be noticing.

During the meal they chitchatted over various light topics. Sergeant Barientos regaled them with humorous tales of police happenings accumulated from his years in the service of protecting the infantile and egomaniacal element of the Beverly Hills menagerie, as he described the population. He knew how to be the charming raconteur. EhEh found himself enjoying the conversation, and added some of his own choice tidbits from teaching days, revealing the same propensity among his academic colleagues as displayed by the Beverly Hills indigenes. Elena carefully chewed and swallowed her healthy organic salad of mixed greens and raw vegetables in a bemused manner listening to the two old men swap stories, displaying their man-talk prowess, while between words, the sergeant ripped into his roast sirloin of beef with enormous gusto.

After coffee, they went out onto the terrace to digest their food and take in the salt breeze flowing in from the ocean. The sea was calm, the midday air warm, the distant sound of gulls soothing, too nice a day to be dwelling on grim matters. Nevertheless, the topic was uppermost on all three minds.

"I can give Marty – that's Lieutenant Moore – the Russians' names and we can then do a thorough search. Anything we turn up, we'll share with you. How's that for cooperation? So, the names?"

"Zaslavsky," EhEh said without hesitation. He had grown to like the retired policeman and was willing to trust him. "Boris and Efim."

"Can you write that down for me?"

Elena extracted a notepad and a ballpoint from her purse and handed them to EhEh who wrote down the names, tore out the sheet and handed it to the sergeant, his hand shaking just a wee bit.

"So, Sergeant Barientos, now that we have helped you, can I ask you a few questions for which your answers might help us?"

"Señor Escudero, I'm at your service. Shoot."

"After studying the police report, it struck me that the murderers had to shoot open the door, which meant that the door was locked. Do you agree that the door was locked? And if it was locked, what could be the reason? After all, this was a beauty parlor, and presumably open for business. Why lock the door? These were questions I asked myself. And my only conclusion for the door being locked was that the people inside must have been having a meeting and didn't want to be disturbed by anyone wandering into the establishment. In other words, why else would there be three men in a beauty parlor that obviously catered exclusively to women? Do you have anything you wish to comment about this theory?"

"Well, Escudero, I see you have the investigator's instinct. Is this what a professor is like? And a pretty sharp theory. Believe me, Marty and I discussed this very idea. And you know what? We drew two conclusions. One, the same as yours. And the second idea was in reality a variation of the first, namely, that the killers wanted to make it appear that the door was locked."

"Why would they do that?" Elena wanted to know.

"Believe me, we scratched our heads over that question. I spent one whole night not sleeping trying to figure it out. But it was a question Marty raised, so we had to plumb it to the depths. And in the end, it was Marty who came up with a semi-reasonable explanation."

"And?" EhEh was thoroughly intrigued.

"Okay, picture this," Barientos sucked in his breath. "You are absolutely correct, Escudero, it had to be a special meeting. But of what kind? This is the core issue. Picture this. The people inside have been called to a meeting. For what reason they may not know. That is to say, they may not know the real reason. They have been called for a phony reason, but they do not know that. The three men who drive up and smash in the door with their bullets and spray the interior do their dirty deed in such a way as to make it appear they are from an opposing force, if this was indeed a drug war killing. They make it appear like an attack from an enemy gang, let's say. But in reality, it is not an attack from another drug gang. It's a staged attack. Interesting theory, eh?"

"A convoluted theory, but interesting, yes." EhEh admitted.

"But why?" Elena asked.

"To make it look as if it was a gang war. You see this theory hangs on the idea that this whole business had nothing at all to do with drug wars, etc."

"Then what did it have to do with?" EhEh wanted to know.

"That's the problem with this theory. We couldn't take it any further. After one day, the case was taken out of our hands. We had no authorization to carry on our investigation, meaning no funding, etc. So we couldn't explore this question with the customary footwork. Maybe from your angle you could come up with something relevant?"

EhEh shook his head. He hadn't a clue. But Elena was bursting with a pregnant thought.

"Could it be the Russians staged this fake attack?"

"Bingo!" Barientos' eyes sparkled. "Not bad. Not bad at all. We might have come to this idea if we had known about these Russian brothers. What more can you say about them?"

"They had a bad reputation among their own people. Their people considered them gangsters." EhEh shook his head in wonderment. "If they staged this killing, why kill their own cousin? It was said that Rachael married one of them. And I assumed that her daughter was the issue of the marriage. Why would a man kill his own wife?"

"Happens all the time, Escudero. And what you say reminds me. We never had any reason to think there was a child in the mix. We found no indication of a child. How is it that you have a child in your story and we don't?"

"My God, this is all totally baffling. You don't have a daughter figure in your scenario, but we do." EhEh shook his head.

A long pause ensued, all three running around in their brains pursuing these unanswerable questions.

Finally, EhEh opened his mouth.

"I have another line of questions, if you don't mind Sergeant."

"Yes?"

"There were four dead bodies. You were the first examining office to view them. What can you tell us about them? And how is it that two were identified and two were not?"

"Okay. We found one man with a wallet in his pocket. His papers indicated he was the Julio Valladares you are interested in. The other two men had no wallets in their pockets. The woman's purse, Rachael Valladares' purse was behind the front counter."

"But didn't you take photos? Couldn't you have identified them from their photos?"

"Of course, we took photos, our forensic team performed all the customary tasks. But the case was taken out of our hands. And what made it doubly difficult was the fact that all four of the victims had had their faces obliterated. All shot up. Their faces a bloody mess."

At these words, both Elena and EhEh went queasy. EhEh could see their blown-apart bloody faces in his mind's eye, his imagination causing his stomach to churn. He thought he would vomit on the spot. This was a piece of information he hadn't expected. It hit him like a bus smashing into him.

"This was another reason we thought the whole thing had been staged. If it had been just a routine drug gang killing, why go to all that trouble of blowing off their faces?"

"But why make it certain that two of the victims could be identified?"

"Exactly, another piece of the mystery, right? This is the conundrum that opens the door to all kinds of speculation."

A second wave of silence followed this last empty statement.

Time had marched on while the three of them had been talking. A slight chill in the air prompted Elena to check the time. She looked at her watch.

"It's past three. We need to get going," she said.

"Leaving so soon?"

Barientos seemed disappointed. EhEh couldn't tell if he were mocking them or not.

"We need to be some place else," Elena explained. "And if we leave now, we'll avoid the heavy traffic."

"Oh? Seeing someone else? And who might that be?"

Barientos was all ears. He had that policeman's knack of grabbing with his teeth like a bulldog. Elena's face went red. EhEh jumped in hoping to turn the cop off the scent.

"This is another matter entirely, Sergeant. You see Elena has an appointment to see a psychic. It's about problems with her daughter. She's embarrassed to admit she goes to psychics." EhEh surprised himself by his ad hoc invention.

"Her daughter? Another daughter?"

"Yes," said EhEh. "In fact Elena's daughter had been a childhood friend of Rachael's."

"I see…"

"Yes," interposed Elena, finally getting her wind back. "My Dora and Rachael spent a lot of time together until they were about ten. But Dora is not at all involved in what we are exploring here. No, my Dora is another matter altogether. She is married to a plastic surgeon, you see, and they are, well, how shall I say, trying to have a baby, and…"

Barientos, obviously losing interest, broke in stating that they should all stay in touch, giving the same pep talk the lieutenant had peppered them with earlier that day. They parted on the terrace, the man in the wheelchair going one way, the two Mexicans the other. At the car, Elena and EhEh gave each other a warm hug, each confiding in the other how well they appreciated their performances. EhEh's lips brushed her cheek. She looked up with a sweet smile, took his face in her hands and kissed him tenderly on the lips.

"I'm getting to like you more and more," she said.

"It crossed my mind," he murmured, "and I must tell you, you have enchanted me."

Barientos was on the phone.

"Two Mexicans, immigrants from Russia. Brothers. Cousins to the deceased Rachael Valladares. One suspected of being her husband. Boris and Efim Zaslavsky. They may be the other two bodies. What can you find out about these Russians? By the way, I think these people are who they say they are."

"We already know that," Moore replied.

"Fast work," Barientos felt a bit jealous.

"Yeah, nothing beats the Internet. Our surveillance photos were excellent. He's a retired professor all right, lives in Guaymas. She's a widow, was married to a prominent businessman, lives in Mexico City. I don't believe they are drug runners."

"No question. But then, what are they looking for? You believe their story, wanting to heal an old man we have listed as dead?"

"It's just possible they're speaking the truth. And yes, there's also the granddaughter and the idea of money to be found. It may be the granddaughter story is just a smoke screen, the real issue being the money."

"Well, I don't think there's any money. That's why those people got murdered. They wanted money. The got machine gun bullets instead.

Lieutenant Moore chewed on this last statement of Joe's for a moment, then he said, "I think my theory holds water. A staged killing to make it look like an attack, a get-away, and a hidden place somewhere, these Russians and the money hiding somewhere."

"And the woman? The wife presumably? They killed her? And the old man who would be the father-in-law to one of them? And where did they find, how did they get the other two victims? Where's all that fit into your theory?"

"They could have taken her with them. And the old man as well. They could have planted the old man's papers on the victim we think is Valladares. Three bums, they could easily have picked up three bums."

"You mean four, a woman bum as well. God, what an ugly picture you're making. It's too gruesome, even for me."

"Ah come off it, Joe. You know as well as I do how far people can go these days. These days? Just take a quick review course on human history."

"So, you think you have enough to re-open this case?"

"No, of course not," the lieutenant laughed. "I've got enough official business on my desk already. No, Joe, I consider this a hobbyist's preoccupation. I don't have the time or the energy to look for these phantasy Russians. You've got time. Why don't you surf the net? See what you can dredge up."

"Maybe I will. Maybe I won't. I'll think about it. Say, you got this Escudero's local number? I forgot to get it."

"Sure, you klutz. I'll email it to you. Gotta run."

At this same time another quite similar conversation was taking place in a BMW convertible heading east on I-10 toward Beverly Hills.

"In two days we've learned a lot," EhEh was saying. "A lot of details that don't add up. In other words, we know nothing. How do you see it, Elena? Are these two policemen telling us everything they know?"

"I think they are, EhEh."

"I wonder what we could learn from the FBI? I wonder how we can get to them?"

"I don't want to deal with FBI people. That's a whole can of worms that just frightens me. Look at me, I'm already trembling. I'd rather just know what we know, and go with that."

"Perhaps you are right. I don't feel we're as much in danger as I thought a few hours ago. I prefer that. If we were for some reason able to penetrate deeper, we might then be in serious danger. So, what do we know? Do you give much credence to Moore's theory? As crazy as it sounds I think I'm leaning in that direction. The one problem, however, sticks out like a sore thumb. Why the lack of identity papers for the two male bodies. No passports, no drivers' licenses. If something like this was so carefully planned, how is it that this very important feature is missing? How else to throw off the scent? They could have been skimming drug money, stashing it somewhere, a carefully planned attempt to thwart the cartel people."

"And the other strange anomaly," Elena added, "the missing daughter. Adriana believed at the time of the killings that she was kidnapped. I wonder if she still does? We can assume, it seems to me, that she believes the dead bodies were the Valladares and probably the Zaslavskys. This is why she thinks the girl was kidnapped. But if Moore's idea is true, how does it happen that the girl and Julio turn up at the Sea of Cortez?"

At this point, as if on queue, Elena's cell phone did its singsong tingle. This time, EhEh was quick to fetch the instrument. Doing so, his eye fell on the pile up of cars around them, and he wondered if they were really ahead of the heavy traffic. It seemed like there was only heavy traffic in this town. And while Elena fumbled with the phone, he glanced behind them and thought he saw a car purposely following them. Believing a car was following them played havoc with his nerves. He had to get a hold of himself, slow down the paranoia. It was just his adrenaline working overtime, he told himself.

The party on the phone was Adriana stating she was running late. She wanted to skip having dinner with them, she really didn't feel like eating any way, but yes, she would be there, arriving some time after 7, maybe a half hour later, rest assured, she would be there.

"I wonder what's that all about," Elena said, handing back the phone.

They decided to grab a bite at a bistro on Rodeo Drive.

Adriana arrived shortly after eight. Elena met her at the door. The woman was obviously agitated. Elena guided her to a comfortable chair opposite the pale green sofa where EhEh was sitting, offered her something to drink. Adriana said she'd have water thank you, no ice.

EhEh smiled across the room watching Adriana with keen anticipation as she sipped her water. She was wearing the same kind of shift she wore in her store, only a different pattern. This one showed a Japanese garden with a lily pond under a small arched bridge surrounded by bamboo. And over that, she had on a padded cotton jacket to protect her against the chill of the evening breeze coming in from the ocean. The jacket was light blue in color with an oriental stitched design. To EhEh, it was an eccentric costume.

He noticed how her hand trembled that held the glass of water. While with the other hand, her red painted fingernail nervously played with her hair. He could tell, this would be a grueling hour for her. By her side sat a large velvet bag of deep purple. It was stuffed with something, and the way it leaned against her thigh it gave the appearance of something alive, a lapdog perhaps. It seemed to him as though weeks had passed since they last talked yet it had been only the day before.

Elena sat down beside him, took his hand, and heaved a deep sigh.

"I don't know where to begin," she said, offering Adriana a gracious smile. "I assume you've decided to trust us, that we are genuine people, and that you want to tell us something. And yet I can see it is not easy for you to speak about…this thing that happened ten years ago. Painful, yes?"

Adriana nodded, and heaved a sigh. She set down the glass of water on the glass-top table beside her, and leaned forward as if attempting to close the gap between her and the two people who looked at her with sympathetic expressions.

"She was my very good friend," she sobbed. "The best friend I ever had. She was like a younger sister I never had."

"That's exactly the way it was between me and Hannah. Rachael's mother." Elena explained. "We were like sisters. We raised our children together, and we fought together for women's rights."

The mention of Hanna's name produced in Adriana a tone of reverie.

"Rachael," she murmured, her eyes fading. "Rachael named her baby Hannah, said it was a family tradition, like braiding two strands of hair, that's how she described it, said she had been named Rachael after her grandmother Rachael, and so on back to who knows how far, Rachael to Hannah and Hannah to Rachael, every other generation, all on the mother's side. Isn't that precious?"

EhEh's eyebrows arched. He wasn't accustomed to the word, "precious."

"I was at Hannah's deathbed," Elena spoke matching Adriana's mournful voice. "The Hannah who was Rachael's mom," she added, to make it clear of whom she was speaking. "Her very last words to me, 'Watch out for the Russians.' Does that mean anything to you?"

"Them," Adriana blurted, an edge of scorn in her voice. "Oh, I knew them all right. Nothing but trouble, those two, pure poison. It wasn't long after we became good friends when Rachael admitted how awful they were toward her; how she wished in the first place she had never gotten sucked in by their superficial charm. She told people she was married to Boris. But that wasn't true. You wouldn't know it anyway seeing how the younger brother, Efim, carried on with her."

"Yes? Go on."

Little by little, Adriana poured out her story, picking up the glass from time to time to take a sip of water, then pausing to dab her eyes with the tissues EhEh brought from the bathroom. Her face, puffy and flushed, turned more in the direction of the sliding balcony door, her eyes projecting onto the glass all the ghostly images that had haunted her during those years of waiting, and more waiting, until someone had finally arrived, someone for whom she could unchain the rusty gate guarding her hidden chest of treasured wounds.

EhEh and Elena sat like two spikes nailed into the sofa's cushions their ears wide open. Adriana's words filled the room with a growing concentration of pain and sorrow expanding like a bubble that held them suspended inside the hotel room high above the noise of the ordinary world. EhEh could actually feel he was breathing some kind of smoky substance. A strange sensation traveled up his spine.

The family, she said, had lived in a rented posh four-bedroom house on the other side of the Hollywood Hills in Van Nuys, a large place with a swimming pool, even a separate wading pool for the baby. They lived comfortably there until the grandfather arrived around '94 or '95, she couldn't remember exactly when. His presence had become a kind of flashpoint for the brothers. Before then, their belligerency was occasional and not as severe. There was some kind of bad blood between the Russian Jews and Rachael's Catholic father, something to do with Isaac, Hannah's father, the Rabbi. They blamed Julio for everything that had gone bad in the Ytzhak family, including what had happened to the Zaslavskys as well.

Adriana's body, stiffening as she told her tale, unexpectedly softened.

"She was a beautiful woman in her own distinct way."

"How so?" Elena inquired.

"She had lovely black hair, very thick. Her eyes were the same intense black. Her face was round with a strong jaw, manly in a way. Her slender shape gave the impression of tallness, but she wasn't really. When she stood up straight, the top of her head came only to my chin."

For the first time, Adriana smiled.

"Her movements were very lithe. When she walked, her body swayed the way a giraffe's neck sways. I loved watching her move."

Then a frown came to her face.

"Rachael had to put up with a lot of crap from them, because of her father's presence. She wasn't at all thrilled to see him in Los Angeles. He brought with him a lot of family baggage that would have been better left behind."

Adriana emphasized how nervous the old man acted, how his jittery nerves played on every one else, he was always looking over his shoulder as if expecting to see some vicious creature pounce on him. But this was only the surface of a very dark situation. And here, she sucked in her breath before plunging further into the story she had gotten from her friend, Rachael Valladares.

The fact was, Rachael had confided, swearing her to absolute secrecy, these two Russian devils were involved in the drug racket. They were members of a cartel. Their job had to do with laundering drug money. They used Rachael's beauty parlor as a front, making deposits of cash in many different banks. The amount of money deposited in any one bank did not exceed the normal amount expected from a business like Rachael's.

"She knew about their racketeering?" Elena expressed surprise. Her knowledge of her husband's business activities had been practically nil.

"Of course she knew."

They didn't put much effort into hiding their criminal activities. They knew they had complete control over her. She had learned from many beatings not to question them. And she tried to ignore the danger she felt. But the fear never went very far away. It was there when she got up in the morning. It was there when she went to bed at night. It followed her to her work. She knew they faced disaster at all times. She had no blinders. She was totally aware of how the drug wars ruined lives. It was like an obsession for her, keeping track of all the killings and blatant battles that took place in broad daylight across the border, and even on this side. You have no idea how much these thoughts drove her mad."

Adriana became teary.

"Excuse me for crying so much," she mumbled, holding a tissue to her nose.

And at the same time, she continued, Rachael seemed to be held captive by an odd fascination. She felt transfixed as if sitting on top of a huge bomb ready to go off. It could happen any time, she used to say to me. And yet she could never stop feeding her mind with all that horror of those news reports. It filled her life. And it got worse when she found out the two Russians were skimming money from the cartel. It totally freaked her out. She had all she could do to maintain a calm front at her place of business, pretending her life was a bowl of cherries, not to mention keeping her father blind to the whole thing.

"And how did they do this scam?" EhEh broke in.

Adriana stared at him, her eyes registering waves of fear, as if she herself had become possessed of Rachael's embattled mind.

"They were doing the unthinkable."

The moneys were delivered to various places, always a different location, Rachael had explained to her. The younger brother usually made the collections. Boris, acting as the head of the firm for the beauty parlor business, made the deposits. How the cartel people were able to remove the money from these accounts, Rachael didn't know, or at least she never revealed this detail to Adriana.

The brothers figured out a way, apparently, to skim a certain amount of cash off the top of each delivery, and hide it somewhere. They managed to do it without being detected by their overlords, but in the end of course it caught up with them, getting them all killed. They had spent hours over the dinner table working out this scheme constantly altering their methods so as to avoid detection.

But Rachael closed her ears as much as possible. She wanted no part in the details. And when her father showed up, the tension became worse because everything had to be kept strictly secret. The Russians complained to Rachael, they weren't free to talk about their affairs in their own house.

"Amazing, isn't it?" She remarked, breaking in on herself as if by way of an aside. "How greed only expands, never diminishes? Just like spoiled brats, they wanted everything their own way."

"And you never revealed any of this to the police?"

"No." She was wringing her hands now. "I was too frightened. Rachael's fears over the drug lords had by now seeped into my own mind. She was gripped by a premonition something horrible was about to happen. She begged me to stay home from the shop that day when it finally did happen. She came to me the night before. She knew something crazy was in the making, but she wouldn't tell me. She made me promise to stay home. And I did."

"And so the next day, when the FBI came to interview you, you could honestly say you knew nothing, you weren't there to witness anything?"

"Correct."

"But you told them about the child. You told them you believed little Hannah had been kidnapped."

"Well, she wasn't there. It made me crazy. She was nowhere. I had gone to their house the night of the killing not knowing that it had happened. I wanted to talk to Rachael, try to help her in some way. But no one was home. And then, driving back to my place, I heard the news on the radio. And suddenly the news was everywhere, every station on the dial screamed into my ears. Rachael, my Rachael was dead, gunned down in cold blood. I jammed on the brakes, collapsed behind the wheel. I just collapsed."

She broke into tears again. Apologized, and looked at her interlocutors, her eyes searching for some sign of understanding.

EhEh stirred nervously, cleared his throat.

"Who do you think could have kidnapped her?"

"I don't know." She looked into her lap. "Maybe the cartel people took her for ransom. Maybe to rape her and throw her into some ditch never to be found. Evil people do such things. My mind wasn't thinking clearly. And then the guy from the FBI didn't believe me anyway, told me I was crazy. Crazy, crazy, crazy," she pounded her fist into the armchair's cushions.

"And you didn't tell the FBI anything else, like where the family lived? No address on the driver's license in Rachael's purse, or in Julio's wallet?"

"They used the address of their business as the official address on their IDs. I certainly wasn't going to tell them where their house was. I didn't want to tell them anything. I figured they wouldn't believe anything from me after the way they denied Hannah's existence. I even felt they might be in on the whole thing. You know, in the pay of the cartel. Crazy to think that way, I know. But you see, I feared for my own safety. The less said the better," she said bitterly.

"And now we show up."

"Yes, ten years later you show up and tell me Hannah is alive and well. What am I supposed to think?"

She sat in silence for a long time, staring at them, as if they had come to drop more pain into her well of sorrow. She stared at them, her puffy face twisted in torment.

"Rachael…," she groaned. "You can't imagine how much she suffered," pointing a finger at EhEh and Elena, tears rolling down her cheeks.

Elena came to her side, placing a hand on her shoulder, and pulled the woman's shaking body to her breast. EhEh lost control of what was left of his composure, his eyes watering. He took a tissue and passed her the box.

"I loved her," she sobbed, dabbing her eyes. "I loved her so very dearly. I loved her more than anyone could ever be loved. You can't begin to imagine."

"You were lovers?" Elena asked. Her uncanny intuition startled EhEh.

Adriana's eyes burned fiercely.

"Yes, we were lovers. It was our only consolation. She was my whole life. She and little Hannah. Those bastards didn't give a damn about her. They only used her for their own gains."

"Boris had no feeling for his daughter?" EhEh was shocked.

"That bastard? No! Absolutely not! He wasn't her father anyway. Hannah's father was in Mexico somewhere. They were lovers just long enough to make the child. When Rachael told him that she was pregnant, he quickly vanished. Happens all the time, doesn't it?" She looked grimly at them

The three sat in silence absorbed in their own thoughts.

Finally, Adriana lifted her glass and drank the last of her water, and then asked for more. Elena took the glass saying, "So Rachael ran off to Los Angeles with her cousins, wanting to avoid a scandal. Is that the picture?"

"Yes," Adriana said, blowing her nose. "That's the long and the short of it. She never actually married Boris. Little Hannah was always Hannah Valladares. They only pretended they were married for appearances." Her voice grew embittered. "But he took his pleasure of her, nevertheless. It was brutal sex and beatings he gave her for her troubles."

EhEh cringed, remembering all the profiles of abusive households he had read. He could well imagine the dysfunctional features exhibited in this story. But this was not an academic exposition. This was emphatically visceral for him. He felt all the sadness that now shook her body with an intense intimacy of his own. Long forgotten pictures of his own dismal childhood before his grandmother had rescued him marched across his inner screen. It all came crashing back. Both parents lost in the delirium of alcohol, himself left alone most of the time, always half-starved, a perpetual swollen belly, never fully understanding the cause of his filthy life. Had it not been for his grandmother, who knows what kind of an existence he might otherwise have had? Now suddenly he could see why he had been so touched by Miguel's role in Manuela's life, another rescuing grandparent. Until now, he hadn't fully made the connection.

Adriana's sorrow affected him to the core. He fell to his knees by her side, his head almost touching her lap, and sobbed for the child he once was.

And without thinking, warm and generous as mother earth herself, she soothed his bare head with her soft hand, murmuring consoling words. And Elena, returning with the water, and seeing them weeping together, felt her heart go out to them—she knew without a doubt why she loved this tall lanky baldheaded man who was able to cry.

It was Adriana who eventually pulled them back from their wretched state. She lifted EhEh's head pushing him so that he could stand up and pull himself together. Her voice resuming a more normal tone, blowing her nose, she spoke as one accustomed to dealing with practicalities.

"And do we actually know if we are talking about the same kid and the same grandparent, Rachael's father and child?"

"They have different names now," EhEh rose to his feet replying, wiping his face with a tissue, "but I believe they are the same people."

"I have photos here," she reached for the velvet bag, her body fluttering with unleashed anxiety. "These pictures should settle the question. I brought them hoping I would find you sympathetic."

By now, Elena and EhEh were back on the sofa. Adriana stood up, bringing the bag with her. She settled into the cushions, fitting herself between the two. It was a tense moment for all three, as she removed from the bag a gaily-papered, thin cardboard box— the kind, EhEh recognized, that used to contain chocolate candies when he was a young man and was interested in such things. This one had lost its shape, crushed by much handling. It was held together with a thick rubber band.

Under soft yellow light cast by a floor lamp, its brass neck bent over the green sofa in a long graceful arc, EhEh and Elena observed Adriana pull away the brittle elastic band that had kept the worn candy box intact for so long. She removed the lid to reveal its contents: a handful of photographs and a fat business envelope, itself wrapped with a thick rubber band.

She held one photo to the light so they could all see it. EhEh was the first to breath a huge sigh of relief. There was no mistaking. He was looking at a younger version of Manuela, a little girl of five or six. But she was unmistakably the same person. She was leaning against an easy chair where sat Miguel. Both child and grandparent stared into the camera's lens without much expression.

If anything, they appeared to be nervous, or unhappy. There was no need to look at any of the other snaps, and Adriana did not offer to show them. The first one revealed everything they needed to know.

"That's them," EhEh lifted his voice.

"You are certain?" Adriana's eyes penetrated his.

EhEh nodded.

"Oh thank God! The baby is found!"

A face full of joy looked from EhEh to Elena. She reached over and hugged the older woman, whose own radiant smile almost blinded EhEh with a touch of awe, observing the scene as if he were in a saintly church.

"May I have this photo?" EhEh asked after they had regained some composure.

"Yes, of course, if you think you will need it. The others I want. They are my only treasure. Only a handful of photos taken during happy times."

She heaved a sigh, and then continued to speak while she picked up the bulging envelope.

"There is more to tell. In here is money. I've been holding onto this all these years never knowing if a time like this would ever arrive. Rachael gave it to me to hold for Hannah's future." Her voice broke, mixing joy and sorrow. "She just assumed that if something happened to her, I would be there to keep Hannah. You can't imagine how desolate I've felt all this time unable to fulfill this wish of hers to protect her daughter. There were days I thought I was going crazy filled with anguish and despair over the child, never knowing what became of her. You have no idea how relieved I am. You say she is about to have a baby? She can't be more than sixteen. Well, she certainly will need this money. Here," she extended her hand, "I gladly give it to you for safekeeping. Don't worry. It's not tainted. Rachael saved this from her business. It's all beauty parlor money, every bit of it."

She handed the envelope to EhEh who pulled off the rubber band and drew out the bills. They were all one-hundred-dollar bills separated into five piles of twenty. EhEh quickly counted ten thousand dollars. He restored the bills to their tattered envelope and handed the money to Elena.

"I hope you don't mind taking charge of this," he said.

Elena nodded, took the envelope, and then turned to Adriana, who had moved back to the easy chair.

"Rest assured. We will hold this money in safe keeping for Manuela. Yes, that's the name she now uses. In good time, I will tell her about you and how you preserved her inheritance. She ought to find it easy to remember you. A child of six retains much, I'm sure. Now, you must be exhausted, and probably hungry. Can we get you something to eat? A sandwich or some soup?"

"Thank you, no. I couldn't possibly eat anything right now. You've been most kind letting me get all this out of my system. Funny, I don't feel at all embarrassed. It's been helpful believe me. I do feel much better now."

"You have helped us very much," said EhEh. "We now have irrefutable information that will help our friend recover from his sickness. He will be healed now. I have no doubt. When things get sorted out, you may want to come visit Hannah. Is there a photo in that group of you and Hannah that we could show to her?"

Adriana shook her head. "I don't know if that would be useful to her. I can't imagine what she might want to remember of her childhood. It wasn't something a person tries to remember." She paused, and then gathered her velvet bag. "I should go. It must be terribly late. I know I'll sleep better tonight, better than I have in a long while. I feel so much lighter."

She rose to her feet and shook EhEh's hand. He bent down and lightly planted a kiss her on her cheek. Elena, with an arm around Adriana's waist, accompanied her to the door, EhEh following closely behind. Looking weary, Adriana paused briefly and offered them a wan glance, then quietly slipped out into the hallway. The old couple stood in the doorway side by side, watching Adriana's wobbly gait, her rusty hair bobbing up and down with each step as she walked to the elevators.

"I need a drink," he said. "I'm totally shattered from all this…." He had no word for it. "Is there any liquor in that bar?" EhEh went to the small island bar, and rummaged through the cabinet.

He was looking for brandy, what he had gotten accustomed to drinking when he lived in England and needed a dollop to brace himself. He found instead something even better, a bottle of Jalisco Tequila. "Would you like some?" He called out, fumbling with the sealed cap, his back to the sofa, where she was already curled up and snoozing. A long and strenuous day for both of them, their bodies no longer had the resiliency of younger people. He saw himself growing older—even older than he now was—but now with her by his side, and he smiled inwardly thinking he was beginning to know his mind. He went looking for a throw blanket and covered her, then slumped down into the easy chair Adriana had vacated.

Lounging comfortably, his long legs stretched out, he sipped his Tequila and studied the sleeping form of this woman who had become rather important to him. In only two days much had passed between them. He was amazed at how easy it was for him to feel an intimate tenderness with her. There had been times during this long day when he felt so connected he could read her thoughts, as though their minds had merged the way they had merged their bodies the night before. He hadn't tasted passion in so long, he had forgotten sensations that now bubbled to the surface without bidding. Thinking of her, he felt a bit giddy. He wondered if this is how one feels when in love. Was he in love with Elena? How could he tell? What were the signals that would tell him without a doubt his true feelings?

His eye traced the gentle curve of her jaw, lingered at her chin marked by a minute dimple. He felt a longing to kiss this tiny, seductive crease until he was almost dizzy with desire. He watched her full lips quiver ever so slightly from the tranquil snoring her body produced and imagined he was hearing the distant ocean he loved so much, the Sea of Cortez, breathing in his ear. A lock of silvery-brown hair curled around her ear almost close enough to tickle her pert nose and he felt his own nose twitch with pleasure. Even in repose, her charming features were alive in his mind's fancy. He so admired the animated person she was whose face easily showed mirth or delight, dismay or consternation, no fixed expression ever to hide behind. Not like him with his stony intellectual facade.

She was a marvel to him and he recognized quite frankly how much he liked her. And just that moment he wanted to go over and brush her cheek with his lips, if only it wouldn't disturb her. Did this mean he was in love? He wasn't certain how to know. It was too difficult a question to have to grapple with at the end of an arduous day. He was too tired to plumb his feelings any further. Instead, he polished off the last of his drink and lowered his eyelids.

Soon, the sitting room filled with the sound of two souls breathing a soft duet.

They lay entwined in each other's arms, still fully clothed. Sometime during the night, they had stumbled into Elena's bedroom and crashed. In the dark, EhEh's eye opened to take in the clock sitting like a silent observer on the bedside table. He read the numbers 3:25, and sighed a blissful sigh, snuggled closer to the body beside him. He felt her warm breast against his chest as she softly breathed. He felt the beat of her heart penetrate and entrain his own heart. The rhythm and strength of this unified beating filled his brain. He was ecstatic.

He felt the same stirring sensation that had come to him when he had watched Consuelo feed the tiny rodent those magical seeds that day in the secret grotto. He remembered the sudden shift that came over his perceptions. Once again in his mind's eye the scene played out before him: A shimmering light surrounding their bodies as the bony bruja squatted before the tiny creature and offered the sacred food, while behind them the ancient tree stood watch, itself a blurry form wrapped in a smoky substance. And a sudden prophetic vision came to him. He saw himself and Elena kneeling before the curandera receiving a blessing that seemed to signify something quite momentous, like an official recognition: they truly belonged together. And finally, the answer came to him. After all this convoluted processing that was his style of opening his mind to an understanding, he finally knew, without a doubt, that he was in love. And the feeling was glorious.

As if she had heard his mind cogitating, visioning, processing, Elena awoke and pressed her lips lightly against his. EhEh, in return, gripped her tightly, kissing her passionately, his tongue stretching to its utmost in its desire to plunge deep into her being, his voice, between kisses, hoarse with feeling, uttering: "I love you, Elena. I love you so very much."

"Dear man," she replied, "You are the one I have been waiting for all my life."

She ran her hand down his back, caressing his thin body, then slipped her delicate fingers inside his trousers in search of his swelling manliness. They lay together thus until they drifted back to a peaceful slumber.

With the first light of dawn, Elena awakened to hear him singing in the shower. She jumped out of bed and tore off her clothes to join him. They laughed and crooned together like a couple of teenagers, seductively lathering each other's skin. Who said two over-the-hill people couldn't enjoy their bodies together?

Not until they were eating breakfast on the balcony terrace overlooking the Hollywood Hills did they turn their attention to the realities of the day. There was much to talk about. They needed to sort things out.

But instead, a heated discussion developed. EhEh began by announcing he was eager to get back home. Their work in Los Angeles, he declared, was finished. They had all the information they needed. It was time to leave. This town, he proclaimed, was no place for a decent person to inhabit any longer than necessary. His arm made a grandiose sweep toward the distant hills studded with white and pink homes of opulence. "Nothing but wealth, arrogance and crime." Elena, who considered Los Angeles one of her favorite spots on the globe, showed displeasure at his words. Her feelings stiffened. She disagreed. There were still glaring anomalies in the facts they had gathered that could stand being more closely examined. EhEh refuted: they had sufficient facts to satisfy Miguel's needs, which caused Elena to laugh in his face, telling him he was acting simple-minded. The facts they had were inconclusive. They led only to more questions, questions they should be probing now, this very moment. And besides, it was unkind of him to speak like this about her favorite town. What had gotten into him, she wanted to know? Was she seeing a Mr. Hyde popping out all of a sudden? What happened to the gentle lover she had allowed into her heart? Maybe he could revise his exaggerated conclusions? Los Angeles? What had happened to the dispassionate sociologist? EhEh was not inclined to apologize. Exaggerated? He bristled with disdain. What haven't they been witnessing in this miserable life Rachael endured but raw brutality? Look at the cruel, bloody, thoughtless destruction of lives, people's happiness trampled to death. And that poor woman tortured with anguish all these years of not knowing. Isn't that sufficient to make your stomach turn? Did he and she need to torture themselves any more with further probing? Here in Los Angeles? But such things happen all over the world, came Elena's resolute reply. Every city has its dark side. Los Angeles was no different. You could say the same for El Ciudad, and even

Guaymas. EhEh winced at this remark. Not Guaymas. No, he insisted, Guaymas was a different kind of place. Did he really believe so? Her eyebrows went up.

Elena refused to soften. She saw how easily EhEh crumbled before the suffering of others. A muddle of feelings overcame her. He was not like other men she had known. He was a gentle soul. And for this she admired him, yes loved him. But also she was seeing an emotional sloppiness in him that alarmed her. His empathetic nature did not match her concept of mature compassion. And now she was unhappy with herself as well for having judged him in the first place. All this confusion caused a frustration that scorched her throat, and she cried out, "Enough of this arguing!" She pushed herself away from the table and stormed into her bedroom, slamming the door. EhEh stood up, dumbfounded, his napkin falling to the balcony floor. Only then did he realize their discussion had become more than a discussion, the kind of academic back and forth he was used to. This discussion, he saw, had become something akin to a lover's quarrel. And he searched his mind for ways to make up with her. He felt miserable. He didn't want to see their life together come to an end before it even got started. He was willing to take the blame for causing this barrier that had come between them, although for the likes of him, he had no understanding of why or how it had happened. Were they so different from each other? A half hour elapsed while they sat brooding in separate rooms. Elena blamed herself for storming out. Gradually, she calmed down, went to the bathroom and washed her face. Her thoughts spoke to her reflection in the mirror, she should have more patience with her lover, they were still too new to each other, and needed more time to blend their auras. She put her face together with new makeup, and then went back to the sitting room.

"Forgive me for getting angry," she said. She sat down on the sofa beside him and took his hand in hers.

Already, they looked like two doves ready to fly off together.

"I shouldn't have spoken the way I did," he murmured, flapping his eyelids. "I practically accused you of having no sensitivity. I guess I've gotten distraught over all this. Ever since last night, experiencing that poor woman's heartache, I've felt devastated. There's such ugliness in life. But I guess I should grow up, eh? At my un-tender age I ought to be able to look at these anomalies that concern you. What is it we ought to be discussing?"

"This is one of the reasons I have grown to love you so, EhEh, your feelings for others. And this is why I need your help. I've been waiting for you to come into my life for the longest time. When we finish this Miguel business, there is something I'd like to discuss about a future collaboration."

"What do you mean?"

"I don't want to go into details now. But I'll tell you this much. I want to start a foundation. With all this money I have, I see no reason to keep it idle in a vault. I want to make it work for the good. Will you help me start a foundation? I want to do something for the children."

"Oh my, yes, a wonderful idea, Elena." His eyes lit up. "Count me in. I want to do this with you." He was tremendously relieved that he hadn't had to figure out a way to gain back her heart.

Elena smiled, happy she had quickly reconnected. EhEh declared himself prepared to stay in Los Angeles for as long as necessary. Reconciled, they leaned into each other and kissed with ardor. EhEh absorbed her sweet fragrance. It took him back to his garden at home. He wondered what she would think of his simple cottage.

By now, it was close to noon. Elena called room service and ordered sandwiches and coffee. While they waited, they gravitated back to the balcony where they could sit in the warmth of the midday sun and feel the touch of a slight breeze coming in off the ocean many miles to the west. EhEh felt calm and peaceful, not the slightest bit agitated the way he had been earlier. Elena lounged in her chair silently gazing within, it seemed to him. Evidently, she was marshaling her thoughts. He welcomed this pleasant interlude, for he sensed the mood would change abruptly once their food arrived. And such was the case. The knock on their door by one of the bevy of handsome young men that staffed this establishment, utterly polite and civil in its intention, brought with it a noisy, unruly world that rushed into their tranquility with the flurry of a marching band. Only God knew how this tanned, blond figure spent his nights, was EhEh's passing thought. He was much too hungry to further speculate, however. And evidently so was Elena. They both dove in with as much gusto as Sergeant Barientos had demonstrated the day before with his outsized grilled steak. The two gobbled their sandwiches. EhEh wasn't certain whether he was chewing chicken made into a salad with celery and onions and mayonnaise or some other concoction with more exotic flavoring, his hunger overriding his taste buds. He mused over this while sloshing hot coffee between bites. Elena, with her mouth full, launched into the heart of the anomalies that, all morning, had been pressing her mind to its limits, even when occupied with anger and remorse over her reactions and treatment of her beloved EhEh, now bringing them up for examination, one by one, the salient points of what had been bothering her.

The big question in her mind was Adriana. She couldn't say for sure, it had been so many years since she had seen Rachael, and that was when she was a child of eight or nine, the last time she had laid eyes on the girl. She, Rachael, hadn't even come home to El Ciudad to be at her mother's side at the dying bed, she, Elena had had to hold Hannah's hand and make excuses, lies if you will, in order only to protect the poor dying woman's heart from the truth, whatever that might have been, whatever the real story, which may or may not had been softened by some kind of fib Julio might have told his wife.

"What is the point you are making?" EhEh interrupted.

"I'm saying this, dear man, that I think Adriana is actually Rachael herself."

"What?"

"Yes. And why not? Who else but she would hold on to the candy box of pictures and that wad of cash all these years, if she weren't the mother? And surely you noticed that box contained a bunch of photos. Why didn't she want to show any of them to us? If she really is Adriana and not Rachael, wouldn't we then see two women standing side by side in some of the photos? But she chose not to show us any pictures. And why so, I ask. Because we'd see only one woman. I bet you."

"I think this is a preposterous notion. Why are you promoting it?"

"I'm not promoting anything. I'm merely stating my gut feeling. I want another look at her. I was haunted all night by this."

Elena didn't stop there. She fortified her argument by rehearsing the scene of the massacre. The obliterated faces. What other purpose was there in that barbarous act, but to falsify identities? The dead woman could be any woman approximating Rachael's appearance. And likewise the two men. They were supposed to be identified as the Russian brothers, obviously. Then why were their wallets missing? EhEh wanted to know. That was a question for which Elena had no answer. And why, EhEh wanted to know, if their wallets were missing, was Julio's wallet not missing, why was it there on the third dead man's body. Who put it there? And for what purpose? Exactly, Elena broke in. Exactly what? EhEh's voice was rising. The whole thing was exasperating.

"We need to go back to her shop and talk to her. I really want to see her again. I want to make sure I am either right or wrong about who she actually is. This is a key point for me. I really believe I can tell, even after all these years. She's a hairdresser. She could easily alter her appearance just by the way she does her hair and her makeup. I believe I will be able to see through her disguise now that I know what I'm looking for."

"Okay, let's go now. And then let's call Barientos. I believe we can get somewhere talking about these issues with him."

They were on their feet in an instant. They took the convertible not wanting to waste any time, and within a few minutes after racing out of the hotel's underground garage, they were parked directly in front of the Everything Shop on Rodeo Drive. There was no need for them to get out of the car. From where they sat it was easy to see that the shop was closed, causing Elena to let out an unladylike expletive. Out loud she promised to return the next day, as if she expected Adriana could hear her. However, it was of no use. Elena returned day after day for a solid week. And each day, the shop was closed. She looked for the sign that was usually posted in places of business: "In case of emergency, call, etc." But there was no such sign. There was no way to trace the missing Adriana. After a fruitless week, alone and dispirited - EhEh had already flown back to Guaymas after another day of scraping around in the city he privately labeled wretched - she gave up, and returned to Mexico.

But for now, they went looking for Barientos, first making a call with Elena's cell phone to be certain he was available for a second consultation. He was. The convertible zipped down I-10 as fast as the speed limit allowed, and then some. EhEh wasted no time with social formalities. One point needed to be cleared up, and Barientos, he believed could provide the answer. The question was, had they or had they not – the forensic crew – taken fingerprints of the victims. That was the question he had failed to answer in the first interview. Barientos flew into a rage. Who did Escudero think they were, bungling idiots? Of course they took fingerprints, and those lousy FBI agents confiscated the evidence before anyone had a chance to put the data into the system. "They swooped in quicker than vultures. Those bastards!" EhEh had the devil of a time calming the old sergeant.

The afternoon sun cut an angle through the glass doors of Barientos' room setting his head ablaze, the sergeant's weathered skin a ruby red. He starred at the carpet beneath his missing lower limbs, a look of defeat buried in the wrinkles of his face.

Elena began to talk. "I have reason to believe Adriana is Rachael."

Barientos lifted his head. The eager look of the hunter returned. "What are you talking about? Who is this Adriana?"

Elena rehearsed the meeting they had had the night before. She told everything leaving out only the fact of the money. Barientos chortled with delight at these new details. If she was correct in her assumption, Marty's theory grew stronger, the sergeant stated. The Russians had staged a phony cartel killing after all. At this, EhEh entered the conversation asserting that the missing identity papers constituted a fly in the ointment. Somehow their plan had been marred. Who or what had caused the blemish? Barientos came back with an astounding thought. If the man called Julio was indeed the man in Mexico still alive, then he must have had a hand in the issue of the missing identity papers, otherwise why would his wallet be on the one body and nothing on the other two male bodies? This new idea caused EhEh to dance a jig. "Of course!" He shouted. "Julio took away the Russian's papers. But why? And where was he when the massacre occurred? Another anomaly! Every rock turned over does nothing for us but produce another anomaly! Blast it!" And now it was Barientos' turn to calm down the professor, looking from EhEh to Elena and back, reminding them that each rock turned over got them one step closer. "This detective business is a long hard game," he instructed them. With his mind focused on Julio, EhEh suddenly remembered Alonzo's description of the day when the hair stylist had run into the back room of the beauty salon, a look of terror on his face. The memory caused him to strike his forehead with the palm of his hand. "Of course!" He shouted to the ceiling. "What? What?" Barientos shouted back. EhEh filled the sergeant in with the story of Julio becoming the personal barber to Presidente Salinas of Mexico. With his own features, EhEh demonstrated the terrified return of Julio from the presidential palace, winding up by declaring he needed to do some quick research. "Right away! Now! Come, Elena. Take me to the library. I need to be in front of a computer."

"If it's the Internet you need, I've got it right here," Barientos wheeled over to the desk, and turned on the computer.

EhEh sat down and went to work, Elena and the sergeant on each side looking over his narrow shoulders. The information EhEh pulled up was juicy. He quickly extracted the pertinent sequence of events, all three avidly starring at the computer screen, twice reading the document EhEh had so deftly compiled, he hadn't been a scholar and a professor for nothing.

> Item: 1988 Carlos Salinas de Gortari is elected president of Mexico. Many suspect the election was rigged.

> Item: January, 1992 Carlos Enrique Cervantes de Gortari (a cousin of Carlos Salinas) and Magdalena Ruiz Pelayo (who worked for President Salinas' father) are convicted of drug trafficking charges in the U.S. and sentenced to 15 and 17 years respectively. This is the first established link between drug trafficking and the Salinas family.

> Item: 1992 Carlos Salinas imposes the first written regulations on U.S. drug enforcement officers operating in Mexico, limiting their ability to function.

> Item: 1993 The Mexican newspaper Processo publishes documents that suggest Raul Salinas, brother of President Salinas, was present at a meeting that took place at the Salinas ranch in Nueva Leon in which traffickers made a payoff to Mexican drug officials.

> Item: 1994 Raul Salinas was convicted of ordering the 1994 assassination of leading politician, Jose Francisco Ruiz Massieu, and was sentenced to fifty years in prison.

It was the first time that a close relative of a powerful figure had been prosecuted for serious crime.

Item: December 1993 Jorge Stergis, top aide to Mario Ruiz Massieu, President Salinas' brother-in-law, begins to transport cash-filled packages to a Houston bank account at the Texas Commerce Bank. The money is bundled with rubber bands and tied in plastic. Stergios continues to make twenty-four such deposits in the next thirteen months. The deposits are always cash, and range in quantity from $119,500 to $477,320. The bank is instructed not to invest the money, but to keep it in a checking account so it is liquid. The bank does not investigate the income source.

Item: March 23, 1994 Assassination of Luis Donaldo Colosio. In the early evening on this day, at a campaign rally in Lomas Taurina, a poor neighborhood of Tijuana, Colosio was shot in the head from a distance of a few centimeters in front of a television camera. The finger of suspicion pointed in the direction of organized crime, particularly the Tijuana drug cartel. But it has also been a persistent rumor that Colisio was shot on the orders of Salinas. The mystery surrounding the political assassination remains open to this day.

The three investigators read the document EhEh had compiled a third time, only now aloud, each one taking turns, as if the account they were reading had mesmerized them into becoming a chorus for recitation, all the details solidly embedded in their brains.

"I remember Colosio," EhEh remarked. "He was a good man, idolized in his home town. He was from Magdalena in our state of Sonora. All of us Sonorans were proud of him. I never understood why he got so chummy with that Salinas guy, one of the many faulty politicians we Mexicans get saddled with."

"It doesn't stop on your side of the border," Barientos stated.

Elena questioned, "How does this Salinas affair connect with the massacre?"

They looked at each other in search of an explanation. EhEh jumped to his feet and declared himself baffled. Was this the cause for the FBI's intrusion? Barientos believed it was. Corrupted officials were facing exposure, he surmised. He theorized extravagantly that Julio the barber had somehow learned about the plan by Salinas to assassinate Colosio. We don't positively know there was such a plan, EhEh interrupted. All we know is that Julio fled Mexico City two days before the assassination. Purely circumstantial. Let's assume there was a plan, Barientos retorted, and let's assume that the Russian brothers got wind of this information from Julio, perhaps overhearing a conversation between the barber and his daughter. Further, let's assume that the brothers determined to blackmail the Salinas family. Hence, the massacre. Elena balked at this, stating Barientos' theory nullified the staged massacre theory put forth by the lieutenant. Barientos sucked in his breath and asserted that the two theories could be combined. The brothers could have gotten wind through the grapevine regarding a threat to their lives over this attempted blackmail scheme, and so they staged their own deaths and disappeared. At this, EhEh threw up his hands and shouted, "Enough!" They were spinning their wheels. The two issues, the Salinas affair and the Beverly Hills massacre, didn't necessarily have anything to do with each other. What Julio may have known need not have had anything to do with what the brothers had been about. They may be barking up the wrong tree entirely with these far-fetched theories. He spoke with the authority of the scholarly skeptic. "Let's keep our heads clear." Elena agreed. Barientos grew silent, looked down to where his feet used to be, then smiled at the professor.

"You're right, Escudero. We're wasting our breath over this when we could be interrogating a known and living witness. You need to speak to Valladares."

"I intend to. I'm catching the first plane out tomorrow."

EhEh turned to his beloved

"Come, let's go, Elena."

"One thing before we leave," she replied, turning to Barientos. "If Adriana is really Rachael in disguise, then the two brothers are probably alive and somewhere to be found. And if you can find them, then we know positively that it was a staged massacre, and therefore Julio has been hiding all these years for nothing."

"Unless he's hiding from them," Barientos replied. "You can bet your boots I'm going to chase them down. The Internet is my preferred tool for searching. If they're alive, I'll find them. "

EhEh had his doubts, but on this he remained silent.

Elena smiled, satisfied the sergeant would do his best; then she leaned over and planted a kiss on his cheek.

"I'll be around," she said. "I'm not flying out with EhEh. Call me if you get any new ideas or information."

"And you do the same. Adios amigos."

Walking to their rental, Elena remarked with a chortle how the three of them had become a tight knit investigative team, each with a single assignment, she to stalk Adriana, he to grill Julio, and the sergeant to roam the Internet.

"Are you saying this is all a lot of fun for you?" EhEh asked, not without a bit of surprise in his voice.

"You have to admit, EhEh, as gruesome as it all is, there's a humorous side as well. We must keep our humor, don't your think?"

For this, EhEh had no response. He was learning there were eddies in Elena's makeup that made him a bit uneasy. At times, she exhibited an energy that threatened his composure. He felt agitated by her sudden eruption of humor, and wondered why. He stood with his hand resting on the car door, and pondered for a moment, his gaze facing west. Evening had descended. He was able to stare directly into the sun, now a fading ruby ball slipping into the darkening blue Pacific, its weakened flames streaking across the purpling sky.

This was his last night in Los Angeles, thank God. In his mind, the wretched business of the massacre had become entangled with Elena's city, and with it his experience of falling in love with her. A muddle of emotions swirled in his heart like opposing tints of paint straining for his attention. And in a way, a trace of Elena, like a drop of bright gold, had gotten mixed in with the dark paint. He was glad to be putting some distance between them, if only for a while, just so he could sort things out. He looked forward to some time alone, a chance perhaps to reclaim the EhEh he once knew. But would he recognize the old EhEh after all that had happened in these quick few days, so intense and so full of joy and, at the same time, such utter gloom for him? And would he want to?

For he then wondered with alarm, when would he see her again? And he realized, once more, this woman meant something to him he was unable to say exactly what, and how much, and how long. How long would it last, this feeling of love and passion that had taken him by such surprise at this point in his life, a time when a man ought to be preparing himself for the final days. The words 'love' and 'passion' traveled in his head like a whirlwind. He climbed into the convertible, his heart pounding with thoughts of romance. She had been in the car watching him all this time, waiting for him to get in. Her face turned to him, her smile lit up by the last rays of the sun. He took her in his arms and kissed her fervently.

"This is our last night for a while," he murmured. "Notice I said for a while," he said humorously. "I mean it. I want us to be together for the rest of my life."

"My wish as well, dear man."

"Let's make a night of it."

"If what you mean is what I am thinking," she laughed, "let's start with a fabulous candlelight dinner. And then…"

"And then?"

Her eyelids fluttered with a captivating sidelong glance.

"And then," she whispered, her voice trailing off with a soft alluring breath that came to him like the promise of a warm and fragrant summer night.

My dear Manuela:

I write to you from some great height in the sky.

Yes, I am flying home, at last. It has been only less than a week since leaving Guaymas, yet I feel an eternity has passed. I have news for you. I have facts for you. Yet I doubt you will take the time to read my report, at least for now, busy that you are with making a baby and a life with your beloved Javier.

Nevertheless I write to you. You have become my in-flight confidant. And someday you will read this. I have no doubt. Perhaps, when you have reached Consuelo's age, with all the wisdom she and life will have taught you, you will take out a few days and read this account of your family history. And I believe you will read with compassionate understanding. The trials and errors your immediate ancestors endured, believe me, they need your compassion.

Only now, in my advanced age, am I able to feel the aliveness of true compassion. I thank Consuelo for having opened some hidden resource within me. She and her medicine have made me susceptible to my heart. Without that sensitivity I would have never connected with all my new friends. My old, self-possessed posturing, maintained during my entire adult life, has dissolved – utterly vanished, like the dry and brittle sandcastle it was, love smoothing away, ocean-like, the bulwarks of a façade to which I gladly say adieu. And ultimately, this process began with you, my dear Manuela. Had it not been for you and your grandfather who enlisted me as your tutor, my life would have gone in the same old rut, deadened beyond my ability to perceive it as such. Yes, I can trace the alteration of my life to that time when you were a mere child of eight or ten. That is when it all began.

So, it is you to whom I confess. I confess to you: this old codger, this old used-up, dried-out former practitioner of dispassionate scrutiny into the ways of humankind, has found, without in the least deserving, the mystery we call love. Yes, he dearly loves life at last. And in particular, he finds himself in love with a most charming, wonderful lady. And she has blessed him with encouragement that she loves him as well. Two days ago, I would have not dared make such a claim. At best I would have meekly voiced a semi-fervent hope. But now a transformed heart – I am speaking here of courage, as do the French speak of the heart – allows me to declare from the highest: my love.

Thank you, dear one. Thank you.

Frugal by nature, EhEh surpassed himself by taking a chunk of his savings and purchasing a car. He bought one of those zippy little Fords everyone was running around in, a creamy white two-door, only four years old.

Miguel, almost totally himself again, was nevertheless deemed not truly a safe bet when it came to driving his old Toyota pickup. For the twice monthly run into Guaymas the job fell to Javier, who, nervously gripping the steering wheel with sweaty fists, attended to EhEh's driver-training sessions with the utmost seriousness, his tongue poking out of the right side of his mouth all the way from the shanty fishing town to the outskirts of San Carlos five or six miles one-way and five or six miles back depending on which fork taken. And after a few weeks of training, he was ready to hit the road to Guaymas almost 20 miles away.

A new era was opening for Javier. Becoming a father represented only one part of his new role in the life of the small community. The shantytown's barbershop would soon have a new proprietor. Old Miguel had consented to pass on his tonsorial secrets to the young man, absolutely delighted to find in the promising Javier an apprentice equal to, or even surpassing, the skills of his once gifted student, the now famous Mexico City stylist, Alonzo Morales. All the fishermen and their wives paid close attention to Javier's progress, first hoping and praying, then, more confident in their estimation of the young man's ability (after all he was only a few months under seventeen), gleefully full of anticipation. They began to feel assured the tradition of first rate haircuts would remain a feature in the life of the shantytown.

One person less concerned with the town's tonsorial fortunes was Doña Consuelo who for her part kept an ever-watchful and doting eye on the swelling belly of her young apprentice. Already she knew after only a few weeks the baby was to be a female. Not only that, her mystical vision saw in advance the baptismal name. The girl child would be called niñita Consuelo. Proud and fiercely jealous for Manuela's well being, the curandera felt honored and humble to be gifted with a namesake. Having had no children of her own, Manuela had become her dynastic next in line. A secret tenderness had grown between the two. The young Manuela had come to Consuelo from the unknown world, as though a gift from the sea. The skinny, barren curandera had taken the child to her bosom, patiently teaching her, little by little, the arcane herbal arts, taking her into the garden where the magic began, gradually passing on the ancient secrets of healing. And over the years her heart swelled with love and pride and an increasing admiration for Manuela's intuitive acumen. She felt assured that someday Manuela would take her place as the shantytown's curandera. Nothing happens by coincidence, Consuelo was wont to murmur many a morning in the course of a year, upright in her bed before rising to her duties, as she piously made the sign of the cross beneath the image of Santos Cuates hanging on the white wall above her head, her black and gray hair, untied, fanned out over her shoulders, crackling with blue sparks.

But as well, she kept an eye on the first male student she had ever had, the admirable Señor EhEh himself. Here was a man to reckon with. His intellectual curiosity kept her on her toes. It was a challenge to meet the expectations of this tall gangling old man with the mind of a persistent bulldog. Indeed, in her view, he was too much in the mind, always wanting to figure out how the magic was accomplished, not easily willing to let go and know directly the nature of the thing.

Back from Los Angeles, EhEh walked almost daily with his teacher along the shoreline. He must go barefooted on the wet sand, she instructed him, so that he could be enlivened by the pulsing energy rising from the Mother's body. He took her to be speaking metaphorically. But she assured him she was speaking literally. In due time, she affirmed, with concentrated focus, he would sense the Mother's tingling reality. Another dose of the magic seeds might help. She would soon take him to her secret grotto, and put him through some direct experiences. This, she promised, and EhEh declared himself eager to move forward with the studies.

The first day they spent together on the beach, EhEh rehearsed for Consuelo what he and Elena had uncovered in Los Angeles. She listened attentively, interrupting him now and then with her own perspective. She was not interested in speculating whether the woman Adriana was Rachel or not, whether the Russians were alive or not. The important point to keep in mind was to see through the trauma that had invaded Miguel's soul, and had torn it away from his body.

"You see," she said, "When the natural and the spiritual are torn apart, two entities arise, and the mind loses its balance." She illustrated, turning to face him, and walked backwards, flopping her head from side to side, gesticulating with outstretched arms in imitation of a madman while saying, "The soul becomes lost, disconnected from the body. The human being, you see, has a spiritual nature that dwells in the body, but dwells also in the spirit world. In this way the soul lives in both worlds." She stopped, and poked a bony finger into his chest. "But it is really one world. The body cannot be cut away from the soul and spirit without losing its balance." She took his hand and resumed walking. "And this is what happened to Miguel. His soul began to rip away long ago when his woman cursed her father, the Rabbi."

"He told you about that night?"

"Yes, he told me. What he described was an unnatural act. His heart was pierced by her violent attack, so unnatural to curse a parent. We humans, you see, are members of the natural world - animals, plants, minerals, earth, and all living things found on earth. We are really all one, and our illness occurs when we do not live in harmony with all these aspects of the self that we truly are. We cannot go around cursing this and that with impunity."

She could see, EhEh did not comprehend, for he came back with yet another question.

"That happened so long ago, Consuelo. How does that even connect with what occurred in Los Angeles?"

"Well, that event in the Rabbi's house was just the first slight rip in Miguel's psyche. It was the beginning of the soul's journey of separation. And it was on that night of his breakdown, here at the swirling dark sea, when Miguel came to this realization that something terrible had happened to him beginning with that point in time. A series of events led from then to the present, the tear widening and widening until the illness reached its severity point."

"The night he broke down."

"Exactly. You mentioned the look of terror on his face that day when he returned from the President's Palace. That was Salinas, right? You remember him, yes?"

"Absolutely. How could I forget?" He looked at her with a face of utter sadness. "Some of my friends suffered much from that man, one in particular, a welder I knew who lost his pension because of that crook. I met him when he was working as a doorman at a hotel. He was never able to retire. I don't know what I would do, how I could live without my retirement income."

"This is something I like about you, EhEh. You do not stay aloof from the common man. You have a sensitivity that qualifies you for the teachings."

EhEh's cheeks went red from this mild compliment.

"That terrifying moment," she continued, "marked a further tearing of his fabric. Something unnatural must have happened in that palace."

"I guessed as much when I read the Google search results."

The curandera didn't know what he was talking about. EhEh had to explain, which he was happy to do, and therefore not have to feel so dumb in her presence.

"This is one of the items I want to question him about," EhEh spoke returning to the Salinas affair.

"Yes, it has to do with the massacre," she said.

He gazed at her full of incredulity. Had Barientos been right after all?

"You really think so?"

How could she be so sure, he wanted to know?

She nodded grimly, unknotting her thick salt and pepper hair and vigorously shaking it out by the snap of her head. She proceeded to make a strange ritual dance before EhEh, stamping on the hot sand, her torso gyrating increasingly faster, her grim face transforming into an expression of horror. Without warning, she suddenly seized both his hands and dragged his reluctant body into the tornado of her dancing frenzy, pulling him off balance. He became dizzy and was about to fall when she abruptly stopped, her body twisted into a shape that looked like a gnarled and weathered tree. It happened so quickly, EhEh was taken completely by surprise. A compounded sensation of stupefaction and terror tore through his body, a total body experience, his mind a complete blank. For once, his mind had shut down.

And then, just as suddenly, Consuelo became her usual self. *How does she do that?*

"Yes," she said, "that event tore a gigantic hole in his psyche, which he tried desperately to hide from."

"Until the bursting of the dam." EhEh nodded, caught up in the threads Consuelo had weaved.

"It's coming to you, I'm glad to see. Now you can understand what I mean about the soul. When it is off-balance it is suffering from fright. The soul runs off in fright, and so you see, the healing treatment involves bringing the soul back to the body. We call it soul retrieval."

"But isn't everyone more or less off-balance?" EhEh was back in his mind. "Don't we all have some kind of rip in the fabric?"

"Of course. This is why we are here in the physical world. We come here because we are souls already damaged one way or another. This worldly dimension is the only realm where we can make repairs."

"But we don't all go into comas," EhEh pulled him-self around to face the sea, feeling at a loss over this conundrum Consuelo had insinuated into his mind, as if that vast expanse of empty blue held in its depths all those lost souls she spoke of.

They resumed walking.

"If one's spirit has lost faith in God or the Divine, you see," the curandera went on, "one suffers an illness as real as a physical or mental illness. And without his realizing it until too late, Miguel had lost faith in God, his particular idea of God. In such a case, all aspects of the self will suffer, and one will experience diseases that affect one's body, mind, emotions, spirit, soul, family, community, and nature."

"And so many of us moderns have lost our faith," EhEh ruminated half aloud, half to himself.

"With Miguel, it was his mind and his emotions. We brujas understand this concept of illness. We have knowledge of how to guide the patient back to balance. Miguel blamed himself for the pain he believed he had caused the old Rabbi, blamed himself for the death of his daughter. He showered himself with self-incrimination, and condemned himself into a coma, all because he had lost faith with himself and with his God. He was out of balance."

EhEh stopped walking. He questioned himself about his own faith. His belief in the church had disappeared early in his youth. He remembered the sad look in his grandmother's face when he told his decision not to accompany her to mass. And his faith in science had vanished long before the end of his career. Not that he merely went through the motions as a scholar and professor. His trained mind continued to regard the epistemology of science as his only way of attempting an understanding of life. But he no longer believed in the process as another form of religion. There was no fervor motivating him anymore in his work as when he first turned to science as the new guarantee of truth.

He believed he was without any faith. He believed his fabric was shred through with holes. Perhaps now, with this woman of magic, he could begin to hope for a restoration. He definitely felt changes occurring within him. She was leading him toward a new kind of faith, one that had its foundation in nature, and yet somehow promised to connect him with soul and spirit.

In his mind's eye, he could see the darkness into which Miguel had plunged as that same darkness waiting at the edge of his own consciousness, threatening at any moment to envelop him. The vision made him shiver. He stood with his feet, burning from the hot sand, planted in the cool water for a bit of relief, the noonday sun blazing the top of his balding head, his eyes squinting as he looked deeply into Consuelo's upturned face. She had squatted to examine a seashell and was just rising when he caught her eye. The hot sand, evidently, had no affect on her bare feet. It seemed to him her gray eyes were vacant of any human personality. He felt he was looking deep into an emptiness that seemed to pull him out of his body. And suddenly, he found himself instantly soaring among nebulae and galaxies of sparkling brilliant colors. The sensation lasted only a moment, but it left him disoriented, and he wondered with some trepidation what would become of him when alone with her in the magic grotto. Was this the only way in, the only passage to her brand of faith, a faith that was at the core of her being?

"I just now had the strangest experience," he said.

"I know," she replied.

"Of course. I should have guessed you would. Is this what you did with Miguel, take him out into another dimension where he could meet his soul, so to speak?"

"Not quite. For him a different method was required."

"The poor man. I can imagine how lost he felt, disconnected and blaming himself, lost in a burning sorrow."

"You have empathy. That is good."

"And now you say he is back in balance? You know how much I want to speak with Miguel. I have questions only he can answer. When can I speak with him? Is he still too fragile? Is his faith strong enough?"

"You can see for yourself how happy he has become."

"Are you saying I may speak with him then?"

"Perhaps. It depends on how you will approach him. He is now more positive about his life. However, taking him back to the old memories might cause a relapse. How will you speak to him?"

EhEh paused to ponder this question. Was she testing him? The thought that he could be responsible for a relapse unsettled him. Meanwhile, the incoming tide brought the sea up to above his ankles. He could feel the slight undercurrent pulling at him, as if nature were in some way imitating his feelings of being pulled down by a possible relapse. He was amazed at how quickly he could recognize a synchronistic event. He could sense movement in his psychic awareness, and had no doubt changes were happening because of Consuelo. He came out of the water and they resumed walking back in the direction of the settlement. EhEh spoke with his eyes on the ground observing the impressions of his wet feet in the hot sand.

"Okay, I see how delicate this is," he began. "I will have to think about it. Off the top of my head, my idea would be to walk with him along the beach, just as we are doing now. I would ask him about his present feelings, how he is happy with the way things are, with Manuela and the coming baby, with Javier and his progress with the scissors. I would then tell him about Alonzo and how he has handled the business all these years of Miguel's absence, and of the money Alonzo has waiting for him in a bank in El Ciudad. Then, if he appears to be at ease with the mention of Alonzo, I would continue with the story Alonzo told me about his terrified return from the Palace. I would ask him if he could tell me more about that incident. And so, bit-by-bit, if he continued to wish to speak, we could get to the moment when the massacre occurred, and I could ask him to tell me his version of that event."

He stopped and looked at her.

"What do say, Consuelo? Will my approach work?"

"I feel comfortable with it."

She smiled at her pupil. They hurried back to the house. It was time for lunch. Manuela had promised a special meal for it was a special day, the occasion being her birthday. She was seventeen. Fortunately, EhEh had remembered to bring a present for her from Guaymas. It was sitting in his white Ford, a dress, in a white box and wrapped in tissue paper, of printed silk, long and flowy with straps for the shoulders and a hem that went down to the feet. It was stylish and suitable to wear as her belly enlarged, and it came from the best boutique in town. EhEh had learned much about this sort of thing from shopping with Elena on a brief spree in Los Angeles. Manuela wore the dress at her wedding that took place just a month before the baby arrived. The ceremony was held, in lieu of a church, under a gaily decorated palapa constructed on the beach especially for the occasion. Everyone attended, including Elena, whose role in EhEh's life had at first taken Miguel by surprise. Her presence brought back memories of tortuous times. Were it not for Consuelo's ministrations, that had helped him take charge of his emotions, he might have descended into a gloomy state again. Instead, he was able to disconnect her from the past and appreciate her for what she now really was, a caring, cheerful and vivacious woman.

The wedding party lasted deep into the night. Enormous quantities of food, beer, wine, and tequila punctuated the dancing and prancing, the kids running madly under everyone's feet. For this village by the sea it was the fiesta to end all fiestas.

Elena's decision to give up her apartment in El Ciudad and buy property in San Carlos pleased EhEh immensely. The idea that she would be living midway between Guaymas and his friends in the shantytown caused him to sing for several days. He told Consuelo of the impending move and elicited from her a willingness to take Elena with them to the magic grotto at some point when she thought Elena ready for the experience. As for Miguel and Manuela, he hesitated mentioning Elena. Not for a while, not until after he had his interview with the barber.

Elena came twice, EhEh picking her up at the airport, before a suitable house was found. She was thrilled to unearth the perfect house, situated on a hill with a sterling, unobstructed view of the bay to the southwest. At night from her patio she could see across the bay to as far as the lights of Miramar nestled on the edge of Bacochibampo Bay, the exclusive suburb of Gauymas.

Her house was small, only two bedrooms and a single bath. But it was modern and almost newly built. It had air conditioning for the very hot months, as well as the usual modern appointments. There was a cactus garden on the slope behind the house that looked to the mountains, and the flower garden in the patio looking over the bay.

She easily imagined herself sitting in a comfortable lounge chair sipping an evening glass of wine with EhEh beside her, the two of them talking softly sharing the highlights of their day while gazing at the sparkling lights of the little township across the bay. This romantic vision she had longed to realize all her life. Thinking of it put a twinkle in her eye.

To the east she could see the stark and magnificent desert mountain ranges stumbling one after the other until they faded into the purple distance. She found she liked San Carlos very much. Out of the way place that it was, a colony of Americans and Canadians as well as cultivated Mexicans had made this little seaside town their home. It had once been a simple fishing village, and it still was. And now a layer of culture was added to its quaintness.

Alongside the ordinary establishments aligned on the single thoroughfare running through the town, shops and small grocery stores that supplied the necessities of a working fishing village, there were now sprinkled among them a variety of very decent restaurants, a nightclub or two, and a coffee house with witty entertainment, several art galleries, a theater and dance company, and a quite swanky section at the north end with more cafes and a few hotels and a handsome marina, all the amenities she could ever desire.

When she came to seek out her ultimate home, she stayed with EhEh in his small house on the quiet shady side street in Guaymas. She was delighted by the simplicity in the way he lived. His house was cool and comfortable, his garden very agreeable. However, it never occurred to her that she would want to live with him. And EhEh never suggested it. He voiced his pleasure at the thought that she would always be close by, that they could see each other anytime they pleased. In his house they slept in separate rooms. In her house they slept together. It was a perfect arrangement for both.

Elena was eager to get started with establishing the foundation she had envisioned. The project required a great deal of thought and attention to detail. A good lawyer had to be found. A name for the organization had to be developed, and an overall plan that would benefit children with needs, and what those needs might be would have to be defined. And how money would be distributed was another question. They were enjoying themselves going over these issues.

When she talked about finances, she casually mentioned that she had taken half of Manuela's inheritance and given it to Sadie Melcher. This took EhEh by complete surprise.

"What?" He blurted. "What did you do?"

"Don't shout, EhEh. I don't like being shouted at."

"I'm not shouting. I'm just surprised. I guess I assumed you would put the money in a trust fund. An arrangement of some sort that Manuela would eventually be given control of, perhaps when she would be of legal age. It never occurred to me that you would take it upon yourself to distribute the money according to your own inclination."

"You mean I should have consulted you?"

"Well yes, at least that. Yes, I believe asking me would have been a decent thing to do. Why would you want to give Sadie half the inheritance?"

"You recall," Elena spoke evenly while inside she was fuming with annoyance, "you yourself informed me of her request for finding the money the Russians had stolen."

"That's true," EhEh replied, equally put out, "but that money was not the same money Rachael had set aside for her daughter. Surely you recognize a difference here. You jumped too fast, Elena. I've been intending to discuss the question of money for Sadie."

Agitated beyond endurance, Elena jumped out of her chair and went to the credenza. They had been sitting at the dining room table going over Elena's scribbled plans for the foundation. She poured herself a stiff shot of Tequila and downed it like a soldier.

"Listen EhEh," she said, still standing beside the credenza. "I gave the money to Sadie because she needed it. The poor woman is practically destitute. Her precious Michael has flown the coop. He's taken up with a floozy of some kind, a woman who dazzled the pants off of him."

"How kind of you," he said sarcasm dripping from his tongue. "It's the men, isn't it, who always ruin women's lives. With all your wealth, you couldn't give her some of your own money?"

"When you put it that way, I sound like a horrible bitch, stingy Elena, yes?"

She poured another shot. EhEh bit his lip. He felt himself slipping into a dark hole he would never be able to get out of.

"I'm sorry I said that. I shouldn't have said it that way."

"Is there a better way?"

She came back to the table, stood over him, her lips trembling. How was it, she wondered, how did they so easily fall into such horrible antagonistic traps?

"Yes," he said, drawing upon an inner strength. "I could have asked you why, what was your reason for taking Manuela's money. I could have reasoned you had a reason for doing that. That would have been the better way."

"Oh EhEh, why are we quarreling? This is such a little thing. I know, five thousand dollars must mean a lot to you. Well it is a lot. But it's not so much we need to be quarrelling about it."

He remained silent, gazing up at her. She was still standing over his head. But now she lay her hand on his shoulder seeking human contact.

"Listen, dear man. I never intended taking money away from Manuela. I intend to replace the five thousand with money of my own. I didn't want to give Sadie my money. I thought it only right that she receive family money. Money, so to speak, that carried the stamp of the family colors. That was my only reason for doing it that way. Surely you can see what I mean?"

"Why you dear heart," he softened. "Of course I can understand your point. Why in the world didn't you tell me this in the first place? Why did you not want to talk it over with me to begin with?" He felt remorse at his early outburst, and at the same time he felt miffed by not having been privy to her thoughts from the very beginning. Would it always be like this, he wondered? Would she always commit to something unilaterally, never willing to consult with him?

"You know, EhEh, I need to get used to us being more together about issues. Yes, you are right. I need to consult with you more. We can't just be lovers. We need to be partners."

"Yes, partners. I like that word. Let's be partners. May I have some of that Tequila? Let's drink to our partnership."

"Gladly!"

She skipped across the room and filled a small tumbler. He stood up to receive the drink, they clinked, they embraced, they kissed, declared they would never argue again, they drank some more, got tipsy, moved into the bedroom, tore off their clothes, made love as if, from all the emotional energy they had dispensed, thirty years had dropped from their frames.

And afterward, EhEh grinned to himself. This pattern they had fallen into would always be acted out. He might as well get used to it.

The several weeks it took to get Elena settled into her new home distracted EhEh from following through with his wish for a conversation with Miguel. He was completely absorbed in the many hours required going around with Elena exploring the art galleries for beautiful things to hang on the walls of her new house, whole days spent driving all over Sonora in search of talleres de artisanos in search for sturdy handmade rugs and furniture of quality and elegance, all the many details necessary for outfitting a home, details that Elena never tired of tackling until she had everything exactly the way she wanted it, as if for her the house was intended to fill two center pages of an interior design magazine, all of which bemused EhEh to no end as he went with her from place to place mindful of his own home, which by comparison had come already very simply furnished through years and years of his grandmother's lifetime of living in the same tiny cottage.

Although he possessed no similar inclination he nevertheless took keen pleasure being with his beloved, enjoyed watching her pert figure wriggle this way and that testing an armchair or a sofa, was transported by the sight of her tossing her body onto a mattress, her hand patting the surface inviting him to lie beside her so she could see how well they fit together. He loved the way she got excited when she spotted a work of art or a piece of furniture that elicited her awe. "Isn't this gorgeous?" The way she squealed with pleasure when she finally found something she had been hunting for several days. He marveled at her delight in beautiful things, something entirely new to his dry bachelor life. She carried her enthusiasm like a young girl, and the energy spilled over to him to the point where he started playfully wrangling with her over a possible selection for the living room or the bedroom, things he previously had had no interest in whatsoever. But he was careful to catch himself in time before an escalation of temperaments would arise.

Those weeks were a perfect delight to them, and he almost lost sight of his mission. He did, however, drive out to the shantytown each week to spend time with his friends. He took walks with Consuelo, had meals with the family. Manuela always prepared a feast of vegetables of various kinds seasoned with herbs and served with large portions of grilled fish brought in fresh by Javier who went out in his panga early in the mornings to be back at the barber chair in time for afternoon appointments. And with every visit Manuela invited him to pat her swelling belly to bring good luck, and he did this with fervor, a tear welling up in his eye. He was amazed at how sentimental he was becoming.

Eventually, normal life had settled in again, and he grew restless with the questions that had been running around in his head for a long time. One afternoon, he found himself sitting outside the shack alongside Miguel. Javier had finished cutting the hair of the last customer of the day, and had taken Manuela in the pickup for a pleasure ride. The two old men sat side-by-side taking in the scene on the beach. They could see the kids playing on the flat part near the water's edge, kicking an old beat-up soccer ball that thumped flatly on the sand, and behind their flashing legs, they could see the men closer to the water hanging their nets to dry, repairing some, laughing and joking while they cleaned fish, throwing scraps to the many pelicans swooping in impolitely grabbing their share of the catch. The cloudless sky reflected the blue of the sea bringing an invisible breeze to the old men's cheeks. The day was sliding to a soothing end.

EhEh sensed the time had come.

"Care for a stroll?" He asked turning to Miguel whose chin had fallen to his chest. EhEh thought he might be snoozing.

Without a word, smiling, Miguel rose to his feet. He led the way down a path through the grassy dunes. EhEh didn't know it, but they were heading for Miguel's place of rendezvous with his Hannah. He noticed how his friend tilted a bit to the left as he walked, and wondered if the old barber hadn't suffered a stroke or some form of brain damage resulting from his coma. He considered taking Miguel to see a neurologist, and then thought better of it. Neither Miguel nor Consuelo would necessarily welcome consulting scientific medical models. He was probably the only person in this shantytown who wavered between the two worlds, the one irrationally rational and the other rationally irrational. Lines from the 19th century English poet came to him. "Caught between two worlds; the one half dead, the other unwilling to be born." Was this his problem? Was he just simply stuck in a 19th century model? He felt provoked with himself finding it so difficult to shift his mindset. He bet no one else in this village had such a problem.

They came to Miguel's favorite spot. The tide was out. They could sit on exposed rocks now dry from the sun.

"Do you mind resting here for a while?" Miguel softly inquired thrusting his chin toward EhEh. EhEh took note: he hadn't seen Miguel demonstrate this mannerism before the illness. "I feel most comfortable sitting here." Miguel went on. "This is where I talk with the ghosts in my life. You want to ask me something, I can tell. My Hannah is here. She's holding my hand. I feel I can tell you things."

EhEh hadn't expected Miguel would come straight to the point like this. He seemed to fathom EhEh's reason for the walk. Had he become prescient? Maybe some of Consuelo's uncanny gifts had rubbed off on him?

"You take my breath away, Miguel. I remember a time when you found it quite difficult to talk to me about matters you obviously needed to get off your chest. Back then you were leading up to some revelation about yourself but always not quite able to get it out. Something that was driving you to despair."

"I am no longer in despair, my friend. Consuelo has done wonders for me. Finally, I am at peace with myself. It's a glorious feeling. I'm free."

"What did she do?"

"I don't know," Miguel looked bewildered. "It seemed that she slid her hand into my body and pulled something out of me. It seemed like that. But such a thing is impossible, no?"

"I'm not sure," EhEh replied, half whispering. "With Consuelo, anything is possible. Of that I am certain. There is something sacred in her touch." His mind wandered off for a moment, then a smiled crossed his face. "And I am so grateful to her for this healing she has accomplished. You really had us worried, Miguel. I don't know what Manuela would have done had she lost you."

"And I owe you too, EhEh. You traveled far to dig out facts, as Manuela put it, to ease my mind. Yes, she told me you were investigating my life. But that was really another life. I'm not that same person anymore."

"Well," EhEh took in a deep breath, "if you are not that same person, perhaps you can talk about him as an impersonal observer."

"Yes," the barber smiled, almost wistfully, EhEh thought. "I am detached from all that stuff that was burning in my head."

"That's good."

"So, now you know a great deal about that life. Consuelo told me a bit about your detective work. She wanted to prepare me for this inevitability."

Miguel reached over and patted EhEh on the knee, as if to imply this inevitable moment had come at an okay time.

"You know, in the beginning I really had her wrongly pegged. I saw her as nothing more than an interfering busybody." His head drooped, his face revealing embarrassment. "To tell the truth, she got on my nerves with all her bruja nonsense. I thought all that was nothing but a bunch of crap. But look at me now." His voice bore a trace of amusement. "I'm a believer. You bet your life."

EhEh had winced at the word "detective." He didn't want to come across now as the "investigator" drilling Miguel for information. It would be a torture for both of them. And he was wary of Miguel's actual condition. He speculated again whether a brain specialist should be consulted.

"I notice, Miguel, how you tilt to the left when you walk."

"Is that so? You think I tilt?"

"I wouldn't say so if it weren't true. I'm wondering if you've suffered some neurological damage."

"Does it matter that I tilt? Actually, I haven't noticed."

"Oh you would not notice it. I've read some of the literature about this. Typically, the person is totally unaware of his condition."

"I feel fine. I'm not interested in seeing a doctor. Consuelo is my doctor. Shall we drop the subject?"

The look of anguish on Miguel's face alarmed EhEh. He bit his lip. He shouldn't have raised the subject. Nevertheless, he had an inkling he had touched on an important issue, and promised himself to discuss it with Consuelo, even though he might be stepping on her toes in the process.

"If you wish. Of course."

EhEh stood up and stretched. The jagged rock was digging into his meager rump.

"You know," he said, suddenly shifting the tone in his voice and the topic as well attempting to sound cheerful, "Alonzo is running your salon in El Ciudad with great success. He's piled up a huge amount of cash that's sitting in a bank in your name, the name you went by in the old days, Julio Valladares."

"That was my name. I didn't make it up, you know." Miguel laughed, rising to his feet wholly unaware of his very noticeable tilt. "Good for him," he laughed impatiently. "He doesn't have to think about me. You can tell Alonzo for me, he can keep the damn money. When I left the business to him, I left it for good. I want no part of it now," he spat out. "All those years I plugged away. All precious time wasted." A bitter look stole into his face. "I know that now. I thought I was bringing happiness to people's lives. All I wanted was to find happiness and share it with others. I didn't know how impossible a task that is." He stepped to the edge of the water. "Isn't that so, Hannah?" He shouted into the blackening waters, shaking his body the way a wild animal shakes itself in its persistence to get rid of something.

EhEh stepped over and placed a hand on Miguel's shoulder thinking to steady the man. He was concerned the old and disabled barber would fall into the sea, or worse, go off the deep end again.

"Sure, Miguel, sure. Ease your mind. I'll tell him you don't need the money. I'll tell him you've found a new form of happiness."

"That's right!" He turned his face to EhEh. A stream of tears flowed from the corner of his eyes. "I don't mind showing you my deep feelings, old friend. I'm happy now. You can see that can't you?"

"Sure, Miguel, sure," EhEh repeated, but his mind was not willing to believe the barber's assertion.

"And I'm relieved. Enormously relieved. And I know Hannah is happy for me. Isn't that so, Hannah?" His face bore the mark of a puzzled man. "I cry out of pure joy."

Abrazo came to EhEh's mind. He gathered the smaller man into his arms and hugged him with great feeling.

"I know you are," he said, and felt comforted himself for the human contact. Feeling the barber's aliveness, he sensed that Miguel's nervousness was mainly due to the impending questions he would be asked. It was only normal, EhEh told himself, for Miguel to feel nervous. And this thought somehow reassured him that it would be fine to go on with the interview.

EhEh urged Miguel to walk with him along the beach. Night was creeping in. A wind, sweeping across the sea, chilled his bones. Slowly, they walked along the strand, staggering a bit and bumping against each other, as if they were a couple of drunken sailors. But EhEh felt no concern. He had decided to dismiss the tilting issue. It was not such a serious matter, he thought.

"So, what do you want to know from me? Shall we deal with that? Isn't this why we are here?" Miguel lifted his face.

"Okay, let's talk about it," EhEh stopped and looked into the other's eyes. "Alonzo told me of the events of that day when you ran into the salon in a fit of terror. You had just come from the President's Palace. He said it was your first and only instance as barber to the president."

"That's true."

"Something happened at the palace that frightened you, yes?"

"Yes."

Despite attempting to not make it so, EhEh felt he was acting the part of a prosecuting attorney in a court of law the way this question and answer routine was going. But he couldn't help himself. He saw no other way of dealing with the matter.

He complained to Miguel, "Look, I don't want you to feel I am acting like a prosecuting lawyer badgering you for a deposition."

"You don't have to think about it that way, my friend. Just ask me what you want to know."

"Fine," he shouted nervously. "Just tell me what happened that day at the palace. That's all I'm asking."

"No it's not. You want to know everything. Well, I will tell you everything. I have no secrets anymore."

Miguel began his tale. He started by speaking about how proud he had been to finally achieve his life's ambition. His hand made a gesture duplicating a billboard. 'Julio Valladares, Barber to El Presidente.' His face beamed. It was a smashing day. He had put on his best clothes and arrived at the Palace exactly on the dot. Julio was charmed to discover a special room set aside exclusively for haircuts, complete with an actual barber's chair. He had with him his bag of equipment, and as he opened the case, the president stepped into the room. And with him a number of men, maybe three, maybe four – he couldn't tell because his back was to the door when they arrived, and while he was engaged in cutting the president's meager hair, he sensed that one of the men stayed always in the shadow of a drapery.

Engrossed in his work, he paid little attention to their conversation. The president spoke a great deal, getting rather agitated, wriggling his body and shaking his head. It was difficult to perform the task. He took in that they were discussing the upcoming elections, but he paid little attention. Politics was not really of special interest to him. He found politicians not easily satisfied; they weren't prone to true happy moments in their lives. His only real desire was to be the hair cutter to an important figure in the world, and thus to follow in the footsteps of his family tradition. "What an utter emptiness of purpose. I see that now. Ambition, bah!"

"You were surrounded with men of great ambition that day. They were hatching something?"

"I believe so. The men were talking earnestly. I had the feeling they were trying to convince El Presidente to agree to something."

While he was snipping away, their voices came to him as if muffled, through a veil, so to speak, a veil of his own making. He didn't really care what they were saying. He was focused on the president's wobbling head that turned this way and that as he argued his points to this one or that one. Their voices grew louder, the argument heated. He wasn't paying much attention until suddenly he heard the word 'assassination'.

The word penetrated to the pit of his stomach. Full of alarm, he stopped snipping. The snipping sound of the scissors ceased. And suddenly, there was silence in the room. He tore his eyes from his work, and looked around. Everyone was staring at him. In a trembling fit of fear, he realized, instantly, they had become aware of his presence. He knew that they knew he had heard them talking. 'Assassination' rang in his ears. He had no idea who they were talking about, who the victim was, or was to be.

But he had heard enough to make them take notice of him. His hands trembled as he quickly resumed snipping, and finished the job in record time. That part was not difficult actually, as the president, thank God, had little hair on his head to begin with.

He was frightened. And they knew he was frightened. He could tell by their silence. They had stopped speaking. He could sense them staring at him while he finished the job. Hastily, he packed up his bag and scooted out of the room, not uttering a word, and hightailed it back to his place of business.

"You know from what Alonzo told you how terrified I was," he muttered.

"Yes," EhEh whispered. "And so you fled to Los Angeles."

"I could think of no other place to go to. I was in a state of shock. I needed Rachael for advice. She would know what to do. I drove like a madman across the border. All I could think of was escape. I was convinced my life was in danger. And while I drove, all I thought of was Hannah. If she had been alive, I remonstrated to myself, none of this would have happened."

"Hannah was a political sore thumb. Because of her, you never got the honor you so desired. Not until she died did you get the chance to cut the president's hair."

"Yes, very true. As long as she was alive I was safe from the disaster of my ambition."

"Are you saying you blame her?"

"Absolutely not!" A chilling laugh erupted from his throat. "What an absurd idea! What do you take me for?"

"Forgive me." EhEh tried to explain. "I'm looking only to understand what embers might be smoldering."

"Nothing is smoldering. I've already said I am free. Nothing remains hidden."

Both men fell silent, disgruntled expressions staring into the sea.

Confusion, laced with panic, gripped EhEh mercilessly. Why was he probing Miguel's psyche like this? What was he attempting to get at? For a split second he wondered if this was his way of testing Consuelo's healing powers. Was he trying to show she hadn't fully succeeded? What a sacrilegious idea! He felt ashamed for challenging his teacher like this. How cynical of him! He scoured his mind for its roots, and in an unexpected moment of clarity, he knew it for what it was: the habit of scholarly skepticism, which he now saw as nothing more than an academically accepted guise for cynicism. Probing

Miguel had stimulated this former tendency. He didn't want to be like this anymore. He wanted the new innocence he was reaching for. His mind called to Consuelo for support. And when he turned his attention back to Miguel, he felt anew the sorrow his empathy had aroused, his sadness over the barber's shattered life. It scorched his soul, this enormous fire that had lit their love, but then had turned that love into a tragic conflagration, that had burned to ashes the lives of their loved ones. All this he felt, glancing at his old friend who stared into the darkening waters in search of his beloved Hannah with frightening intensity.

After a while, he opened his mouth. "Miguel, do you want to go on?"

"Yes. I want to finish this, tell you what I had wanted to tell so long ago when we first met. I always sensed your sympathetic nature."

"It is because of you, dear friend, that my heart has opened."

They started walking again. Miguel laid his hand on the tall man's shoulder, partly to show his warmth and partly to steady himself.

"Yes, I fled to Los Angeles. Rachael was happy to see me. She didn't ask me why I had come. But I had to tell her my reason for coming, and she assured me everything would be all right, that no one would come after me, I was safe with her. She soothed my nerves like a doting mother. Besides, she said, she could use my talent in her beauty salon. Her business would increase. And little Hannah charmed my heart. Her love for me soothed my nerves even more. That first year was balm to me. Whenever we had the chance, I took Hannah to the beach. The child loved the sea. I could sit on the blanket for hours and watch her play by the water, digging holes in the wet sand, her body turning like the brown of a walnut. She giggled and danced in the shallow surf, beside herself with pleasure from seeing the holes she dug fill with gurgling ocean water."

But soon trouble began for Julio. The two Russian brothers, distant cousins of his dead wife, had evil eyes for him. He didn't know why. And Rachael looked away with a sad shrug when he asked his daughter about this. In the end, he concluded they had been infected with the Rabbi's animosity.

So he stayed out of their way as much as possible, and concentrated his attention on the child. They showed her no affection. Julio held this against them. He assumed Boris was little Hannah's father, Rachael never told him otherwise. He thought it cruelly unnatural for the brothers to treat the child like this. And although he tried not to think about it, it bothered him not knowing what their business was. He knew they couldn't have regular jobs. They came and went at odd times, were often gone for several days. And when they returned, they always had strange haunting expressions in their eyes, as if some demon were at their heels.

"They were part of a drug gang," EhEh interrupted.

"A drug gang?" Miguel looked incredulous. "What kind of a drug gang?"

"They worked for a Mexican drug cartel. Their role was to launder large sums of cash, and maybe other assignments as well."

Miguel let out a loud whistle, his hand tracing on his chest the sign of the cross.

"¡Dios mío!"

"Of course, you didn't know," EhEh speculated aloud. "The people who came for them, who came to murder them were not after you. You believed you were the target, didn't you?"

Miguel began to tremble. "Yes…yes. I believed they were after me because of what I had overheard."

"You knew Colosio had been assassinated. That was the man you thought they were talking about in the Palace that day, correct? And so, it seemed logical to believe your time had come, yes?"

"No, I didn't know. I didn't read the papers. I didn't watch the news on the TV. And I didn't know who they were talking about in that room. I knew nothing!" He protested.

"Nevertheless, you assumed the killers had come for you," EhEh repeated.

"What else to believe? The threat of danger stalked me everyday. Only when I was at the beach with little Hannah did I feel safe. Otherwise, I feared for my life. Sooner or later, they would find me. I was convinced."

"But you couldn't leave Rachael and Hannah. You didn't try to keep on the run, so to speak." EhEh bit his tongue for using that term.

"No. I couldn't leave. I was terrified to leave. I felt I would have gone off the deep end. I clung to them. They were my anchors. And then when the inevitable happened, I saw how my vile selfishness had destroyed my family. And I lived with that pain ever since."

"But now you can see, the massacre happened not because of you. You are not at fault. You never were at fault. You need not blame yourself anymore."

Miguel appeared perplexed in his attempt to come to grips with this statement of EhEh's. He had for so long convinced himself of having annihilated his family. Because of him, the Rabbi had suffered egregiously. Because of him, his wife Hannah had been driven to struggle for her human rights as a woman just so she could fill the gap of losing her father's respect. Because of him she had to die at such a young age from all sorts of unhealthy exposure. Because of him, his beautiful daughter Rachael had been gunned down in cold blood. This was the story he had told himself everyday. And now he was supposed to see himself in a different light? It seemed impossible.

Miguel seized EhEh's arms and pulled himself up, standing on his toes, to look straight into EhEh's eyes.

"You are saying the killers weren't after me?"

"That's right. That massacre had to do with cartel drug wars, not with you. Adriana told us the true story. The brothers were double-crossing their bosses. The gang came and wiped then out. And in the process killed Rachael, perhaps in error, perhaps intentionally. They may have believed she was in on the betrayal. And a fourth man was killed. He had your identity papers on him. How did that happen?"

Miguel let go of EhEh's arms and lowered himself to his ordinary height.

"I can tell you all about that. But first, who is this "us" you are talking about? And who is this Adriana person?"

EhEh quickly gave him the details about Elena's involvement, how it was she who steered him to the salon and Alonzo. Miguel sucked in his breath at the mention of Elena.

He had unhappy memories of that lady, he said. EhEh assured him, Elena was a very nice woman who treasured her friend Hannah. "Don't forget, it was she who came to visit Hannah at her death bed." Miguel said he would take her humanity into account. Then he repeated his question about Adriana.

"You didn't know her? You never met Rachael's best friend? The woman with the shop just next door to the salon?"

Miguel shook his head looking baffled.

"I didn't know this person. Rachael never mentioned her. I never looked inside the shop next door. I was in the salon only in the mornings. Rachael and I and the baby came to Beverly Hills from Van Nuys every morning six days a week, and I would cut one or two client's hair until little Hannah would wake up. She'd fall asleep in the car driving over, and then would sleep half the morning in the back room where Rachael kept a bed for the girl. The back room was like a small studio apartment. When the baby woke up, I would go and make a breakfast for her and have my second cup of coffee. Then by ten or so, we'd be ready to go to the beach, or I'd take her to the park, or to some other kind of amusement, and we wouldn't come back until noon when Rachael made lunch for us. And in the afternoons, I always took the baby to the beach. That was our routine. I don't know why Rachael never spoke about this Adriana woman."

Of course, she wouldn't talk about Adriana, EhEh realized. They were secret lovers. It made sense that Miguel would be in the dark about Adriana.

"So, the day of the massacre you were at the beach with little Hannah?"

"No, we were at the park that morning. We got back just at noon or a little after, I'm not certain. I drove up the back alley and parked behind our shop. It was then I heard the noise. At first, I had no idea I was hearing machine gun fire. I knew something terrible was happening in the salon. I thought perhaps equipment was exploding. Quickly, I unlocked the back door and ran inside, holding Hannah by the hand. I told her to stay in the back room. When I stepped into the salon, my heart leaped to my throat. There, on the floor, were sprawled four bodies, blood pouring from their heads, their faces, their necks and chests. I saw my darling daughter lying there. I couldn't believe my eyes. What had I done? I cried out in pain. My first thought, my only thought was they had come after me. This killing had been meant for me. Not for my daughter. It was terrible. I was shattered. Then I heard sirens, and I knew the police would be there in a minute or two. I had to think fast. My only thought was to escape, to get away before the police found me, and it would follow then that the killers would discover they had not killed me. And that's when the idea came to me. Of course. How simple. All I had to do was change identities with one of the dead men. All their faces had been obliterated, literally torn to shreds by machine gun bullets. That was the noise I had heard. My nerves were shattered, but I steeled myself and reached into the stranger's pocket and took his wallet, replacing it with mine, careful not to get blood on my hands. And then, for a reason I really cannot fathom, I decided it best if I removed the wallets of the two brothers, which I later burned at my first opportunity. I had just finished taking their wallets when Hannah stepped into the room. She screamed. Immediately, I jumped to hide her face from the sight of her mother lying there in a puddle of blood. Quickly, I snatched her in my arms and ran into the back room grabbing up everything I could see that was Hannah's, a few toys, some pieces of clothing, her blanket. I didn't want the police or killers to know anything about her. My only thought was to protect her. I took all her stuff and ran out of the building, jumped into the car holding her in my lap, never mind her safety chair, and drove as fast as I could away from the building, zigzagging through back streets making my way to Van Nuys. Just as I pulled out of the back alley and onto the street leading away from Rodeo Drive, I heard the first police car pull up out in front. My heart pounded as I drove up and over the hill, down into the Valley constantly looking behind me through the rear-view mirror, terrified. It was the same terror that propelled me out of the Presidential Palace only a few years before."

Miguel went on explaining that Rachael had made certain there was no connection between the business place and their house in Van Nuys. The police would not easily be able to trace the family's residence. EhEh asked him if he was certain the dead bodies were those of his daughter and the two brothers.

"Of course they were. I'd know them under any circumstance. I could see in a glance who they were."

"And the third man? You recognized him?"

"No, he was a stranger to me."

"And so you eventually found your way to this remote fishing village."

"Yes, but not directly. I drove to Tijuana and looked up an old family friend. He was the grandson of Poncho Villa, the man my father was barber to. The grandson was a lawyer with many underground connections. We had known each other as children and we stayed in touch over the years. He helped me become Miguel Guzman, provided me with papers, got rid of my car for me, and found the pickup Javier now operates. Poncho and my father were good friends. Poncho was a good leader. He controlled a vast territory. He gave the peasants a fair shake, decent housing and decent wages. He established schools for their children, hospitals and other social services. His own sons became well educated. My father and he were good friends. And my father was with him the day he was assassinated. With tears he often told me the events of that day. It's no wonder I reacted the way I did cutting El Presidente's hair. Funny, isn't it, how these things repeat themselves? In less than a week, I left Tijuana with my new identity, and with Manuela. She had just turned six, and was doing remarkably well under the circumstances. The trauma of what she may have seen was buried deep inside her. I fibbed by explaining to her we were going on a long vacation in Mexico, and that we would have a lot of good times, that her mom had agreed, it would be good for her little girl to get to know about the place where her mom was born, even though her mom couldn't go with her. My story seemed to satisfy the mind of a six year old. The last thing I did before leaving Tijuana was to buy a barber's chair."

Miguel stopped talking. His jaws clamped shut, his lungs heaving. EhEh took the man's hand, then moved in closer and hugged him. He could think of nothing to say. He put an arm around Miguel's shoulder, and together, they walked back to the settlement.

"Not my fault," Miguel murmured. "Not my fault," he repeated. "It had nothing to do with me. My God, nothing to do with me."

His step seemed to be lighter. His face showed itself, damp with tears, blissful and at peace.

Night had long since arrived. A full moon swathed the beach and the sea in silver light. They made their way across the shining dunes. Lanterns and bare light bulbs glowed through the windows of the small houses and shacks. People were finishing their evening meals and were settling down for the night, another day slipping gently into an indistinct past, each day much like the other.

Inside, they found Manuela and Javier at the table, and Consuelo was there as well. They were already eating. Javier went into the bedroom to get a fifth chair for EhEh so that all five might sit at the table. The family looked intently at the old man, ascertaining his state. And finding him obviously at peace, shaking his thick white hair, and remarking how hungry he was, Consuelo turned her gaze from Miguel to EhEh, a broad warm and softening smile on her bony face.

"It is done," she said. "Let us give thanks for God's Grace."

Dutifully, and with quiet piety, the children bowed their heads. And so did Miguel. And so did EhEh.

The months slipped past in quick order. The night came when Manuela went into labor. The whole village was full of anticipation. Javier drove to San Carlos to phone EhEh, who in turn phoned Elena, then picked her up in his white Ford and together they drove to the shantytown. The place was buzzing. Toasts were being made. A few who knew how, strummed their guitars, softly crooning songs seldom heard on the radio. It was a warm night, everyone in the most pleasant mood while they waited for the new member of their community to arrive, the one everyone already knew as little Consuelo.

And finally, the day came when Consuelo consented to EhEh's request. He had met with his teacher many times, taking instruction in the magic grotto where he learned and practiced the secrets of shamanism. And Consuelo was pleased with his progress. Yet, it would be a long time, she predicted, before he would be willing to call himself a brujo.

He was eager to share this new part of his life with Elena. He desired that she experience the magic of Consuelo's grotto. This was the request he made. And so a time was arranged.

It was morning. EhEh was about to leave his house to fetch Elena, when his phone rang.

"Bueno?" He shouted, a tone of irritation in his voice.

"Escudero?" A man shouted back. EhEh didn't recognize the voice. "Barientos here."

"Ah, Señor Barientos! You just caught me. I was on my way out. It's been a long time."

EhEh was itching to go. Elena was waiting for him. Consuelo would wonder what was keeping him. And now this unexpected interruption threatened his patience. But an inner voice spoke to him. It was his newly established brujo instinct, and it told him to calm himself and pay attention.

"You have news?"

"That's right, amigo, I have news," Barientos chortled. "I've found them!"

"You what?"

"I've found them. It took me months, but I found them."

"What in the world? Are you telling me they are alive?" Uncanny as it was, EhEh knew exactly who Barientos was talking about.

"Hold off a second, Escudero. Let me unfold my story in my own leisurely way. You have no idea all the hours I spent surfing the Internet. I searched hundreds of online newspapers. I googled for hours with inquiries. And in the end I succeeded. I found them."

EhEh sat down in the chair next to the telephone table. This was going to take a length of time. He would have to phone Elena when it was over to tell her why he was late.

"Please go on, Barientos."

"Thank you, my friend. Okay, so picture this. I found a newspaper story in the San Francisco Chronicle, not front page stuff mind you, but lurid enough to get printed. This is a brutal story, so brace yourself. The story was about a murder trial, a woman by the name of Sonia Ruiz on trial for murder. She was living with her husband, Emilio Ruiz, and his brother Lorenzo in the Mission District, a Latino barrio. Two men and a woman. How does that strike you?"

EhEh shrugged, "Does that make them our threesome? My guess, not very likely."

"But that's not all. Listen, the woman was a hairdresser, worked in a local beauty parlor. And the men had no visual means of support. No jobs. They loafed around, drank a lot, she said. Also they beat her regularly. She claimed they both sexually abused her, until she finally couldn't take anymore. This was her defense. Her lawyer, a public defender, made a half-hearted argument stating she was driven into temporary insanity. He based the insanity claim on the fact that she had blasted the brothers in their faces at close range with a sawed off shotgun. Only a person with a crazed mind would blow off their victims' faces like that, he argued. On the stand, she testified the weapon belonged to her husband, and that she pulled it out of the closet in a moment of cold fury after the brothers had raped her. But the investigating officer proved she had gotten the shotgun from a nearby pawnshop. This definitely showed cold-blooded premeditation. The jury brought in a conviction of murder in the first degree. She was sentenced to life in prison. This happened six years ago, four years after the massacre on Rodeo Drive. These were the people we've been looking for, no doubt in my mind. What a nasty, nasty ending. Whaddya think, my friend?"

"All very well," EhEh hedged, he felt dismayed by Barientos' story. He didn't have the heart to think about more tragedy. If he could, he would just softly say goodbye and hang up. But he wasn't wired for committing impolite gestures. So, he replied to the sergeant's question. "Admittedly, several distinct parallels. However, I'm not sure I'm convinced."

"Wait a minute, Escudero, we can't so easily dismiss the similarities. Imagine the state of her mind, this Sonia Ruiz. As Rachael, she is no doubt forced into their ruse of staging a massacre that, among other things, would cost her her daughter. That alone is enough to build resentment. Then she is forced to work to support the household. Those bums certainly must have had money they stole from the cartel. But they prove to be stingy as well as mean spirited, abusing her so inhumanly. She is driven to despair, and finally, she blasts them off obliterating their faces, just as they had done to the four innocent victims, the people they got off the street no doubt, four homeless and vulnerable victims. Do I make my case?"

"In your mind, your argument is convincing, do doubt about it. But your initial assumption has no basis in fact. We don't know if the massacre was staged or not. You are basing the Ruiz connection on an improvable theory. We can just as easily see the massacre as a stroke of the cartel killers. And besides, I've spoken with Julio and he assured me the victims in the beauty salon were his daughter and the Russians. He said he couldn't possibly mistake them."

Can't you tell from my voice, I don't want to talk anymore about this?

"Yeah, that would be the simpler explanation. And I would accept it; only the cartel people don't ordinarily wipe out peoples' faces. That's not their MO. And Julio could be wrong. Many times witnesses are wrong."

For a moment, EhEh remained silent. He thought about the woman in prison, and imagined he too could be wrong. Perhaps she was indeed Rachael. He could feel her immense sadness. The loss of her child. A life ruined. And it came to him; there was something he could do. If the Ruiz woman were Rachael, then her heart might be lightened knowing the fate of her daughter. He should go and see her, find out for himself who she really is, tell her about Manuela.

"Are you there, Escudero?"

"Yes, I'm here. Tell me, Barientos, where is she imprisoned? If she is indeed our Rachael, I would like to visit her and tell her about her daughter. This ought to ease her mind to a degree. I can imagine how much she is suffering. This is the least we can do for her."

"I'm sorry to have to tell, my friend, I told you this is a brutal story. You won't be able to do this." Even the hard-boiled cop breathed a sigh of sadness. "Because she is dead, my friend. Believe me, I thought about going to the prison myself, even though in my condition that would have been a real hardship. But she is dead. She died in the prison hospital two years ago from an autoimmune disease."

Another expanse of silence wormed through the telephone wires. EhEh felt his heart contract. He felt this woman's sorrow as if it were his own. Whether she was Rachael or not didn't really matter. The effect was the same. He had gotten so intertwined with this tragic family's history; his emotions had become an instrument for sorrow, and not just for this family alone. He felt the enormous weight of a world drenched in sadness.

"Escudero?"

"Yes?"

"Listen, I didn't call with the idea of bringing you a happy ending. I just thought you ought to know. You can take it whatever way you so wish. But for me, this information closes the case. It's over now, and we can go on with our lives. At least for me it's all tied up now. No lose ends. I hope it's the same for you and Ms Navarro."

"I'll have to think about it. I'm grateful you called me, sergeant. You deserve our thanks for all the work you did."

"Thanks, friend. It was a team effort. You and Ms Navarro did your share in putting this all to rest. I'll say goodbye now, and good luck to you."

"Goodbye, Sergeant Barientos. Take care."

EhEh hung up and sat for a while waiting for his feelings to quiet down. There was too much suffering in the world, too much for him to hold. He mulled over the question of how much he could share with Elena. He knew immediately he had no interest in repeating this conversation to Consuelo, and certainly not to Miguel. Why stir them up over nothing more than supposition?

He thought about Elena's role in all this, and came to the conclusion he really was not interested in telling her this dreadful story either. We cannot hide from the sordid things of this world, he acknowledged. But we don't need to spread it around either. Let the past be done with. Anyway, she was fully engaged in her children's foundation. This was her only real concern now: the future of the children. Why distract her with questionable information, with unnecessary speculation, with yet another family tragedy? He let out a sigh, and wondered when the taste of this bad news would wash out of his system.

He slowly dialed Elena's number. When she picked up the phone, he asked for her patience. He would come by to get her in an hour or so. He needed some time get his mind settled. By the tone of his voice, she knew something had happened, and that he wasn't willing to talk about it. She didn't press him. Then mentally, he sent a message to Consuelo hoping she would pick up the signal of his regrets for not arriving at the appointed time.

EhEh drove slowly down Avenida Serdan, his mind gradually draining itself of Barientos' dreadful story. In its place, he turned his thoughts away from pain. He thought about his own life, and all the changes. In less than a year, a whole new sense about things had come to him. In his mind's eye he looked back at his old life, which, when he lived it, seemed comfortable and appealing in its uncomplicated simplicity, but which now he saw as resembling something more like a misshapen, dried out gourd. For one thing, there was no Elena then, no idea even that companionship, particularly a woman's warmth, could be so important an element for a contented life. Nor in his wildest dreams did he ever sense he could feel the awesomeness of nature that now permeated his very being. He felt himself, now, every moment, immersed in an aliveness that penetrated to his depths. His eyes saw the world as a shimmering substance of constantly shifting colors making his body tingle with excitement. And at times he would find himself dizzy with wonderment at the sight of a vibrant sunset as its fires shot across the sky in ribbons of dancing colors, or seeing the leaves of his backyard trees vigorously orchestrating the song of the wind. And this alteration had come about in the strangest, most unlooked for way; himself never expecting another man's misfortune would pluck him from so mediocre an existence as had been his, sitting day after day in the library pouring over abstract theories that made the soul brittle, as compared to a life now that so surprisingly transported him to the portals of ecstasy. It was this ironic twist of fate that caused him to marvel at the mystery that now filled his life.

And when he came to the road that led to San Carlos, he had to stop at the top. The road had taken him up a steep hill to the peak of a smallish mountain that offered a sweeping view of the coastline below. The blue sea splashed against the black pockmarked rock of the mountain. The white beaches, glistening in the distance under brilliant sunlight, traced a graceful arc around the bay. EhEh paused here for a while by the side of the road, and gazed at the glorious scene, his mind empty of all thought. Then, gradually emerging from a near trance state, he resumed his drive down the mountain and into the outskirts of San Carlos.

The one main road running through the town skirted close by several beaches before approaching the first row of houses that marked the beginning of the town proper. EhEh glanced to his left, and noticed the many people on the beach. Only then did he realize it was Sunday. After church, many of the working class families were accustomed to visiting this particular beach. EhEh remembered coming here when he was a kid with his grandmother many a Sunday after mass. Seeing the clusters of people lying and sitting on their blankets, or resting on beach chairs under umbrellas, seeing mothers applying lotion on the brown backs of their children, seeing the small kids splashing in the water, the older ones, boys and girls walking along the surf ogling each other, seeing the families enjoying their day of rest in this simple, natural manner stirred EhEh's sensibilities.

An impulse to join them got him out of his car. He took off his shoes and socks, and trudged across the sand toward the water's edge. Out of the corner of his eye, he saw a group of boys working the strings of their kites. And suddenly, a long forgotten memory surfaced. He couldn't have been more than ten when he had the strangest experience on this very beach. A shy kid, he stood on the side and watched as a group of older boys and some girls as well guided their kites pulling the strings to make them dance across the blue sky. It was a busy day for kites. Kites of all shapes, sizes and colors filled the air amidst the hollers and joyful screams of the kids. He remembered, how the kites looked like alien visitors from another planet hovering over the crowd. It was a time when his imagination was filled with science fiction ideas.

And maybe what he remembered seeing that day was in actuality the product of his imagination. And then again, maybe it was real. At the time, he was convinced that what he saw really happened. It was the weirdest thing. His eyes saw a stream of pelicans sweeping across the sky right above the kites. That in itself was not unusual. Pelicans inhabited the sky in great numbers. After all, this was their natural habitat. All day long, they dove into the sea with uncanny accuracy, their pouchy beaks, like powerful swords, penetrating the water just deep enough to pluck out a fish, taking it into their pouches with a single gulp. They were so much a part of the place, the human population tended to ignore them.

    He saw it with his own eyes. Suddenly, one of the pelicans grabbed a kite and attempted to fly off with it. It seemed to young EhEh that the bird wanted to join in the fun, just as he wanted to, only he was too shy to do so. But then, what could have been a moment of fun between the two species turned into something more serious. The boy whose kite it was, screamed with alarm and excitement when the pelican grabbed his treasure. He tightened his grip on the piece of wood that anchored the string, and a tug of war between him and the pelican began. The boy grimly pulled on his kite. But the pelican wouldn't let go. To EhEh, it was a very amusing sight. But also, he sensed something like a cosmic event happening between man and bird, although he had no words for it, as if two worlds, the human one on the ground, and the pelican one in the sky were clashing, contending, vying for ownership of the air. And as he watched full of wonder, the most unbelievable thing happened. Two other pelicans came to the aid of the first. Now three pouchy beaks had hold of the fragile kite whose paper skin was tearing. The kite disintegrated, the pelicans flew off, and the wounded false bird fell out of the sky, landed on the sand in a jumble of splintered wooden strips and torn tissue. The crowd of children groaned in defeat.

    But EhEh, the child, felt elated. Always feeling himself a puny specimen, he looked upon the other kids, more agile, more muscular, more aggressive, as beings approaching the heroic stature of demigods, whom he envied no end, but also whom he found in their arrogant ways unbearable. In his early life, he had no words for these feelings. It was later that he found the language that fortified him. All he knew at the time was that he was glad to see the pelicans win the battle.

    And now, all these many years later, remembering the incident, EhEh, old and as ungainly as ever, was brought to tears. He suddenly recognized the significance of that incident in the formation of his character. He saw that boy whom he had been, as someone who had secretly become an enemy of mankind, pretending, as the scientist that he became, a desire to study and understand his fellow man. But now he knew, he had opted to be an alien, a human only in name, a human in disguise. A lonely one. He was crying for that lost boy.

"That's changed now!" He cried out to the sky, crying openly before the entire world. And some of the people on the beach took notice. They stared at the crying man. "I'm not that person any more!" He declared to them, as if he were on trial. And having said that, he felt as though he had expelled something vile from his body. He felt clean of rancor. For the first time, he felt truly ready to enter the magic grotto.